KE

SECRETS AND MALICE

CHAPTER 1

June 1980

Anthony Scalini's world was suddenly spinning out of control as a blurred, black and gray panorama of trees and dark skies swarmed furiously around and above him. His forearm shook as he gripped the door handle and fought against the centrifugal force that threatened to unseat and launch him onto the driver's side. Even in its frantic state his mind resolved the high-pitched screaming in his ears to the shriek of tortured rubber grinding against the asphalt beneath them. His one clear and disturbing thought was he had forgotten to buckle his seatbelt, the top was down and he hoped like hell they didn't roll over.

Suddenly, as quickly as it had all begun, it was over.

The mustang came to an abrupt halt in the middle of the road, facing almost a hundred and eighty degrees from the direction it had been traveling only moments before; the only motion a gentle side-to-side rocking as the car settled back onto its suspension.

Sitting in his seat stunned and afraid to move, he noticed his legs were fully extended and still trying for all they were worth to push a hole through the floorboard, and he wondered if he had actually thought he could stop the spinning automobile with his feet like one of those characters on the Flintstones. His body's sudden demand for oxygen reminded him he was still holding his breath and he exhaled loudly, immediately replacing it with a fresh lungful, but it did little to calm him.

As he stared straight ahead and tried to compose himself he could see that something was clearly wrong with the windshield. It appeared as though there was something lying against it but as he leaned forward he could see that it was actually a spider web of cracks that started on his side and extended its tentacles almost the entire length across. They were so dense you could no longer see through the glass and most of his side was caved in toward the dashboard. Even the steel support rod was bent. They had hit something hard. Or something had hit them.

"What the hell just happened, Brett?" he asked in a nervous voice that sounded strangely like someone else's.

When he received no answer he leaned over to silence the stereo that continued to blast AC/DC screaming about some girl having *the jack*. The sudden quiet was both eerie and unsettling and he wished he had just turned it down instead.

"What happened?" he repeated, now looking toward the driver's side.

Brett Mitchell, the driver of the mustang and Anthony's best friend for the past two and a half years they had been attending law school together looked, at the moment, like a poster child for a drivers' education school. His hands were at ten and two, his posture was straight, he had his seatbelt buckled and his eyes appeared to be cautiously watching the road even though they were no longer moving. He also looked perplexed, as if his mind was campaigning for all it was worth to convince him that what his eyes had just seen could not possibly be true.

"I don't know . . . I think we hit . . . someone," he replied without looking at him. The unexpected calm in his voice contrasted starkly with Anthony's own roller coaster emotions.

"Hit someone? How could we have hit someone? Who the hell would be out here at this time of the night?" He knew they had, though.

A momentary flash of wide, terrified eyes framed in the mustang's headlights, a sickening thud that sounded like a wool blanket soaked in puss being hurled toward a brick wall at high speed, and that horrifying feeling of hair brushing against his own as whatever it was they hit had slammed into the windshield and then passed over the top of him. Even now it made him want to paw wildly at his head to rid himself of the sensation that still lingered. He was certain that that sound and feeling would visit him often in his nightmares in the years to come.

The mustang's right headlight had shattered from the impact but the left one was working fine as it continued to illuminate a small stretch of road they had just traveled. It was also illuminating something else.

"Is that what we hit?" Anthony asked, nervously pointing around the useless windshield to a spot a few yards up the road from where they sat. "There's something in the road, Brett. Does that look like a body to you?" He could feel his heart racing and was finding it difficult to breathe. He also knew he was on the verge of panicking, but recognized it wasn't going to do him any good unless somehow the act of running around a cornfield raving like a lunatic was going to miraculously put them ten miles further down the road versus being here, stalled in the middle of some no-name country road with the smell of burned rubber lingering in the air, and God only knew what was lying up there in the road. He didn't think it would.

Suddenly Brett came to life. "I don't know, Anthony," he said as he unbuckled his seatbelt and stepped out of the car. "I think it was a girl, but it happened so fast I'm not sure."

"Where are you going?" Anthony blurted in a high voice he barely recognized.

"We need to go check it out. Whatever it is, we can't just leave it laying there. And why don't you relax. Even if it *was* a girl we hit, is it our fault she was walking in the middle of the road?

"No, of course not. It's *her* fault that we weren't watching where we were going."

Brett ignored him and said, "I don't know for sure what I saw, Anthony. I do know, however, that whatever or whomever it is may still be alive so we need go check it out."

Anthony agreed and they began walking slowly toward the motionless mound. When they were within a few feet of it, the question of human or (or what?) was answered definitively; the blue jeans cleared that up. Also, the long brown hair and slight build made female a pretty safe guess. Whoever it was lay face down in the road in a large pool of what looked like motor oil in the thin light. Of course it wasn't oil; it was blood, and a lot of it.

"Oh, shit!" Anthony said weakly. He was standing on the dirt shoulder of the road and lurched toward the ditch to be sick. When he was finished he stood up, running one hand through his wavy, brown hair while simultaneously wiping his mouth on the sleeve of his cardigan sweater. He saw that Brett was kneeling down next to the...

"Is it a girl?"

"Yes," Brett responded, his fingers checking for a pulse.

"How old?"

"I'm guessing fourteen or fifteen. It's hard to tell without better light but she's young. There's also a lot of blood on her face and that makes it tough to tell as well."

A moment or two passed with neither saying anything as they both stared at the girl laying lifeless and broken before them; trying to come to terms with the fact that they had done this to her.

"Is she dead?" Anthony finally asked; already knowing the answer but feeling a desperate need to trump the silence that had descended on them.

"Yes . . . I'm pretty sure she's dead. I can't find a pulse."

"Shit." He leaned over with his hands on his knees as his stomach convulsed again. This time all that came up were slimy tendrils of mucous that burned with stomach acid and partially digested scotch. Brett waited silently until he was done, not wanting to embarrass him. Finally he said, "We need to figure out what we're going to do here, Anthony."

"Maybe there's a phone around here we can use?"

"I doubt it considering we're out here in the middle of

Hicksville surrounded by a few thousand acres of corn. However, on the off-chance we could find one, who do you plan on calling, the police?" Brett asked, as he stood up and began pacing the immediate area around the body, eventually walking over to the other side of the road and bending down to retrieve something.

"Well, yeah, I think that would probably be a good place to start, don't you? What is that?" he asked, gesturing toward the thing Brett was now holding.

"It's a backpack. Looks like she may have been hitchhiking which could mean that she's not from around here." He looked over at him. "I don't think the police are a good idea, Anthony.

"Are you crazy? What are you proposing; that we just kick her off into the ditch and drive away? It was an accident, Brett, but if we don't report this it's going to become a lot more than that."

"Alright, look, let's think this through. Under normal circumstances I would agree with you about the police, but these aren't normal circumstances. Both of us have had a lot to drink, and even if we hadn't hit anyone and had just been pulled over for speeding, we'd already be in a lot of trouble if they gave us a Breathalyzer test.

"We're not drunk," Anthony said defiantly.

"No, maybe you're right. Maybe we're not crawling through the paw paw patch puking up our liver drunk, but I know I had at least four drinks tonight, and it might have been five, and I didn't see you exactly sandbagging. Do you think you're going to blow something below the legal limit? Because anything above that – *anything!* – and they're going to take one look at this girl and we're both getting in the back of that police car with handcuffs on."

"I'm not saying this to hang you out to dry, so don't take it that way," Anthony said, "but I wasn't even driving. What are they going to do to me?"

"Maybe nothing," Brett responded, looking directly at him. "On the other hand, they could very well go after you for involuntary manslaughter since you knew we'd both been drinking and did nothing to prevent either of us from driving. Do you want to take that chance?" When Anthony didn't respond he continued.

"Look around you, Anthony," he said with a sweep of his hand. "Look where we are. Do you want to risk being put on trial and have your fate rest in the hands of a bunch of Indiana hillbillies who don't want us here anyway? How sympathetic do you think these farmers will be toward two irresponsible college boys who have never shoveled shit out of so much as a single horse stall in their life?"

"I think you're exaggerating," Anthony said, with more conviction than he felt.

"Well I think you're being naïve because we just killed this girl and that's *exactly* what it would be like."

Anthony shifted his gaze from Brett, to the dead girl and back to Brett again, nervously folding his arms high across his chest and then immediately unfolding them and placing his hands back on his hips. His lips were pursed tight and his nostrils flared with each shakily drawn breath as he contemplated the unavoidable connection between their current dilemma and their future. "So what are you proposing?" he asked, finally.

"We put her in the trunk, I take you back to Bloomington and drop you off at the campus, and I will take care of getting rid of the body tonight. It's as simple as that. You don't have to know where she is. As a matter of fact, it's better if you don't. Starting tomorrow we just move forward with our lives as if this never happened." Brett stated all of this in his calm, matter-of-fact way, as if he were merely explaining to Anthony the fundamentals of a new chess strategy he had learned recently.

"Just like that . . ." Anthony stated flatly.

"Yep, just like that."

"What do we say if someone asks about the damage to the car?"

"We just tell them we hit a deer, that's all. Look, Anthony, the odds are this girl isn't even from around here so no one will be looking for her. Why should we throw away our lives because some runaway wants to walk down the middle of the road at midnight and we happened to be the unlucky sons-of-bitches who hit her?

"You have her backpack in your hands, Brett. Look and see if there's some identification. Maybe she's not a runaway. Maybe she lives on one of these farms around here. Maybe she's the goddamned local Sheriff's daughter or something."

"The Sheriff's daughter?" Brett echoed sardonically.

"How the hell do I know? I just know that she belongs to *someone;* runaway or not."

"Is it going to change what we do?"

"But don't you want to know?" he pleaded. "Aren't you the least bit curious whose life we took tonight?"

"No."

"No?"

"No," Brett answered firmly. "It won't help and it could just make what we have to do that much harder. If we attach a name to her it's going to make it personal."

Anthony closed his eyes and turned his face up toward the dark, shadowy sky, pausing for just a moment as if to say that he was now willing to accept any divine intervention being offered that evening. When none was forthcoming he exhaled slowly, opened his eyes again, and looked at Brett evenly . . . "I don't ever want to speak of this again, do you understand? Not ever."

"Trust me; it'll be as if it never happened."

"How ironic is it that two law students are about to commit a crime as heinous as this so they can continue to pursue their dream of arguing the guilt or innocence of others?

"Look, Anthony, I've heard it said that the worst day you can possibly imagine *outside* of prison is still infinitely better than the best day *inside* of a prison. I'm not interested in finding out if that's true, are you?"

"No, I'm not," he answered quietly. "But I feel like we're making a pact with the Devil, and I can't help but wonder what he'll want in return one day."

"The Devil's got nothing to do with this. Now come on and let's get it over with," Brett said, bending over and placing his hands under the dead girl's arms.

With a sigh of resignation Anthony stepped forward to help.

CHAPTER 2

February 2003
(Twenty-three years later)

Terri Ranes was torn from the comforting abyss of sleep by a painful, choking pressure on her throat and a hand placed roughly over her mouth.

"You scream or fight me, bitch, and your mother won't recognize you when I'm done, do you understand me?" This threat was delivered in an unmistakably male voice and emphasized with a measured increase in the pressure being applied to her throat by his forearm. "Just nod your head if you understand," he said, leaving little doubt that full compliance was expected.

Terri nodded just once, and though her eyes were still adjusting, she could now make out that the man leaning over her was wearing a ski mask. She was also struck by how his eyes appeared to have a greenish glow to them; almost luminescent.

"Just when you thought it was safe to go back in the water, huh?" he taunted with the gleeful satisfaction of a bully who had finally forced his way into the secret clubhouse he'd been excluded from joining.

Terri didn't respond as her breath moved rapidly through her nostrils, sounding too loud to her, and she knew that in direct contradiction to those stories you read where a person in a life-threatening situation is moved to feats of superhuman strength and uncommon heroism, her fear was immediately debilitating. She was afraid to move and doubted her body's willingness to respond had she even tried.

"I'm going to take my hand off of your mouth now, sweetheart. You agreed to keep quiet so I'm expecting you to keep your promise, ya hear?" She nodded again, eyes filled with terror.

When he was fairly certain she wasn't going to pose a problem he let his hand slide from her cheek down to her breast and the mind-numbing revulsion she felt started from somewhere deep within and emanated from every pore, causing her to shudder beneath him. She couldn't have been more repulsed if she'd had a thousand disease-ridden cockroaches crawling on her, and every hair on her body seemed to take on a distinct and separate existence of their own as the hideousness of what was happening slammed a million volts of electric current through every nerve in her body.

"Don't worry, baby, we'll consummate our newfound relationship soon enough," he said, vainly mistaking her physical reaction as a sign that she was getting turned on. The lasciviousness in his voice terrified her, and she fought against the emotional riptide of insanity that threatened to pull her under. A small moan of disgust left her throat and suddenly she knew she was going to scream. It came rushing up like a freight train she was helpless to stop, and in the split second before it erupted from her vocal chords she jerked her head violently to the side and bit down on his arm. It was involuntary and she didn't mean to do it, but she doubted the truth would help her right now as he slowly looked up at her. Even through the mask she could see the anger, and something else . . . something . . . dark.

"I didn't mean to," she pleaded.

"You didn't mean to?" he said, looking at his bleeding arm.

"I – I was going to scream." she said in a pleading voice.

"Shhhh," he whispered as he reached out and gently, almost lovingly, wiped away the incriminating blood from her lips. "You will, sweetheart," he said softly. "I promise that you *will* scream before this is over."

Something sinister flashed in his eyes and without warning he reached down with his left hand grabbing her by her hair, and as he jerked her head off the pillow toward him he delivered a vicious punch to her face. The blow was devastating and lit up her head like molten lava being poured into an abscessed tooth as it drove her violently back into the pillow. She blacked out briefly, just long enough for her synapses to recover from the shock and begin allowing the firing of nerve impulses again. Through the fog of pain enveloping her she recognized that the situation had just gone from bad to worse, and she raised her arms in a feeble attempt to ward off another blow as she saw him leaning toward her again.

"Waith, I'mm sthorrhy," she pleaded. Her head felt thick and there was a loud ringing in both ears. She was also pretty certain that more than one of her teeth had been knocked loose. "I did int do it on purfus," she said, pleading to be understood. "Did int mean to make hew mad."

"You didn't mean to make me mad, huh? Well, it's a little late for that now ain't it, sweetheart?" He again grabbed her by the hair, only this time he jerked her violently to her feet, pivoted with her away from the bed and delivered another crushing blow to the left side of her face. He felt bone structure disintegrate beneath his knuckles and was consumed by a feeling of power and invincibility. His arousal was immediate and predatory.

Terri's head and torso flew straight back as she was literally lifted off her feet and she slammed down onto her back, her head bouncing off the thinly-carpeted floor with the sound of a half-rotted pumpkin being dropped from a roof. Her head exploded with pain and the shock momentarily paralyzed her, but her instincts were telling her she needed to get to her feet so slowly, painfully she attempted to roll over to her hands and knees.

Apparently her attacker didn't agree as he stepped forward and delivered a powerful kick to the back of her thigh, causing Terri to let loose her first real scream of pain as she collapsed back down to the floor. As she reached back to grab her throbbing leg a second kick landed in the same place, and this time she felt the bones in her hand shatter. Her scream of agony was cut-off abruptly as he dropped his two hundred plus pounds of weight directly onto her ribcage, knee first. The air was forced violently from her lungs with an audible whoosh, and she felt her entire side give with a sickening crunch.

"You've really brought out the worst in me tonight, sweetie-pie. All I wanted to do was come over and have a little date with you." He shrugged his shoulders as if to convey to her that he just didn't understand how things could have gotten so out of control. "But that's alright, we'll do it your way," he said with a sick finality. He made as if to stand up and suddenly, his eyes flashing malevolently, he dropped back down and delivered a ferocious punch to the side of her head.

This time there was no pain and Terri found the comforting blackness she so desperately sought as she drifted softly to a place where her pain could no longer follow, and it welcomed her in its embrace like a mother caressing her infant child. There were no bright lights and there was no one waiting to guide her to an eternal place of promise. She slept.

CHAPTER 3

Sarah set a bowl of corn flakes and a glass of orange juice on a tray and started up the stairs with breakfast for her husband who, up until a year ago, had been a healthy, vibrant man in his late forties with a thriving law practice and a passion for living everyday to its fullest. Of course, that was all before the "C" word had crept silently into their lives and began hungrily devouring him from the inside out.

"Hi, Sweetie," she said as she entered the bedroom. "How's your appetite?" She set the tray down next to his bed and walked over to open the blinds on both windows. It was a typical February day in Indiana with overcast skies, blustery winds and dirty, week-old snow covering most of the ground. Spring had yet to mount any real challenge.

Brett Mitchell was a pitiful sight to behold. He had lost over seventy pounds and had the sticks masquerading as his legs been able to support him on a scale, the needle would have struggled to reach one-twenty. A steady flow of oxygen was delivered through his nose by a cannula and his skin had a sickly, yellow pallor to it from too many unsuccessful chemo and radiation treatments. With any hope for remission conceded months ago, his doctors had finally sent him home to die, prescribing him a personal pharmacy of drugs intended to eek out as many extra days of life as possible. The terrible twilight of his suffering was made tolerable through a morphine drip that provided temporary relief from the agony of having one's internal organs feasted on by a blind, ravenous thing with a mindless lust for tissue and blood; a disease that would not be satisfied until it took its final, wretched breath in perfect synchronicity with its host.

When the pain became too intense the morphine was self-administered by squeezing a rubber ball attached to a tube that was inserted into his vein. There were supposed to be limitations to the number of times the ball could be squeezed in a given hour, but toward the end the pain offered no reprieve and besides, no one cared if a dying man died a junkie if it meant they didn't have to listen to those God-awful screams at night that eventually trailed off to a low agonizing moan. Sarah couldn't have told you which one was worse.

Brett opened his eyes and attempted to focus on his wife. "Not hungry." he said weakly.

"Of course you're not, but you need to eat anyway to keep up your energy level, so there's no use fighting with me about it. Besides, I think I'm a tad stronger than you these days, skinny-minnie, so don't make me put you in a head-lock and force-feed you," she said, with feigned sternness.

He grinned at her weakly and sighed, signaling that he'd tolerate a bite or two just for her, but after that it was going to be war.

When the doctors had told her there was nothing else they could do and were sending him home, she had gone out and purchased one of those electric beds that had something like twenty different position settings so he wouldn't be stuck lying flat on his back all the time. She had also had a TV mounted on the opposite wall so he could watch CNN and Discovery Channel, which were his favorites. She reached for the bed controls now and as she raised him to a semi-sitting position, he thought for the thousandth time that although he was eternally grateful that she had stuck by his side though all of this, he hated the sadness and fatigue that was so deeply etched in her face. If not for her suffering he would have been able to find peace with dying.

"Open up now and let's get some food in you," she said in that maternal voice she occasionally adopted with him. She wondered when it was exactly that she had made the mental transition from loving wife to motherly caretaker. Of course, with men, there probably wasn't much differ-ence, she thought. The slight grin on her face betraying the humor she found in this kernel of wisdom.

"What's funny?" he asked

"Oh, nothing," she said, not wanting to explain. "Your sis-ter Rose called and said she needs to come by and see you. It sounded urgent."

"Did you tell her it was okay?" he asked.

"I told her you hadn't been feeling very well and should probably rest."

"I have terminal cancer," he said softly.

"You have what?" she asked, bending down to hear him better.

"Terminal cancer; that's why I don't feel very good." he said, displaying the most serious look he could muster.

"Oh, we're in a sarcastic mood today, are we?" she asked, pulling the spoon of cornflakes away from his mouth just as he bit down on air. "How would you like to change your own bedpan today, Mr. Smart Guy?" she threatened.

Brett smiled at her. "I love you."

"I love you too," she said, meaning it.

"Call and ask her to come see me, okay."

"You know I told her it was alright. She'll probably be here any minute."

"Good. Can I have my cornflakes now, please," he asked, offering his best puppy dog look.

"Sure, but you better control that sarcasm or I'll spoon it into your nose," she threatened.

After a few bites she set aside the cereal and lifted him up to fluff his pillow and smooth the sheet beneath him. Once that was accomplished she sat on the bed next to him and took his hand in both of hers.

"Do you think you'll ever tell me about it?" she asked him, fixing her eyes on his.

"About what?" he asked, knowing very well where this was heading and wishing they were talking about anything else.

"About whatever it is that sometimes causes you to disappear to that place in your mind where no one else can seem to follow. At least I've never been able to."

"I think you're imagining things," he said, trying to lighten the suddenly serious tone of the conversation.

"I'm not imagining anything, Brett," she said, refusing to let him. "I see it in your eyes. I've always seen it; the pain, the regret, maybe both. It hurts me as well because you've never felt comfortable sharing it when we've shared everything else together. I just don't understand why?"

She could see that whatever it was, he wasn't going to divulge it to her right now and decided to drop it. As she stood up she said, "Brett, you're a good man and you and I have had an amazing life together. I just want you to know that nothing you could tell me would ever make me think less of you. But we can talk about it later . . . or not at all if that's what you decide, but right now you should rest. Your sister will be here soon."

CHAPTER 4

Rose knocked lightly on the open door before entering her brother's room. "Hi," she said, offering a warm smile that more often than not she reserved only for him. Brett opened his eyes slowly and looked toward the door. "Hey, Rosie," he said. He was the only one she let call her that.

When she reached his bed she bent down and kissed him on the cheek while simultaneously rubbing his head. "Your hair feels nice and clean. Get a bath yesterday?" she asked.

He nodded.

"Were you sleeping when I came in?"

Brett took a deep breath. "It would be a stretch to categorize what I do as sleeping." he said, making a painful attempt to adjust his position. Every time I doze off this thing inside me decides it's snack time and starts chewing on one of my organs. This, of course, scares the bejeezus out of the sandman who runs away screaming like a little girl, leaving me lying here hating myself because I don't have the guts to reach over and squeeze the hell out of that little rubber ball until I go marching straight through those pearly gates stoned out of my mind."

Rose just looked at him, knowing there was nothing she could say to make it better.

"I'm sorry, Rosie," he offered. "It's good to see you. You look beautiful as always," he said, reaching out his hand and tracing one finger down the faint shadow of a scar that ran from her cheekbone to her earlobe. She had a couple of smaller ones on her forehead but those stayed mostly covered by her hair. A car had hit her when she was ten years old as she'd been riding her bike to school, though she had no memory of the accident and Brett said it was because she'd suffered amnesia from the head trauma. The scars had mostly faded over the years and they certainly didn't detract from her natural beauty. She had always caused a lot of heads to turn with her large, dark eyes and long, raven hair.

Rose studied him closely, her eyes projecting a portrait of the enormous sorrow she felt for what he was forced to endure. She had made a pact with herself that although she cried often for him when she was alone, she would try her damnedest to never let herself cry in front of him. He had always been the strong one for her and she was determined to be that rock for him in the end. However, she feared she would be sorely tested on this visit.

"You always did have a flair for the dramatic, big brother," she said, summoning a wry smile for him. "And it's good to see you, too," she added. "Sarah told me you've been a little out of control this morning and suggested I take you for a little jog to burn off some of that excess energy. Are you up for it?"

"That would be like some macabre version of the Tortoise and the Hare, don't you think?"

"Yes, I suppose you're right," she agreed.

Suddenly her eyes welled up with tears and she looked away quickly. Alarmed, Brett found her hand with his. "What's wrong, Rose?" After a few seconds and no reply he said again, "Please tell me what's wrong?"

"Toby's been arrested!" she blurted, wiping her eyes and looking at him.

"Arrested? For what?" he asked. She looked hurriedly down at the floor as the tears came harder. "For what, Rose?" he repeated, very concerned now.

"Rape," she said, barely audible. She kept her head lowered.

"What?" he exclaimed, hoping like hell he had misunderstood her.

"For rape!" she said again, expelling the word from her mouth as though it were a piece of putrid, rotted flesh. "They've arrested my boy for rape, Brett." She began to cry openly, her shoulders moving up and down to the rhythm of her sobs.

Brett was absolutely stunned. Sure, she'd had some problems with Toby over the last three or four years, but they'd been problems that most parents encountered with their teenagers; drinking, smoking cigarettes (probably a little pot, too), a couple of fights . . . but rape?

"Who are they saying he raped?" he asked, his years as a defense attorney now taking over and dictating his thought process.

"Well if you asked the police, who *didn't* he rape would be a more appropriate question," she answered bitterly.

He thought about that for a second. "Are you saying that they are alleging he raped more than one person?" he asked incredulously.

"Thirteen," she said in a voice that was barely above a whisper.

"No," he said in disbelief, suddenly feeling nauseous from something other than the eighty some odd pills he took each day just so he could survive to play squeeze-the-ball one more day.

"Thirteen counts of rape; thirteen different women," she confirmed. "What am I going to do, Brett?"

"When was he arrested?"

"Yesterday."

"Where are they holding him?"

"At the Monroe County jail."

"Why there?"

"He lives in Monroe County, remember?"

"That's right. When is the arraignment?"

"The day after tomorrow. What am I going to do, Brett?" she repeated. "I can't bear the thought of my baby sitting in a jail cell."

Suddenly he was hit with a horrible thought. "Do they think he's the French Lick rapist?" Since he had nothing to do but read, watch TV and squeeze his wonder ball while he waited to die, he'd been following the story as closely as anyone and was well aware of the terror this sexual predator had been spreading. The press began calling him the French Lick rapist only because that's where the first rape had occurred. It immediately picked up national press coverage, though, because French Lick was the hometown of former Celtic great Larry Bird. He had hoped they'd catch him but... Toby? She nodded her head and cried harder.

"Well, there's nothing you can do about him being in jail right now, Rose. The earliest he would be released would be the day of the arraignment, and that's only if the judge sets bail. I can tell you that it's highly unlikely he'll do that under these circumstances since we're talking about multiple felonies here."

"But he didn't do it, Brett. You know he didn't do it. He's not capable of raping anyone, let alone thirteen different women," she said, her eyes pleading for him to agree with her.

"How did it happen?"

"What do you mean?" she asked, swiping at the tears on her face.

"The arrest; how did they come to arrest him? What evidence do they have?"

"Apparently one of Toby's neighbors at his apartment complex saw him come home a couple of nights ago with what he apparently thought looked like blood on his shirt. The next day he saw on the news that a woman had been attacked the previous night so he called and reported his suspicion to the police. They showed up at Toby's apartment later that night with a search warrant and took some of his clothing and other things."

"They arrested him right there and took him to jail, Brett. Oh, God, I can't lose you *and* my boy. You two are all I have left. I just can't," she cried, laying her head on the mattress next to him and sobbing.

Brett could hear Sarah busying herself downstairs as he absently stroked Rose's hair and closed his eyes; unable to believe this was happening but already contemplating what to do about it. The pain in his abdomen and chest was starting to worsen but for now he ignored it. He needed to figure out what to do and he couldn't think clearly in a morphine-induced haze.

After a few minutes Rose stopped crying and sat up. Nodding toward the phone on his nightstand, he gave her a number to dial and told her to hand it to him. When it was answered on the other end he mustered a deep breath and said, "Hi, Karen, this is Brett Mitchell. Do you remember me? Yes, that's right. Well, I've been better but I'm hanging in there, thanks for asking. How are things in the prothonotary's office? Good, good. So, I just heard through the grapevine that they think they've arrested the French Lick rapist."

He felt sorry for Rose when he saw her visibly flinch.

"Uh huh, yeah I agree, I think it's great as well. I hope they have the right guy and that this is the end of it. Listen, who's the judge assigned to this? Oh, Judge Scalini?" he repeated, raising his eyebrows. "No kidding. Well, he's a competent judge so hopefully they'll put this guy away for good." He avoided looking at Rose as he said this. "Yeah, I know you do. Well, listen, it was good talking to you and you take care. Okay, I will. Bye now."

"Is that Anthony Scalini, your friend from law school I've heard you mention a few times over the years?" she asked as she took the phone and set it back in the cradle. He looked completely worn out right now and she could tell he was in a lot of pain.

"One and the same," he said, grimacing slightly and placing his hands on his stomach.

"Does that help? I mean, are you and he still close? Have you stayed in contact over the years?"

"No. Right after graduation he got hired on with the DA's office down in Monroe County and I ended up practicing here in Indianapolis so our paths never really crossed over the years."

"So it doesn't help us?" she asked, disappointment already spreading across her face.

"I didn't say that."

"So it does help us?" she said, perking up.

"I didn't say that either, Rose," he said, hating the anxiety his ambivalence was causing her.

"Listen, I need some time to think about this so why don't you go home and try to get some sleep. Come back here tomorrow morning around eight and hopefully I'll have a better idea of how we should proceed. I just need some time to think it through, okay?"

"Okay," she said. She took his hand in both of hers as she stood up. "I can't lose both of you, Brett," she repeated. "First I lose my parents before I'm old enough to even know them, then you with this damn cancer, and now . . . I've just lost too much."

"Trust me, I of all people understand, Rosie. Just give me tonight to think through our options and we'll discuss it again tomorrow, okay? By the way, make sure you bring me a copy of the search warrant they served on him."

"Okay, I will. I love you," she said as she headed out the door and toward the stairs. He could see that the limp she'd been left with after the childhood accident was more pronounced today than normal. Over the years it had become practically unnoticeable, but it tended to return when she was tired or under a lot of stress.

"Love you too, Rose. I'll see you in the morning. Please ask Sarah to come see me after she's shown you out, okay?" he called after her. This extra exertion caused him to emit a small groan and immediately a thin sheen of sweat covered his forehead. He reached over and gave the ball one quick squeeze and after the pain had subsided somewhat, he began to go over in his mind what she had told him.

Toby, a rapist? It didn't seem possible. There had been the occasional problem but for the most part he had always seemed like a pretty good kid. Was it possible he had really done this? He didn't know, but he did know that Rose would never survive losing him to cancer and watching her only child get sent to prison for life, or worse. By the time Sarah arrived he knew what had to be done. Unfortunately it would involve breaking a solemn promise he had made many years ago.

"Rose looked upset. What's going on?" Sarah asked when she came into the room.

"Hi, Sweetheart," he said, offering her what he hoped was a comforting smile. "Sit down, please." He patted the mattress next to him. She did as he asked and he began bringing her up-to-date on the news Rose had delivered.

Sarah was silent as she pondered this. "Do you think he could have done it?" she asked after a few moments.

"I don't know. The police must have found something pretty compelling when they searched his apartment or they wouldn't have him in custody. However, the Governor has been taking a beating in the press over all these women being raped and the cops not having so much as a single suspect, so it's possible they're just looking for a scapegoat and setting him up; wouldn't be the first time, that's for sure."

"Well what did Rose want; from you, I mean?" she asked him.

"She wants help. She wants me to fix it, that's what she wants. She's going crazy with the thought that she might lose me *and* her son."

"I understand, Brett, but under the circumstances I don't know what you're going to be able to do. We're talking about rape here. Does she want you to represent Toby or something? I mean, you can't even walk to the bathroom on your own right now."

"Thanks for reminding me."

"I didn't mean it like that," she said, immediately sorry for having said it, "but we both know there's nothing you can do?"

Brett reached over and gave three successive squeezes then sighed deeply and closed his eyes, anticipating the sweet relief from the torment of his disease that was only seconds away. "I fear you may be right, Sweetheart," he said as he began drifting away on a sweet, narcotic cloud.

CHAPTER 5

Toby McGrady was in a foul mood. He hadn't been in his cell twenty-four hours and he already hated it. The food sucked, the guards all had bad attitudes, his cell smelled like stale vomit and feces, and the tiny little mattress that covered the concrete slab masquerading as a bed was not intended to support a two hundred and twenty pound frame and it had played hell on his back last night. This whole thing was like a nightmare he couldn't wake up from.

One minute he'd been sleeping and the next minute the cops were banging on his door in the middle of the night telling him they had a search warrant. After reading the warrant he had let them in and then watched as they pounced on his apartment like a pack of voracious pit bulls on a poodle. They boxed up a number of his personal clothing items as well as his computer, placed him in handcuffs, read him his rights and brought him to this shithole where he'd been since late last night.

The interrogation started at five o'clock this morning and it was a six and a half hour marathon that alternated between screamed accusations, fists pounded on the metal folding table they had him sitting behind, and threats of life without parole, which was generally followed up with the offer of a cigarette, food or drink, and the occasional, *"Help us out here, Toby. Do something for us and we'll let the D.A. know you cooperated."* But no matter how many times he told them he didn't know what they were talking about, it was obvious that they weren't going to hear him until he gave them exactly what they wanted, and so the questions continued. He was actually amazed at how accurately the TV cop shows portrayed law enforcement interrogation techniques. It was so cliché he had to force himself not to laugh at them.

But finally they'd had enough and with a look of disgust on his face, the detective who appeared to be in charge of the whole production ordered a uniformed officer to take him back to his cell with a promise to Toby that they weren't even close to being done with him.

A little later he'd been allowed to make a phone call and he'd called his mom. He explained to her what had happened and directed her to go see his Uncle Brett. He couldn't afford a good lawyer and he doubted his mother could either, and the prospect of being represented by a public defender didn't seem like a great option under the circumstances, so even though he knew his Uncle was dying, he was still a lawyer and would hopefully know what to do.

Anyone else in his situation would be too nervous to even think about eating, but Toby wasn't nervous. Being in jail didn't make him nervous; being charged with multiple counts of rape didn't make him nervous; and the prospect of spending the rest of his life in prison didn't make him nervous either. His perception of the world differed dramatically from what others would consider normal. To him life was nothing more than a game to be played, and in this game unlike in almost every other game, you were allowed to make up your own rules. He had his rules and he accepted that others played by their own, and in the end it didn't matter who won as long everyone played. That's what he'd always done and that's what he would continue to do. He laced his fingers together behind his head and with an almost imperceptible grin behind his lips, he wondered when they were going to feed him again.

CHAPTER 6

"We have a lot to talk about today, Rosie, and time isn't exactly on my side these days so we should probably get to it. Why don't you grab that chair over there and pull it up next to my bed."

Rose hadn't slept at all last night thinking about Toby sitting in jail, and when finally dawn had arrived she'd turned her thoughts to seeing Brett again today, imagining how he would look at her with that quiet confidence that came so naturally to him and tell her that everything was going to be all right; that the police had simply made a mistake. But now that she was actually here reality was setting in and she knew it had been nothing more than wishful thinking.

"Rosie, against my better judgment, I'm going to tell you something that I had made a promise to never tell anyone, and I'm letting you know up front that it's not something I'm proud of, so I hope that as you listen you'll bear in mind that it took place a long time ago, when I was much younger. Unfortunately, the decisions we make when we're young are not necessarily the decisions we would have made today, but until we learn to turn back time we're stuck with the indiscretions of our youth."

When she started to say something he held up his hand and cut her off.

"Don't say anything yet. You may want to hear me out first before you just dismiss the notion that something I could tell you would cause you to change your opinion of me, okay?"

"Okay," she said, settling into her chair. "I'm listening."

"This was during my last year of law school, about twenty three years ago I guess. A friend of mine and I attended a dinner hosted by a Mr. Smythe, who at the time was one of the senior partners of Schumann, Smith and Smythe. Do you remember that firm?"

"Wasn't that the law firm you went to work for right after you graduated from law school?"

"One and the same. Anyway, we were honored to have been invited and we were so excited to have the opportunity to pick the brains of some of the best known litigators in the State at the time. It was a great party and we were on cloud nine as we stood listening to these legal warriors try to outdo each other with their stories of epic courtroom battles and judicial heroism and, well, you get the picture, right?"

She nodded, wondering where in the world this was going.

"Anyway, with both of us still being in law school neither of us had any war stories of our own to contribute, so we did the only other thing there was to do; we drank. And when we finally said our goodbyes a few hours later and jumped in our car – my car actually – to head back to campus, we were an accident waiting to happen. I mean, neither of us had any business driving that night, but back then no one thought much about it. I mean, who'd ever heard of Mothers Against Drunk Driving, right?" he asked, as if still trying to justify it after all these years.

Not wanting to interrupt his train of thought she just nodded again.

"So there we are tooling down the back roads of Southern Indiana in the middle of the night, listening to AC/DC and doing probably seventy miles per hour - can you believe I still remember who we were listening to after all these years?" he asked her, as if that was just the most ridiculous thing to have stick in someone's mind, "when all of a sudden we hit something."

"What do you mean *you hit something*?" she asked him, finally speaking for the first time. "You mean like a tree or a fence or something?"

"God, if only that were true," he said. "But no, it wasn't a tree or a fence. It was a person; a girl actually."

"A girl!" she exclaimed. "You hit a girl?"

"Yes. It happened so fast I didn't even brake until after we had already run her over. Well, we didn't exactly run her over; she hit the front of the car, slammed into the windshield and catapulted over the back of the car. When we finally stopped I could see her lying in the road. Neither of us wanted to believe we had actually hit someone, but we both knew what we'd seen in the headlights." He paused for a moment, reliving the horror of that night just as he had done every day since. "By the time we walked over to where she lay, she was already dead."

"Wait a minute," Rose said. "How is it possible that you killed this girl and I never knew about it? Did Mom and Dad know? Didn't you guys call the police?"

"No one knew but the two of us, Rose, and that's the way we wanted to keep it. And to answer to your question, no, we didn't call the police."

"How could you not call the police?" she asked doubtfully. "I mean, what did you do with the body, bury it in a cornfield?" The comment was intended to be facetious but she noticed with a building sense of dread that he wasn't laughing.

"Something like that," he responded, reaching over to give the rubber ball a full squeeze.

"What do you mean, *something like that?*"

"I mean we got rid of the body," he said, closing his eyes while he waited for the morphine to provide some relief from the burning in his gut that seemed to be constant lately. Rose could see he was in pain so she stopped the questions momentarily and considered what he had just told her. This does not sound like my brother, she thought. He's always been so in control, no matter the situation. She wondered what circumstances could have caused him to do such a thing.

Finally she said, "I can't imagine the burden of having to carry something like this with you all these years, Brett. Didn't you ever have the urge to tell someone; to just . . . I don't know . . . purge your soul?"

"Of course I did, but I couldn't. We were these young college kids who'd had too much to drink, and we ended up killing an innocent young girl because we exercised poor judgment. The drinking would have been a mitigating circumstance and the odds were that they would have locked us up for years. Our lives would have been ruined before they even had a chance to get started."

He paused for a moment to catch his breath and saw her staring at him. "It was too late to save the girl, Rose. She was already dead. So we chose to save ourselves instead. I know that sounds incredibly selfish now but that's the decision we made then. To be perfectly honest my buddy wanted to call the police, but I convinced him not to by giving him the worst case scenario of what could happen to us if we actually had to stand trial out in the boonies. In the end he agreed with me and so we hid her body."

She stared at him in disbelief, knowing she had to ask the question but unsure if she could handle the answer. "Are you going to tell me where she is?"

Brett appeared to consider the question. "We watched the papers and the news reports for months, wondering when we were going to see where someone had reported their daughter missing. That was what we feared most, you know; having a name to go with the body. That would have made it so much more personal."

Another grimace, another squeeze…

"We never heard anything, though. It was like she had run away from somewhere and no one had cared enough to report it. To this day I have no idea who she was, or if anyone besides us even knows she's been missing all these years."

"Where is she, Brett?" Rose asked again.

"That's not important."

"What do you mean it's not important? Then why did you tell me all this; just to clear your conscience? You have an opportunity to make this thing right. You can tell the police where she is and maybe they can identify her through DNA or something. At the very least they can give her a proper burial. I mean, what are they going to do to you at this point?"

Brett looked at her and said simply, "No."

"But, I don't under . . ."

"No!" he said harshly, and then grimaced from the pain brought on by the exertion.

When it had mostly subsided he looked at her. "That is not why I told you. Look, I probably won't live another week, Rose, and I am not leaving that kind of legacy behind for you to have to deal with on your own. I want you to promise me right now that you will never repeat to anyone what I have told you today."

"Brett . . ."

"Promise me, Rose, or this conversation's over right now. There's nothing you could do with the little bit of information I've given you anyway."

She took a deep breath and closed her eyes, exhaling long and slow. "Okay, I promise," she said finally. "I won't speak of it to anyone. Sarah doesn't know about this?"

"You're the only person I've ever told."

"That's what I don't understand, Brett; why you bothered to tell me at all. You could have taken this secret with you to the . . . well, you know what I mean . . . and no one would have been the wiser. Why tell me now?"

"Because the friend who was with me that night is Anthony Scalini." Her eyes grew wide as the implications of what he had just said sunk in.

"He's the judge presiding over Toby's case."

"I know."

"But how does this help us?"

"Believe me, it helps us, Rose. Now did you bring a copy of the search warrant with you?"

"Oh yeah, here it is." she said, pulling it out of her purse. She was quiet while he spent the next few minutes reviewing it. "What time did you say they served this on him?"

"I don't know exactly, but it was after midnight. They woke him up out of a sound sleep, the bastards."

"Hmm, that's interesting. Okay, Rosie, listen closely because here's what I need you to do . . ."

CHAPTER 7

"All rise!" commanded the bailiff as Judge Scalini purposefully entered his courtroom, black robe flowing behind him.

"Please be seated," he said, as he took his position behind the bench.

Anthony Scalini was five feet ten and a fit one sixty five to one hundred and seventy five pounds, depending on how long it had been since the last holiday. He had dark, curly brown hair that he wore very short, and you had to be standing right next to him to notice the hint of gray beginning to encroach on the sides. He had a longish face with deep-set blue eyes, a nose that was slightly too large (a gift from his Italian heritage) and a wide mouth with thin lips that seemed to always be pursed in deep thought. He wore glasses that had been prescribed for reading, the kind with aviator frames, but kept them on whenever he was in his courtroom as he thought they made him look more scholarly; a characteristic that had served him well when he'd argued cases in front of juries first as a young prosecutor for the DA's office, then as the assistant DA, and later when he was elected as the District Attorney for Monroe County.

Now, at forty eight years old, he was the youngest of the four judges elected to the Monroe County, Indiana Circuit

Court, a fact he was very proud of, and he was about to preside over the arraignment hearing for one of the most important cases of his career.

As he slowly scanned his courtroom he noted with some concern that the back two thirds of the seats normally reserved for the public were already filled with reporters hunched together in conspiring little groups discussing everything from the Pacers to the latest gossip on this case leaked by the police and DA's office. The only exception being a pretty woman sitting alone in the corner of the back row who the bailiff had warned him was the defendant's mother. The front two rows of seats had been reserved for victims and their family members, and most of those were filled as well. The circus had begun.

Cameras had been temporarily banned until he ruled on a defense motion to permanently ban them during the trial, (of course, the prosecution vehemently opposed this) and he completed a quick scan to ensure his directive had been followed.

Satisfied it had, he did a quick count of deputies and was relieved to see that there were triple the normal two. He had ordered additional security knowing that emotions would be running high for this hearing and throughout the ensuing trial, and two of the deputies would be posted directly between the defendant and the victims and their family members at all times. The defendant had allegedly hurt a lot of people and the last thing he needed was some angry boyfriend, husband or father getting his hands around this joker's neck and trying to mete out his own brand of justice. The remaining four deputies would be placed strategically around the room to quell any other unforeseen problems.

Although he was known for his thoroughness and attention-to-detail, his preparation for this trial had been especially meticulous. It was way too important for stupid mistakes and he intended to ensure that things proceeded as smoothly as possible. He had boned up on procedure, read and re-read applicable case law exhumed by his clerks from the county's massive law library, and had even placed a call to solicit any words of advice or encouragement from another judge he knew who had presided over a case of similar magnitude a few years ago.

A personal call from the Governor last evening had just served to reinforce the huge interest this case was attracting statewide. Elections were just around the corner and the political implications were loomed large. More importantly, though, assuming the police had arrested the right guy, this animal deserved to be locked away forever.

The fact that District Attorney, Michael Haas and assistant District Attorney, Jay Krump were both sitting at the prosecution table was indicative of the importance of this case to the State as well.

Haas was an interesting character who had an affinity for the spotlight and cameras which, of course, did not make him so different from most other publicly-elected officials. What did make him different, though, was that he had that uncanny knack for being able to stop and mingle with the media, acknowledge one or two of the more veteran reporters, bless them all with a witty quote or two about the latest and greatest case his office was prosecuting, and then, with a dismissive wave of his hand, send them scurrying off in all directions to frantically relay all that had been bestowed on them by the mighty DA Haas.

What was most entertaining, though, was that he would pull all of this off while appearing to be much too important and busy to actually be bothered by their questions. It was an act that never ceased to amaze and entertain Judge Scalini when he would catch a clip of it on the evening news. However, in spite of his headline hounding, Michael Haas was very competent as well as very principled, and the judge expected to encounter no major problems from their side. They would definitely be ready on the first day of trial. Today was just the arraignment.

Counsel for the defense was a different story altogether.

Brandon Spencer Hill, Jr.

The judge was shocked when he'd first been assigned the case and had seen the guy's name listed as counsel for the defendant, primarily because he had never heard of him. Granted he didn't know every lawyer in the county, but he'd been almost positive he would see the name of one of the local, high-profile mouthpieces representing the defendant. Not that southern Indiana had a slew of big-wig attorneys within the confines of its cornfields, but there were a handful who had handled high-profile cases in the past like when the Sheriff's son over in New Haven got busted with over a hundred pounds of marijuana in the trunk of his car, or that mother down in Evansville who killed her two kids last year by setting their mobile home on fire so she could collect on a lousy ten thousand dollar life insurance policy. Then there was that judge over in Hamilton who got busted in a child pornography sting. Certainly any of those attorneys would have been more qualified to represent the defendant than this frightened-looking young man sitting in front of him. Heck, a couple of them probably would have taken the case pro bono just for the publicity.

Anthony sighed as he noticed that Mr. Hill had what looked like five times the normal paperwork spread before him on the table than was practically needed for an arraignment, and he wouldn't have been at all surprised if some of it was his notes from law school. He had asked his clerk to do some research on Mr. Hill, thinking *(hoping)* that perhaps he was an experienced attorney from out-of-state, but what his clerk came up with didn't exactly set his mind at ease. Mr. Hill had only held his license to practice law in the State of Indiana for eleven months. Their search of the local schools produced transcripts from the School of law at I.U. Bloomington, the judge's alma mater, which ordinarily would have alleviated some concerns since it was a well-respected school. However, Mr. Hill had graduated three years prior to having passed the bar exam eleven months ago. He'd passed on his first try but it was concerning that he'd waited three years to attempt it. The rumor was that the defendant's mother had found him and that Mr. Hill had been properly mortified by the prospect of representing her son in such a serious matter. She had apparently been very persuasive, though, as here he was in full cheap suit regalia, ready to wage legal war or, if his pasty complexion was any indication, vomit all over his shiny new briefcase. The judge hoped it was the former.

This was all very distressing as he did not intend to facilitate a trial that could be overturned on appeal due to incompetent representation for the defendant, and he intended to ask this young man some questions just as soon as he had an opportunity.

"Is the State ready to proceed, Mr. Haas?" he asked the DA.

Standing, the District Attorney said "Good morning, Your Honor. Yes, the State is ready to proceed."

"Is the defense ready to proceed?" he asked, looking warily at Brandon Spencer Hill, Jr.

Rising quickly and almost tipping his chair over to the amusement of the press, Mr. Hill said, "Yes – ah, Your Honor. We . . . uh . . . we're ready to proceed, Your Honor."

Anthony nodded and taking a final glance around to ensure that his courtroom was in order, he turned to the bailiff and said, "Bring the defendant into the courtroom, please."

The bailiff immediately poked his head through a side door and spoke to someone on the other side. The sudden silence in the courtroom was deafening, and the air was thick with a mixture of anticipation and fear. The media was about to see for the first time the man who had been terrorizing the southern half of their state for the past nine months; the man *they* had labeled the French Lick rapist.

In the front sat nine of his alleged thirteen victims, all of whom were about to see their attacker for the first time in the light, and without a ski mask. A couple of the women began to cry silently and were quickly consoled by those next to them.

A few seconds later two deputies entered the courtroom escorting between them a tall man of about six foot two who looked to be in his late teens or early twenties, blonde hair, a nice face with rugged, square features and what appeared to be a muscular build beneath the orange jump suit.

His most striking feature, however, was his eyes. They were a brilliant aqua-green color and seemed almost to emanate a faint glow as they scanned the room.

As they guided him to the chair next to his attorney he calmly searched the faces in attendance, smiling pleasantly at those who had the courage to look back. Many of the family members met his gaze with their own look of unbridled hate and anger, though any thoughts of vigilantism were nullified by the presence of the deputies. He found his mother in the corner and offered her a wide smile, which she returned along with a quick wave as he took his seat.

"This is the arraignment hearing for the State versus Toby McGrady. For the record, who is counsel for the defendant?"

"Uh, Brandon Spencer Hill, Jr., Your, uh, Your Honor," he stuttered, obviously caught off-guard with the question. The defendant was looking at his attorney as if he had just walked out of an alien spacecraft, and it was obvious to the judge that this was most likely the first time the two had met. This certainly didn't do much to calm his misgivings regarding Mr. Hill's suitability to provide adequate counsel for his client.

"Who is counsel for the State?"

"District Attorney, Michael Haas, Your Honor."

"Very well, let's begin," the judge said, surveying the courtroom one last time.

"Mr. McGrady, you have been charged with thirteen counts of rape, eight counts of deviant sexual behavior, to include sodomy, as well as two counts of aggravated assault. How do you plead to these charges, sir?"

Hearing their horrifying experiences laid out in the courtroom in the form of criminal charges was too much for some of the victims who became visibly distraught. One so much so that, much to the delight of the press, she fled the courtroom in tears, causing them to grab their pens and quickly lower their heads in perfect unison as they began scribbling on their note pads.

Toby's attorney stood up and motioned for him to do the same. Once he had him on his feet he leaned over and whispered to him. "You need to address the judge and tell him how you plead to the charges."

Toby turned toward the front of the courtroom and said, "I plead not guilty to all those charges, Judge."

"Bullshit!" someone said from the gallery, drawing gasps from some, and broad smiles from the press, who once again began to scribble in perfect synchronicity.

The judge picked up his gavel and pounded it three times in quick succession, commanding the attention of everyone in the room. He fixed them all with a stare and then very deliberately said, "Listen carefully to what I am about to say, folks, because I'm not going to repeat it. I understand the seriousness of the charges against this defendant, and I understand the raw emotions that go along with that. However, this is an arraignment intended only to inform the defendant of the charges against him and allow him an opportunity to enter a plea. No testimony will be heard today; no evidence submitted. In this country, thank God, we are considered innocent until proven guilty and I can assure you that that fundamental, constitutionally guaranteed right shall prevail in my courtroom. If you cannot control your emotions then you need to stay home and follow these proceedings in the newspaper. Anyone exhibiting apoplectic or otherwise inappropriate behavior will be escorted out of this courtroom and banned permanently from the remainder of the proceedings. I can assure you that future incidents of inappropriate behavior will not only earn my ire, but I will close these proceedings to all but the victims. Do I make myself crystal clear on this?" he asked, directing it to the entire room at once.

When no one dared answer for fear of drawing his attention toward them, he said, "Good. Now let's move on. Let the record reflect the defendant has entered a plea of not guilty. What kind of a timeline are we looking at for a trial date?" he asked, looking at the DA.

"Your Honor, the State feels that the evidence is such that this is an open and shut case. Therefore, we can be prepared to try this case within a couple of weeks." DA Haas said.

"Mr. Hill?" he inquired of the young defense counsel. "What are your thoughts for a trial date?"

"Your Honor, that timeline is acceptable to us as well."

"Two weeks, counsel?" The judge asked, incredulously. "When were you retained by Mr. McGrady?"

"Yesterday, Your Honor. Uh, by the defendant's mother," he said, somewhat sheepishly.

"I don't care who wrote the check, Mr. Hill. Are you telling me that you were only retained yesterday yet, in spite of the seriousness of these charges, you feel qualified to prepare an adequate defense for your client in the next fourteen days?" the judge pressed.

"No, Your Honor, I'm not saying that at all. My client has insisted that we not delay the trial for any reason. They, I mean *he,* wants the earliest date offered by the court. I, of course, have advised him against it but he and his family are adamant."

The judge pondered this for a moment before addressing the defendant directly. "Sir, do you understand that a trial resulting in a finding of guilty on charges of this nature would more than likely result in you being incarcerated in the state penitentiary for the rest of your natural life?"

"Yes, I do," Toby stated matter-of factly.

"Then please explain to this court, sir, why you seem hell-bent on rushing to trial versus giving your attorney an adequate amount of time to prepare a proper defense?"

"The constitution guarantees me the right to a speedy trial, judge," he said simply.

This brought another gasp from the gallery and the reporters wrote furiously. The fact of the matter was that Toby had no idea why his attorney was agreeing to the date, but he assumed it must have come from his Uncle Brett so he just went with it.

Judge Scalini launched a stern look around the courtroom, quieting everyone down instantly, and then turned his attention back to the defendant. He was seasoned enough to know better than to let himself be baited in his own courtroom so he ignored the smug response. "Very well, the trial is set for the twenty first, two and a half weeks from today. I truly hope there's a method behind your madness, sir," he said to Toby. "Now let's address the issue of bail."

"Your Honor," DA Haas began, "in the State's opinion, the heinous nature of these crimes makes the defendant a serious flight risk, not to mention a continued threat to the community were he to be released pending trial. As such, we would ask this court to deny bail."

"I'm inclined to agree," the judge said, looking at Mr. Hill. "Your response, counsel?"

Mr. Hill stood and said, "Your Honor once again, against my advice, I have been directed to not ask for bail."

"Good," the judge said. "That makes it simple. The defendant will be remanded to the Monroe County jail until trial." There was an audible exhale from some of the victims and family members, as well as a couple of the female court employees.

"Are there any additional motions we need to discuss at this time?"

When both sides indicated there weren't he said, "Fine, we'll reconvene here at nine AM on the twenty first." And with that he disappeared through a door behind his bench and walked down the hallway to his chambers, glad that the first part was over. His bailiff, Joe Duggery, poked his head in the door a few minutes later.

"Everything okay, Judge? Need anything?" he asked

"No, I'm good, Skull," he answered.

Everyone called Joe "Skull" because of his last name. He was a tough, leathery old man who could have been anywhere from fifty-five to seventy-five years old, but no one knew for sure and he wasn't giving it up. He'd been around for what seemed like forever and had probably seen more judges come and go than anyone working in the Monroe County court system.

"What do you make of that defendant?" Anthony asked him.

Skull stepped into the office and closed the door as he pondered the question. "He's a cold, that one, Judge," he finally said. "Don't have a feelin' bone in his body. Looking at them eyes is like lookin' at the Devil himself. I'd convict him and throw away the key right now without ever hearing any evidence if I was on that jury."

"Well, then let's be thankful we don't get many jurors like you, Skull," he said, grinning at him. "Lord knows attitudes like that would throw our legal system back to the days of the Salem witch hangings."

"Say what you will, Judge, but I don't care a wit. That boy's no good and if he were to walk away free I'd lock my family up tight 'til I read his obituary," he said, with a deadly serious look on his face.

"I don't think you'll have to worry about that, Skull. From what I've heard, the evidence appears to be pretty damning so I don't anticipate the State having a very difficult time proving its case. Of course, as usual, that's between you and me and these walls," he cautioned him.

"Now, Judge, you know I don't go around spoutin' off at the mouth," he said, looking perfectly offended that the judge would ever assume otherwise.

"I know you don't, Skull, I just say that out of habit. You know if something like that were to ever be leaked to the press we wouldn't stand a chance in hell at sitting an impartial jury. They'd file for and receive a change of venue without even breaking a sweat."

"Yeah, I know."

"Okay then, so don't take it so personal," he said, grinning at him again.

"We don't have anything else on the docket today, Judge. You need me to stick around for awhile?"

"No, that's okay. Get out of here and go spend some quality time with that wife of yours."

Judge, Agnes and I figured out a long time ago that there were limitations to how long we could stand to look at one another's face each day. As long as we stick to those limits we get along fine, but as soon as we try stretching 'em we both end up mad and poutin'. No, I guess I'll just head on over to the VFW, down me a couple a frosty ones and make myself feel better by reminiscing with some old codgers who have a harder time gettin' around than me." he said, turning for the door.

"Korea?" the judge asked him.

Skull turned around with his hand still on the doorknob. "Yeah, Korea."

"You've never talked about it. Was it bad?"

"Well, it wasn't a cakewalk, Judge, but I doubt it was as bad as what those poor women out there had to go through with that monster."

Anthony absorbed this for a moment. "I'll see you tomorrow, Skull," he said.

"Okay, Judge. Oh, by the way, I almost forgot. The defendant's mother passed a note to me through that greenhorn lawyer of theirs. Said it was for you. I read it like I do all of 'em but I can't make any sense of it. Maybe it'll mean something to you," he said, handing it across the desk.

"See you tomorrow, Judge."

"See you, Skull," he said, intrigued by the note. "Close that door behind you, will you." He waited until he was gone before unfolding the piece of paper. What he read made his blood turn to ice.

Judge Scalini,

I wish to discuss with you a matter separate from that of my son. It involves a young girl and a mustang with a broken windshield. Please contact me this evening at 574-425-9999 to schedule a time and place to meet.

Yours in the pursuit of justice,

Ms. McGrady

Suddenly Anthony couldn't breathe. It felt as though his chest were in a vise, causing his heart to beat in a frenzied staccato. This can't be happening, he thought. He had spent the last twenty three years trying to forget about that night; trying not to let the guilt overwhelm him, and now . . . now, here it was like some black, slimy thing writhing on his desk; willing to be ignored but refusing to be forgotten.

"How can this be possible?" he said out loud. His mind was working at warp speed as he considered how this woman could possibly know anything about that night. He'd never even heard of her before. I have to call Brett, he decided.

He found Brett's home number through the court directory since, like most attorneys, his number was unlisted to the public. Sarah picked up on the second ring.

"Hello?"

"Yes, is this the Mitchell residence?"

"Yes it is, who's calling, please?"

Hesitating for just a moment he said, "This is Anthony Scalini," choosing not to use his title. After that night, he and Brett's relationship had regressed to little more than a cordial nod when they would happen to run into each other at school; both recognizing that the secret they shared virtually eliminated the possibility of maintaining a normal friendship. After graduation they had both gone their separate ways; him joining the DA's office in Monroe County and Brett hiring on with a firm further south in Dubois County, then a year later going into private practice in Indianapolis with another guy from their class. Anthony had periodically kept tabs on Brett's career over the years, mostly out of curiosity, and he supposed Brett had done the same, though neither had ever made an attempt to contact the other.

After a moment's hesitation she said, "Mr. Scalini, this is Sarah Mitchell, Brett's wife. Brett has spoken of you before, how are you?"

"I'm fine, Mrs. Mitchell," he said, a little surprised that Brett had mentioned him.

"Please, call me Sarah," she said.

"Fine then, Sarah. I was wondering if Brett was available. There's a matter of some urgency I'd like to discuss with him."

"Anthony, I'm not sure if you know this, but Brett has been battling cancer for over a year now. He has fought valiantly but barring a miracle, he will be passing on to the next life very soon. He would not be up to a conversation right now, nor do I expect his condition to improve. I'm very sorry," she said.

Anthony was blown away. He'd heard nothing of this. "Uh, no, Sarah, I had no idea. I'm very sorry to disturb you during what must be a very trying time for you and your children. Please forgive me," he said, fishing just a little and hoping she would confirm or deny whether they had ever had children.

"That's quite alright. How could you have known? And it's just Brett and I. The good Lord never saw fit to bless us with children."

"I'm sorry to hear that," he said. "Well, you have my condolences and please extend them to Brett as well. There was a time during law school when we were almost inseparable, and Brett's courage in facing down this dreadful disease doesn't surprise me at all. It's too bad we drifted apart over the years," he added almost wistfully. "Listen, if his condition was to improve, and only if he felt up to it, I would appreciate an opportunity to speak with him."

"Yes, you said it was an urgent matter; is there something I can help you with?" she asked.

"No, but thank you," he responded. "Let me give you my number and please, if there's anything at all that I can do for you, don't hesitate to call," he said.

After providing his contact information he thanked her again and hung up. He rubbed at the headache that was building behind his eyes, completely bewildered by the combination of the note and the news of Brett's cancer. This is bad, he thought. If Brett dies without me having an opportunity to speak with him I may never know who it was he told. Though it was highly inappropriate for him to speak with anyone associated with the defendant other than counsel, he resolved right then to call Ms. McGrady that evening and find out what it was exactly that she wanted. Besides, given the circumstances what choice did he have?

He leaned back in his chair and sighed heavily. Somewhere he had read that a man who refuses to atone for his misdeeds will forever be haunted by the tortured, agonizing plea for absolution pinging incessantly from within his soul like moral sonar.

He was suddenly scared to death.

CHAPTER 8

Rose sat at a booth in a café across the street from the courthouse where she was waiting on a cup of coffee and a bagel she had just ordered. She gazed out at the light flurries falling lazily from the heavy, overcast sky. The arraignment had just ended and she was meeting Toby's attorney to discuss a very important matter. This would be only the second time they'd met since she'd hired him, and afterward she planned to visit Toby at the jail. She hadn't spoken to him in two days other than his one quick phone call a few hours after he'd been arrested and she was anxious to see him.

Despite the ugly, prison-issue jumpsuit he'd been wearing, she thought he had looked good at the hearing. It had been very difficult to sit there and see the way people were looking at him, though; the hate and the loathing so intense in their eyes. Of course, she felt sorry for those poor women in the courtroom and what they had been through, but she was convinced there was no way that her Toby had had anything to do with it. They simply had the wrong boy. She knew as surely as she knew her own name that Toby wasn't capable of committing such heinous crimes.

When her order number was called she went to pick it up at the counter and as she turned to walk back to her table, she found her path blocked by an older, heavy-set woman she thought she recognized from the courtroom. Standing to the side and slightly behind her was a young girl whose pretty face bore the deep lines of worry and fear that can only be understood by those who've witnessed firsthand man's insatiable capacity to visit evil upon another.

"You're that monster's mother, aren't you?" the woman said accusingly, as if this in itself was a crime punishable by death.

Rose was caught completely off guard and when she opened her mouth to respond, nothing came out.

"Aren't you!" the woman repeated, louder this time. With everyone in the café now watching this confrontation, Rose attempted to walk around her but the woman side-stepped to cut her off and thrust an angry finger into the middle of her chest.

"Tell me something," she said, her voice rising an octave. "What kind of a mother is it that raises a beast who goes sneaking around at night breaking into young girls' homes and violating them?"

Rose could feel the blood rushing to her cheeks partly out of embarrassment and partly out of anger, and she wanted to be anywhere right now but standing in front of this raving lunatic. She again attempted to walk around her and, again, the woman's large body blocked her path.

"Look at my daughter, you bitch!" she said loudly, pointing an angry finger in her daughter's general direction. "Look at what your filthy, disgusting, pig of a son has done to her!" she screamed, now feeding off of her own rage. "She doesn't sleep, she doesn't eat, she's afraid of her own shadow and she cries until there are no more tears to cry because of what that animal did to her." Her personal nightmare being aired in public was too much for the already-distraught girl, who collapsed sobbing into the nearest chair, burying her face in her hands.

"I'm . . . I'm sorry for what your daughter has been through," Rose started. "but . . ."

"You're sorry?" the woman said, leaning back with her hands on her hips and cocking her head as if she hadn't heard her correctly. "You're sorry? Your son rapes my daughter, robs her of her innocence, and all you can say is "You're sorry?" Well guess what? I'm sorry too. I'm sorry that you're such a sad-sack excuse for a mother that you raised a filthy rapist. I'm sorry that your . . ."

"Look!" Rose interrupted firmly, no longer embarrassed but now just angry at this unprovoked assault. "My son did *not* rape your daughter or any of those other women," she yelled back. "Just because a person is arrested doesn't make them automatically guilty. Now I am truly sorry for what your daughter and those other girls have been through, but don't you go judging my boy a rapist just because the police are using him as a scapegoat."

The woman paused for a moment and gave Rose a quizzical look, as if unsure of how to respond, and then suddenly and without warning, she slapped Rose hard across the face. Rose reeled back until she almost fell into the lap of a man sitting behind her, dropping her bagel as she fought for her balance. When she regained her footing she saw that the enraged woman was advancing on her, obviously prepared to deliver another slap - or worse.

Suddenly a man stepped between them and it took a split second for her to recognize that it was Brandon Hill.

"Stop it," he ordered, meeting the stare of the irate, red-faced woman. She stared back at him as if contemplating whether she'd suddenly found a new target for her rage, but finally she backed up a step.

"This may be none of my business but last time I checked, vigilante lynch mobs were illegal in this country," he said, maintaining strict eye contact with her. "Now I'm not going to pretend to know how angry you must be," he said, "nor can I begin to understand the horror that your daughter must have had to endure, but I do know that Ms. McGrady's son has only been arrested at this point, not convicted. His guilt or innocence will be left in the hands of a jury to decide – not you; and *only* after hearing all of the evidence."

After a brief pause he said, "And even if he *were* to be found guilty, which is highly unlikely," he added, only because he thought that's what he should say as Toby's attorney, "he's an adult and responsible for his own actions. Where do you get off blaming his mother?" he demanded. "Maybe I should advise Ms. McGrady to file assault charges against you so you can spend a few nights in jail and get a taste of what her son's going through right now. How does that sound?"

The woman was too angry to be overly concerned with this threat and she continued staring at him, as if considering whether or not to renew her assault. Someone on the far side of the café cleared their throat and it only served to emphasize how quiet the place had become. The other patrons were mesmerized by the drama being played out in front of them and no one wanted to miss a single word.

"He's the one," the woman finally spit out. "My daughter says she'd recognize them demon eyes anywhere. He's the one and I'll be sitting front and center when they convict that animal and send him away for the rest of his miserable life. You just wait and see," she said as she affected the look of a person who is perfectly comfortable within their own judgmental, self-righteous skin; even when it's stretched over a three hundred pound frame. And with that she gathered up her distraught daughter and started them both moving toward the door.

"Don't count on it," Rose spit right back at her.

"Oh, I'm counting on it, missy, and you can take that to the bank," her fat face huffed over her shoulder as they exited the café.

When the door closed Brandon lowered his arms which were still extended from when he had first stepped between them, and watched as Rose bent down to retrieve her bagel from the floor. She tossed it into a trashcan as he led her to an empty table amid the stares of everyone. This angered Brandon who turned around and said, "Don't you all think she's suffered enough indignity for one day? How about going back to whatever it was you were doing. How does that sound, huh?"

His admonishment caused most everyone to look away in embarrassment and return to their food, though most simply resorted to the occasional ill-disguised glance over their forks or newspapers.

"Thank you," Rose said when he had sat down across from her.

"My pleasure," he said with a slight grin. "Nosey people get on my nerves."

"No. I mean for putting that big-mouthed woman in her place. You didn't seem nearly as nervous then as you did in court a little while ago," she said, grinning at him slightly as she reached up to touch her cheek. It still burned from the slap.

"No problem," he said, grinning back. "On the one hand I feel sorry for what she's going through with her daughter, but on the other hand she had no right to attack you like she did."

"Well, thanks all the same."

"What was it you wanted to see me about?" he asked her.

"I don't really want to discuss it here," she said, aware of how people still had an ear cocked toward their table. "Can we go for a walk? I've lost my appetite anyway."

"Sure, let's go," he said, standing up and helping her with her coat.

They walked a few blocks down from the courthouse to a small city park that was popular in the summertime with the younger crowd of rollerbladers and skateboarders since most of the paths were paved. Right now, though, it was mostly deserted since the combination of winter and school kept the little daredevils away; winter probably more than school.

Brandon was quiet, giving her a chance to regroup as they walked slowly past a large fountain depicting a man that resembled Neptune, surrounded by four playful dolphins. It waited patiently for warmer weather until it could once again mesmerize onlookers with its majestic cascades of water. He stole a glance toward her and was struck by how beautiful she was. Her profile was perfectly proportioned with a small, upturned nose, full lips and high aristocratic cheek bones.

"Let me ask you something, Ms. McGrady: How did you come to hire me in the first place? I mean, I'm not exactly a household name in these parts, you know."

"First of all call me Rose, okay? You make me feel like I'm old or something," she said.

"Fair enough," he said, grinning sheepishly.

"I found you by calling the Indiana Bar Association and getting a list of attorneys who had passed the Bar within the last year. Then I narrowed it down to only those practicing in Monroe County. Did you know there are seventy-three of you?" she said, looking over at him.

"Seventy-three, huh?" he repeated, slightly amused. "So how did you come to choose me out of these seventy-three lawyers?"

"I liked your name the best. It sounded very upper-crust," she said matter-of-factly, as if everyone knows that that's how a person should choose their attorney.

"You liked my name?" He pondered this logic for a moment. "I'm still confused, though. Why choose anyone from that list? I mean, why would you want someone who has little to no experience? You have to know that your son is potentially in a lot of trouble, and regardless of whether or not he did anything wrong, you still have to convince a jury of that, right? I just can't figure out why you wouldn't have hired someone who's handled big cases like this before, that's all."

"I'll answer that when you answer a question for me, okay."

When he nodded she continued, "Why did it take you so long to pass the Bar exam? I mean, it's been almost four years since you graduated but you just passed it eleven months ago."

"My mother became very ill right around the same time I graduated," he began. "My father passed away a few years earlier and I'm an only child, so the responsibility of caring for her was left to me. Luckily my father had a hefty insurance policy so that allowed me to care of her full-time without having to work. When she died last year she left everything to me and I suppose with some wise investing and frugal spending I wouldn't have had to go to work, but I knew I'd be bored out of my mind so I decided to cram for the Bar and see if I was any good as an attorney."

"How old are you?" she asked him.

"I'll be thirty-five in a couple of months. Hello middle age," he said with a grin.

"That leaves some unaccounted years, though," she pointed out. "And by the way, it pisses me off that I'm older than you," she said, feigning indignation.

"I was in the Marine Corps for four years after high school, then it took me a year of college to figure out what it was I wanted to be when I grew up. See, all perfectly elucidate. And by the way, you look pretty good for an older woman," he said, grinning at her, though he knew she couldn't have him by more than maybe two or three years.

Ignoring him she said, "Do you mind me asking what your mother died of?"

"Cancer," he said softly.

"I'm very sorry," she said, struggling to maintain her composure.

"Thank you. Now I thought you were only supposed to ask me one question. I think you've managed to sneak in a couple of extras so now you have to answer mine. Why would you bother choosing anyone off of your list of wet-behind-the-ears, no-experience-havin' lawyers?" he pressed.

"Two reasons. The first is that you are a heck of a lot cheaper than a veteran lawyer, and I can't afford much right now. The second is that there isn't going to be a trial so the experience thing is moot. Oh, and there is one other thing: I was told to let you know that this case will probably jumpstart your career years ahead of most other attorneys with similar experience."

"Which basically amounts to no experience," he said. "Well, thanks for the vote of confidence, but I'm just as confused now as when we started this conversation. What do you mean there isn't going to be a trial? Do you know something I don't?" he asked her.

"My brother is an attorney, Brandon. He and a friend of his from law school, Jerry Brenner, have had their own practice for over twenty years."

"Brenner and Mitchell? I've heard of them. So why doesn't your brother represent Toby?"

She took a deep breath before responding. "Because he's dying of cancer," she said, looking off into the distance.

Brandon was floored. "I . . . I'm so sorry, Rose. I had no idea . . ."

"How could you," she said, dabbing at her eyes with the sleeve of her coat.

"You and he are close," he said, more a statement than a question.

"We lost our parents when I was very young and he's the only father figure I've known."

After giving her a moment he said, "I'm sorry for all that you are going through. I happen to have firsthand experience with it and it's a lot for anyone to have to cope with. If you ever want to talk - about anything . . ." He left the invitation hanging between them.

"Thank you, that means a lot to me."

"So tell me why you, or your brother anyway, doesn't think this case will go to trial."

"My brother, Brett's his name, reviewed the search warrant and concluded that it was served improperly."

"Improperly?"

"Yes. Are you familiar with the differences between *reasonable suspicion* and *probable cause* in the context of search warrants?" she asked him.

"Seeing as how I just passed the Bar exam a few months ago, and most of it's still fresh in my mind, I think I do," he said, a little embarrassed. "Probable cause is a more stringent standard than reasonable suspicion."

"Right, and do you know on what basis Toby's search warrant was issued?"

"Reasonable suspicion based on a tip from a neighbor, wasn't it?"

"Right again," she said. "And do you remember when they served it on him?"

"Uh, sometime after midnight, I believe."

"Actually, it was closer to one-thirty a.m.."

Suddenly Brandon stopped walking and turned to look at her, finally comprehending what she was saying. "And a warrant issued on the basis of "reasonable suspicion" can only be served in daylight hours," he exclaimed triumphantly.

"Exactly. At least that's the way Brett explained it to me. He also said that since they conducted their search at night, none of the evidence they claim to have would be admissible. Personally I don't believe they found anything, but since I do believe they're setting him up as a scapegoat, even something they may have planted would be inadmissible. They're stuck, and with no evidence there won't be a trial."

Brandon thought about this for a minute. "I don't know, Rose," he said, "we may have a tougher time getting that to fly than you think."

"Why is that?" she asked him.

"Because it isn't always as cut and dried as it may first appear. There are a number of things the defense could come back with. For instance, they could say that in their opinion they believed the suspect posed such a danger to the general public that they felt it was prudent to make an exception. The court does allow some discretion in extreme situations, and an argument like that could absolutely be allowed. I mean, let's be honest, there's a serial rapist out there somewhere. Now I'm not implying it was Toby but the public is terrified, and if they have strong evidence that points toward him then they are not going to be inclined to release him on a weak technicality. I don't want to burst your bubble but I wouldn't hold your breath on this. I haven't seen the evidence yet but the prosecution has to disclose everything to us and I should have it by this afternoon. I can tell you that the D.A. caught me in the hallway after the arraignment and told me that what they had was very damning and that he'd be expecting a phone call from me to discuss a plea bargain once I'd had a chance to review it."

"Don't count on it," Rose said as she turned and they began walking again.

"How can you be so certain?"

"I really don't want to get into all the details with you right now, Brandon, but Brett told me to instruct you to file an emergency petition today for a motion to dismiss based on police misconduct and lack of evidence. He said that the judge will hear it within a couple of days and he'll dismiss the case once you point out the problem with the search warrant. Then we'll all get to go home and resume our lives, and you'll be the hot new defense attorney in town for getting the trumped-up case against your client dismissed on a technicality."

Brandon took her arm and turned her toward him, searching her eyes with his.

"Is this on the up and up, Rose? I mean, how can you be so sure the judge will see things our way?"

"Because Toby didn't do this, Brandon, and since I know he didn't do it I know that whatever the evidence is they claim to have against him, it has to be fabricated. Because of this, I'm convinced they would never get a conviction even if it went to trial. All I'm trying to do is save everyone a lot of time and money and get it over with sooner rather than later. My brother knows this judge from way back and he has assured me that he's as fair as they come and that he'll let common sense prevail. Just trust him, Brandon. File the petition today, okay?"

"Alright, I'll get it filed and we'll see what happens, but I still say you shouldn't count your chickens so soon. You could be setting yourself up for a huge disappointment."

Rose's cell phone began to ring and as she searched her purse she said, "Just file it, Brandon. It'll all work out, you'll see."

"Hello?" she said into the phone. "Yes, Sarah. Oh . . . um . . . how bad? Okay, I'm leaving right now and I'll be there as fast as I can." She hung up and gave Brandon a worried look. "I'm sorry but I have to go. My brother's not doing well and I need to be there with him. Can you do me a favor and stop in at the jail and tell Toby that I will visit him tomorrow, please? He's expecting me within an hour and he'll be worried sick if I don't show up."

"Sure. No problem," he said. "Listen, I hope your brother is okay. Are you alright to drive or do you want me to get you a cab?"

"No, I'll be fine. Thank you for your help and please don't forget to tell Toby, okay?" She reached up and gave him a quick peck on the cheek and began hurriedly walking back toward the courthouse parking lot. "I'll call you tomorrow," she called over her shoulder.

Brett watched as she walked away, his cheek tingling where her lips had been a moment before. She seems like an honest person who adores her brother and has a blind loyalty to her son, he thought. And she's beautiful to boot. So why then, he asked himself as he shoved his hands in his pockets and began heading to his car, do I feel like there's something smelly in Denmark?

CHAPTER 9

Rose's first glance at Brett caused her to suck in her breath sharply. He lay on his back with his eyes closed; his gray, ashen skin and sunken cheeks combined to give him a corpse-like appearance. I'm too late, she thought, sagging against the doorjamb. Thankfully it was short-lived, though, as Brett slowly opened his eyes and turned his head toward her, offering a smile.

"You look like you saw a ghost," he said weakly.

"You scared the hell out of me," she said, straightening up. "You were so still and I thought . . ." she couldn't finish the sentence.

"You women aren't getting rid of me that easily," he said. "Can you come over here and raise me up, please?" It was obvious he was laboring each time he spoke.

"Don't say stupid things like that," she said, walking unsteadily across the room to raise his bed. "I know you think it's funny but it's not."

"Sorry."

"Well, you should be," she said, still trying to recover from the initial shock of seeing him like that. After raising him to a semi-sitting position she spent a couple of minutes busying herself with the numerous medicine bottles on his nightstand, letting him think she was pouting. Finally she said, "Sarah tells me you've had a rough day."

"I've had better ones," he said. "The pain's almost constant lately."

"I'm sorry, Brett," she said, taking his hand in hers. "I'm so sorry." Tears filled her eyes.

"Don't cry, Rosie," he said. "You're going to make me cry and I'm too tired to cry."

"I . . .," she stumbled for the words. "I just hate this, Brett. You of all people don't deserve it."

"Even after what I told you?" he asked, watching her face.

"Not even after what you told me, silly-boy. That was a long long time ago and you were young. Besides, I have no doubt the guilt you've lived with all these years has been a punishment far worse than that which any court would have ever meted out. You are a good man, Brett. The best I've ever known. You've been the only father-figure I've ever had in my life."

"Thanks, Rosie. That means a lot to me."

"You've always been my hero. Nothing will ever change that."

He gave her an embarrassed look. "So tell me what happened at the arraignment."

Rose wiped her eyes with a tissue. "Everything happened pretty much as you said it would. He pleaded not guilty and the judge denied bail."

"How was Toby?"

"He looked good," she said, her face brightening considerably. The orange jumpsuits aren't very flattering but he seemed to be in good spirits. He smiled when he saw me."

"That's nice. Did you get the note to the bailiff?"

"Yes, I'm hoping he'll call."

"He'll call. And you told your attorney to file the motion to dismiss?"

"Yes, I explained to him your reasoning but he said he didn't think it would be as easy as we thought."

"Under normal circumstances it wouldn't be but, of course, he isn't aware of our ace-in-the-hole," he said, looking at her. "He's not, right?"

"No, of course not," she said. "He was definitely fishing, though."

"Let him fish," he said dismissively. "Do you know what you're going to say when Anthony calls?"

"I think so. I've been rehearsing it in my mind ever since we spoke about it."

"Don't get cold feet, Rose. This is your best chance to get Toby released. Even if you're convinced he's innocent, a jury trial with something like this is always a crapshoot. You don't want to take the chance, believe me."

"I'll pull it off, don't worry."

"That's my girl," he responded, grimacing as fiery tendrils of pain shot through his stomach.

"How are you two doing?" Sarah asked as she entered the room. "Can I get you something to drink, Rose?"

"Some tea would actually be great, Sarah, thank you," she said.

"Coming right up," she said, reaching around her for Brett's water pitcher. "I'll fill this up while I'm at it, Sweetie." she said, bending over to plant a kiss on his mouth. "Need a squeeze?" she asked him. When he nodded she reached over and gave his morphine ball two full squeezes. The time to be concerned about administering too much was long past. His time was drawing near and they both knew it.

"She and I should have had more time together," Brett said when Sarah had left the room again.

"I know."

"Rosie?"

"Yeah?"

"I want to say something and I don't want you to get mad at me, okay."

"He didn't, Brett."

"What?"

"That's what you want to ask me, right; what if Toby really raped those women?"

He looked at her for a moment. "How do you know for sure?"

"Because I just know, okay? Call it a mother's intuition. I mean, don't you think I would know if my only child was prowling the streets at night attacking women in their sleep?"

"I'm not saying you're wrong, Rose, but let me ask you something: What if you use what I told you to get Toby off the hook and you find out later that he really was guilty?" he asked. "Can you honestly tell me you haven't thought about that?"

Of course she had thought about it. She'd hated herself for it afterwards but she had definitely thought about it. Toby had become more aloof since moving out on his own a year ago and he would sometimes go for two weeks or more without calling her or stopping by. There was no disputing that he had always assigned the lion's share of the blame to her for the divorce, and then later for his father disappearing without so much as a goodbye, but the tension between them had seemed to get better as he got older, and the last couple of years they had managed to avoid even talking about it. She assumed he had simply matured and moved past it.

"If I don't believe in my son, who will?" she said, with an anguished look on her face.

"I understand, but I've been thinking about this and I want you to do one thing for me before you talk to Anthony. I want you to go see Toby, and I want you to look him straight in the eye and ask him if he raped those women. If he tells you he didn't and you honestly believe him, then do what we talked about and protect your son. But if you have any doubts about him, Rosie, any at all, then you need to think long and hard before you put your neck on the line, because whoever it is that's attacking these women, he's evil and needs to be locked up in a cage like the animal he is."

She considered this. "Alright, Brett. I'll go see him if it will ease your mind, but only because you asked. I know he's innocent."

"Thank you," he said, closing his eyes.

"Here you go, guys," Sarah said as she returned with their drinks.

"Thanks," Rose said as she took the glass from her.

"How did it go in court today with Toby?" Sarah asked Rose.

"So far so good. I'm actually getting ready to leave to go see him. It shouldn't take too long and then I'll come right back to help you nurse tough-guy here back to health. He's not looking all that energetic today," she said.

Brett gave no indication that he heard her. His breathing was very shallow and the rise and fall of his frail chest was almost imperceptible beneath the sheet. She and Sarah looked at each other and their faces confirmed what the other was thinking.

"Are you sure you have to leave right now?" Sarah asked her.

"Believe me, if I hadn't promised to do something I wouldn't." She then stepped close to Sarah and said in a whisper "We're losing him, aren't we?"

"I'm afraid we are. I honestly don't think he's going to make it through the night, Rose. Please hurry back, okay?"

"I will, I promise." Bending down, she gave Brett a kiss on his forehead and told him she loved him, pausing momentarily for a sign he'd heard her. After a heart wrenching few seconds in which she found herself holding her breath, he opened his eyes slowly and looked at her.

"Go do this, Rosie, but then hurry back," he said softly, winking at her as he had done for as long as she could remember.

She nodded then stood up, flashing a nervous smile to Sarah. "I'll be back as soon as I can." She then grabbed her coat and hurried down the stairs. When she got outside the house she felt like screaming. Everything was happening too fast, dammit! If the judge was calling her any day but today she wouldn't have to leave Brett just so she could go see Toby and confirm what she already knew. She jumped in her car and sped off, and after calling Brandon to inform him that he didn't need to go see Toby after all, she began to wonder what it was going to be like to talk to her son through four inches of bulletproof glass.

CHAPTER 10

Sarah pulled a chair over so she could sit and watch him as he lay quietly resting. Loving him as she'd always loved him; deeply and completely.

When the doctors had first sent him home with her she had known in the back of her mind that at some point she'd have to deal with not having him around any longer, but it had always been tomorrow, never today, and the fact was that she had simply avoided dealing with it. But suddenly tomorrow *was* today and she was terrified. She leaned back and closed her eyes, trying to squeeze back the tears that had seemed to be almost constant the past two days.

"Why are you crying?"

When she opened her eyes again she saw him looking at her, the concern clear on his face, and it wasn't lost on her that although he was the one dying, he still found the strength to be worried about her.

"I'm crying because I miss you," she said, no longer even trying to avoid what they both already knew.

He slid his thin arm toward her, inviting her hand into his. She took it and could almost feel his strength draining away.

"I'm not gone yet, freckle face," he said, using the nickname he'd given her years ago because of the cute smattering of freckles she had on both of her cheeks. They had faded over the winter months but they would darken considerably come summer.

"You're not fighting anymore."

"Oh, that." He gave her a small, wistful grin. "Well, it was all posturing anyway. We knew the ending half way through the movie, didn't we?" He grimaced and closed his eyes tightly for what seemed like a long time and she reached across him to give the ball three hard squeezes. She hated the evil thing inside him that asked no quarter and gave none.

"Your bravery is amazing, Brett. I can't begin to tell you how much I respect that quality in you," she said, waiting for him to relax again as the infusion of morphine, the anti-C as he sometimes called it, worked its magic. He had beads of sweat on his forehead and upper lip, and she wiped them off gently with a tissue.

"I'm not brave, Rose," he said. "I have no idea what's next and that scares the hell out of me."

She said nothing, knowing the living were pitifully ill-equipped to offer any reassurances where death was concerned.

"I don't think I'm going to make it until Rose gets back."

"I know," she said, crying openly now.

"She'll be mad at me."

"I think she'll understand."

"I tried to be there for her."

"You were. She adores you."

"In a thousand lifetimes I couldn't have found a better mate than you to share my life with."

"Brett . . ."

"No more talking, Sarah," he said, his hand tightening its grip on hers.

She leaned over and placed her lips softly against his mouth, her tears cascading from her cheeks onto his, concluding their journey at his pillow. She didn't know when it was exactly that he had stopped squeezing her hand but at some point she had released it and placed her hands on his shoulders, laying her head on his now still chest. She knew she should call Rose but she felt an urgent need to absorb the last remnants of warmth still emanating from him. She was thankful his suffering had come to an end but his death was so much worse than anything she could have ever imagined.

Another hour passed before she could bear to separate herself from him and finally place the call to Rose.

CHAPTER 11

Rose's conversation with Toby had gone pretty much as she'd expected. After signing in, having her purse pawed through and being unnecessarily delayed while two cretin guards ogled her, she was led to a small cubicle with a chair and a shelf about twelve inches wide jutting out from the wall. Just like on TV they sat across from one another, separated by glass and communicating through dirty, red phones mounted on the wall next to them.

There'd been small talk about things like the food (disgusting) and living conditions (severely inadequate in his opinion). She'd asked him how he was being treated and he told her he was like a celebrity but for all the wrong reasons. Everyone wanted to see the guy who was supposed to be the French Lick rapist. Rose saw this as her opportunity.

"Toby, I'm going to ask you something that will probably hurt your feelings and I only hope that you can forgive me?" she said.

Toby studied her for a moment. "You're not really going to ask me if I did it, are you?"

Rose felt horrible; like she was betraying her only child, but she had promised Brett so she forged on.

"I have to know, Toby. I need you to look me in the eye and tell me you had nothing to do with hurting those girls."

"I don't believe this," he said, looking up at the ceiling. "My own mother..."

"I'm sorry, sweetie, but I need to hear it from you."

Toby continued to show his indignation, but the fact was he had been expecting this.

"I had absolutely nothing to do with it, okay?" he said, holding her eyes unflinchingly. "You know me better than that. Do you really think I spend my free time casing women's homes so I can sneak in and rape them?"

Rose smiled at him. "No, Toby, I don't, and I'm sorry I have to put you through this, but I just needed to hear it from your own mouth."

He sighed. "I guess I understand. Hell, if you believe everything the police have been saying you could just lock me away forever and not even bother with a trial."

"I know. I'm sorry. Your Uncle Brett and I have been spending a lot of time talking about how to get these trumped up charges against you dismissed. We've come up with a very good strategy and I'm confident you'll be out of here within a couple of days. How does that sound?" she asked him, excited to have positive news for him.

Toby thought about it for a minute. "It sounds great, but how are you going to do it? I mean, we both know the charges are bogus, but how are we going to avoid having to go through a trial?"

"I don't want you to worry about that right now, Toby. Just trust me and everything will work out, okay?" Brett had warned her that conversations on these phones were not considered privileged information and, as such, were most likely being recorded so she should avoid getting into any detail. And he had also made her promise that other than the problem with the search warrant, which would be brought out in court, she was never to reveal to Toby the details of how they had affected his release.

"We're talking about my freedom here, Mom," Toby said. "Don't you think I have a right to know how I'm going to keep it?"

"Listen, Toby, I can tell you this much: Tomorrow Brandon, uh, Mr. Hill, is going to file a motion to have the charges against you dropped. There's a problem with the search warrant and that's really all I can tell you right now. Don't worry, though, everything is going to work out. I promise," she reassured him.

"If you say so," he said.

"I say so," she responded, smiling sweetly at him.

After they had said their goodbyes Toby was escorted back to his cell where he sat on his bed and thought about their conversation. If what his mother had told him was true, he should be getting out of this hellhole before the week was out. It was a good thing too, because he was getting claustrophobic sitting around like a goddamn monkey in a zoo.

෴

Rose was pulling out of the parking garage across from the jail when her cell phone rang. She saw B. Mitchell in the display and stared at it as her eyes filled with tears.

CHAPTER 12

"How are you holding up, Sarah?"

After spending the last hour saying a private good bye to her brother, Rose had returned downstairs to find Sarah nursing a cup of tea at the kitchen table. "Oh, hi, Rose," she said, looking up at her. "I'm hanging in there. They said they'd be here in a couple of hours to pick him up. Is that okay with you? I didn't know how much time you wanted to spend with him."

"No, that's fine. Do we need to pick out a suit to send with them?"

"I laid it out in the family room earlier today," she said, looking slightly embarrassed. "I just had a feeling, you know."

"I know."

"Can I get you some tea? I'm sorry I didn't ask you earlier but I didn't want to disturb you."

"Oh, that's okay, I can get it," Rose said, just as her phone rang. She thought about ignoring it but then remembered the call she was expecting.

"Hello?"

"Yes, Ms. McGrady?"

"Yes, this is she," Rose said, motioning to Sarah that she was going to take it in the other room.

"This is Judge Anthony Scalini. I received your note earlier today and I'm contacting you per your request." After a slight hesitation he said, "Ma'am, I'm obligated to tell you that this is highly inappropriate given the circumstances. Should anyone other than us know about this I would be forced to recuse myself from your son's case immediately."

"I'm aware of that, Mr. Scalini." Just as Brett had advised her, she intentionally avoided using his title in an effort to keep the psychological playing field level. "But what do you say we avoid discussing the issue of inappropriateness until we've had an opportunity to agree on an acceptable definition, shall we?"

"Alright . . ." he said, not sure what she was getting at but willing to go along until he had some idea as to what it was that she wanted with him.

"Your note said you wanted to meet."

"Yes, that's right," she said. "Unfortunately now is really a bad time. Later this evening would be much better; say about ten p.m.?"

"That's pretty late, Ms. McGrady. Can't this wait until sometime tomorrow morning?"

"No, no it can't. It's very important that we meet this evening, and ten is probably the earliest I can make it."

"Very well," he conceded. "Do you have some place in mind?"

"Yes, I thought we could meet at the Brandywine shopping center in the parking lot of Craig's grocery store."

"In the parking lot?"

"Yes. It's imperative we meet someplace where we can speak privately. However, I recognize that you may be reluctant to meet anywhere that's deserted so I thought this would be an acceptable compromise. Do you agree?"

"I don't suppose I have a choice, do I?" he asked her.

"Not really. Believe me, this will be quick and painless and then we can both move on with our lives, okay?"

"How will I find you?"

"I'll be driving a white Taurus and I'll park all the way in the rear of the lot. When you find me park so your driver's side is next to mine, this way we can talk without either of us having to get in the other's vehicle."

"Very well, Ms. McGrady. I'll see you at ten o'clock then."

Rose hung up and exhaled sharply. The first part was over and she was proud of how well she'd maintained her composure. Then again, she supposed the fact that she had just lost the most important person in her life next to her son was serving to provide at least some perspective. Whatever it was, she was determined to see this through tonight, but right now she needed to get back to Sarah.

CHAPTER 13

The heater ran on high as Rose sat behind the wheel of her car waiting for the judge to arrive. Just as she'd told him, she parked at the rear of the lot, far from the attention of the steady stream of late night shoppers and the bright lights intended to make them feel safe. She was twenty minutes early and if it weren't for the butterflies in her stomach from the anticipation of the meeting, she could have fallen asleep where she sat. It had been a hell of a day and she was as mentally exhausted as she could ever remember being.

Prior to the mortuary personnel arriving she had called the jail and asked to speak with Toby. When a rude guard sarcastically reminded her that her son was incarcerated for rape, not over at a friend's house for a slumber party and that no, she could not just call and speak with him whenever the urge struck her, she lowered the phone to her side and closed her eyes, willing herself to exercise patience with this insufferable moron since he had access to her son and would probably enjoy any reason to make his life miserable.

When she was fairly certain she wouldn't bite his head off she put the phone back to her ear and explained to him that she wanted to inform Toby of a death in their family. Obviously the guard had taken many of these calls over the years and was unmoved. He told her she could either tell him who had died and he'd pass it on, or she could wait and tell Toby herself tomorrow during visiting hours. Imagining the callousness with which this jerk would deliver the news, she told him she'd wait, thanked him and hung up. Now here she was waiting to talk to the man who, if everything went according to plan, was going to set her son free.

A few minutes later a large Cadillac judging by the familiar-looking shape of the hood ornament rolled slowly past her and she could see the dark silhouette of the driver looking in her direction. The car drove on maybe another fifty feet before making a u-turn, and this time when it approached, it pulled in so that both driver's side windows were within a couple of feet of each other. Rose rolled hers down and held her breath as she waited for him to do likewise. He did and finally she was face-to-face with Judge Anthony Scalini. She was somewhat comforted to see that he looked as nervous as she felt.

"Ms. McGrady?"

"Yes," Rose confirmed.

"I'm Judge Scalini, but I guess you probably assumed that." He was struck by how pretty she was in spite of the deep etchings of stress on her face.

"Let's keep this as informal as we can under the circumstances and dispense with the titles, okay? Rose said. "How about if you call me Rose and I'll call you Anthony?'

"Very well," Anthony said. "So why are we meeting here, Rose; in this fashion, I mean?"

She took a deep breath to steady herself. "My son has been arrested for something he didn't do, Anthony, and although

I know this, I'm not interested in trying to convince an impassioned jury of it. Therefore, I need to ensure there isn't a trial."

"Ms. McGrady, uh, Rose, as I told you on the phone earlier, this is highly . . ."

". . . inappropriate." Rose finished for him. "I know that. Unfortunately there's no other way."

"Look," he continued, "even if your son is innocent, and I'm sure as his mother you believe that to be true, the law is a process. Once a person has been arrested and subsequently charged, the case has to be brought to some conclusion either through a conviction or a finding of innocence. A person cannot be set free simply because someone outside of that process believes them to be innocent. Surely you must understand the logic of this," he said, studying her to see if what he was saying was getting through."

"Anthony, you and I will get along much better if you don't patronize me, okay?" She stared hard at him and was encouraged to see him flinch slightly at her admonishment. "I'm not an idiot and I'm not some distraught mother who's lost her mind with grief. I happen to be well aware of the judicial process. However, in your encapsulated explanation of due process you left out one potential conclusion."

"What's that?"

"The one where the case is simply dismissed and everyone gets to go home."

"Yes, that is a valid scenario as well, but in your son's case there are no grounds for such a ruling." he said, somewhat exasperated. "I haven't seen the evidence myself but from what I know, the State has a very strong case against him. There's not a Judge in the country who would dismiss this case under the circumstances."

"Well, you're wrong there, Anthony," she said, "because you're going to dismiss it."

He just looked at her, remembering her note. "Rose, I couldn't dismiss it even if I agreed with you which, for the record, I don't. All that would happen if I tried is that I would be yanked off the case while I was being investigated for misconduct and another judge would replace me and send the case to trial anyway. Given this, I don't know what you expect me to do."

Rose ignored him and continued. "You're going to receive a petition for a motion to dismiss tomorrow. The issue is the search warrant. It was issued based on reasonable suspicion, not probable cause, and therefore could not be served at night. In this case it was served around one a.m., which means that anything they took from Toby's apartment, or more likely planted there," she said angrily. "is inadmissible. Therefore, the State will have no choice but to drop all charges due to a lack of evidence," she concluded.

He paused to consider what she had said. "I hate to be the one to break this to you, but that isn't going to work, Rose. The court is given broad discretion with these types of issues and given the serious nature of the charges, the State will have no problem justifying what time they served the warrant. I'm sorry but I'd be laughed off the bench if I dismissed this case based on that argument."

Rose looked at him hard. "Then you'd better grow some tough skin, Anthony, because I'm afraid you're going to have to endure some heckling. I assume you remember that I mentioned something about a girl in my note, right?" she tested him.

Here it comes, he thought. "Yes, I remember," he said, his heart racing. He forced himself to not say anything more until he could figure out what, if anything, she knew about that night.

"What do you think it would do to your career if that got out?" she asked him. "Actually, I'm guessing your career would be the least of your worries."

"I'm not sure what you're getting at," he said hesitantly.

"Oh, I think you know exactly what I'm getting at. As a matter of fact, I imagine you probably see that poor girl's face every night when you lay down and close your eyes."

She knew. Anthony was stunned and it was obvious by the look of disbelief on his face. "How did you find out?" he asked her in a voice barely above a whisper. He was too ashamed to meet her eyes.

"Does it matter?"

"Yes," he said simply.

She considered whether to answer and decided that with Brett's passing it really didn't matter any longer. "McGrady is my ex-husband's last name. I kept it so I would have the same last name as my son. My maiden name is actually Mitchell. Does that ring a bell for you?"

Of course it did. "You're related to Brett Mitchell?" he asked her. The surprise was apparent on his face.

"I'm his sister."

He thought about this. "But how can that be? He and I were inseparable for almost three years and he never told me had a sister," he said skeptically.

"Oh, I can assure you I'm very much his sister. Brett and I have had our share of family misfortune and he's always been very private and protective where that's concerned, which would probably explain why he never mentioned me."

"I spoke to his wife before I called you. Sarah, I think. I was attempting to speak with Brett to find out about the note I had received from you, but his wife told me he was dying of cancer."

"He's not dying any longer," she said. "He passed away earlier today, which was why I couldn't meet you until now."

He could see the pain creeping onto her face. "I'm terribly sorry," he said.

"Thank you but my grief is selfish. He was in a lot of pain and I have no right to mourn the end of his suffering. He's better off where he is now."

"How much did Brett tell you about that night?" he probed.

"Everything."

He thought about this before continuing. "Rose, assuming you are planning on using this information to blackmail me, I'm going to need to be convinced that you actually know what happened. That is what you're doing, right? Blackmailing me?"

"If it comes to that, yes. Of course, you can simply tell me you'll grant our motion to dismiss and we can both go home," she said.

"I think you know I can't do that so please tell me what Brett told you."

"Alright. In a nutshell he told me you both had left a party after drinking too much, and on the way home you ran down and killed a young girl on some back road out in the country. Then, instead of doing the right thing and notifying the police and her family, you decided to simply get rid of the body. Does that sound about right?" she asked him.

Though he'd had to live every day with this dark memory, hearing a stranger recount the horrible thing he had done all those years ago was almost unbearable. He gripped the steering wheel tightly and leaned his forehead against the back of his hands as Rose watched him. The truth was, if she had forgiven Brett for this one error in judgment made at such a young age, how could she not forgive him as well?

"Anthony, this isn't easy for either of us and I want you to know that I'm not proud of what I'm doing. I recognize that Brett was also with you that night and, in fact, was the one driving the car. However, I can only be concerned with my son right now, so this is the way it has to be. I'm truly sorry."

Anthony sat up and took a deep breath. "Rose, I've been thinking about it all day and though I understand why you are doing this, I'm afraid I'm going to have to decline participation. You see, Brett is the one who got rid of the girl that night. Granted I helped put her in the trunk of his car, but he dropped me off at the campus before hiding her body. Not even I know where she is. There's no way you could prove any of it."

Rose had been expecting this. "That's a good theory, Anthony, and one I'm sure you've consoled yourself with over the years, but it's not entirely true. You see, Brett told me where he put her."

"Even if he did, and I doubt it, there's no way to prove that I had anything at all to do with her death. All you would have is a body," he pointed out. "I'm sorry to have to say this but with Brett's passing you don't even have a witness."

She was prepared for this as well. "Whatever happened to your college class ring, Anthony?"

The question confused him. "What do you mean?"

"I mean, where is your college class ring; the one you were wearing that night?"

"I'm not sure," he said. "I lost track of that years ago. To tell you the truth I have no idea what became of it. Why?"

"You didn't lose it, Anthony. After you two put the girl in the trunk and started back to campus, you saw that you had blood on your hands and you cleaned them with the handy-wipes Brett kept in his glove box. Do you remember that?"

"Yes, I think so."

"Well, according to Brett, you were so concerned with wiping away every tiny speck that you apparently took off your ring and set it in the center console compartment. Do you remember doing that?"

"I couldn't say for sure, but where are you going with this?"

"Brett also said that you were very distraught that night and although you had finally agreed with his plan to get rid of the girl, he didn't necessarily trust that you would be able to stay quiet about it. He felt he needed some insurance." Anthony didn't say anything and though he had a feeling he wasn't going to like where this was going, nothing could have prepared him for the bombshell she dropped on him.

"When Brett dropped you off you remembered your ring, but when you looked for it you couldn't find it. He told you it had probably fallen under one of the seats and that he'd look for it the next day. Do you remember that?"

"Yes, now that you remind me I do remember that. If I'm not mistaken that was the last time I saw it."

"It was, but you didn't drop your ring, Anthony, Brett picked it up when you weren't paying attention and when he hid the girl's body he put your ring in one of her pockets."

Anthony was stunned to silence and his heart threatened to pound its way out of his chest cavity as he tried to get his mind around what she'd just said.

"He wanted me to tell you that he never intended to use it, but he felt better knowing he could if he needed to."

Anthony had seen hundreds of people testify in court, and as he watched her he had no doubt that she was telling the truth.

"This will ruin my career, you know," he stated matter-of-factly. "Does that matter to you? I know what I did was wrong but your brother was right there with me. Why do I have to pay the price for it alone after all these years?"

"Because my son could go to prison for the rest of his life and I can't let that happen, that's why."

"Your son could be guilty, Rose. He could actually be the one who raped those women. Did you ever think about that?"

"He's innocent," she said unwaveringly.

"I don't deserve this."

"Did that girl deserve to die like that?"

He just looked at her. There was obviously no way he could justify what they had done and he wasn't even going to try. Maybe he was wrong and did deserve this after all.

"I have to go," she said. "You'll get the petition tomorrow morning so please call the hearing quickly and get the State to dismiss the charges. Again, I'm sorry it's come to this but there's simply no other way." With that she started the car and looked over at him one more time as she pulled away, but he was staring off in the distance and didn't notice.

CHAPTER 14

Toby looked at her with alarm. "What do you mean he died? What about getting me out of here?"

After possibly the single-most stressful day of Rose's life, she had gotten up early to be at the jail as soon as visiting hours started, which today was nine a.m. She was excited to be able to give him the good news about the hearing but, unfortunately, she also had to tell him about his Uncle and she decided to break the bad news to him first. To say that she was shocked by his inappropriate and somewhat disturbing reaction would have been an understatement.

"Toby, I just told you your Uncle passed away and this is how you respond; thinking only of yourself?" she scolded him. "He treated you better than your own father did, so maybe you should forget about yourself for a second and show some respect. He was an incredibly positive influence in your life."

"I'm sorry, Mom," he said, instantly contrite. "It's just that this whole thing is freaking me out. You know, having handcuffs slapped on you in the middle of the night and being locked up here for the last four days . . . it's just hard. I'm sorry."

"Okay," she said, just wanting to change the subject. "I also wanted to let you know that there's going to be an emergency hearing called so the judge can rule on the petition I told you we were filing this morning."

"Does this have something to do with the problem with the search warrant you were telling me about?"

"Yes, and it's going to get you out of here, Honey, just like I told you."

"That's fantastic. When do you think the hearing will be?" he asked.

"Probably tomorrow, but it could be as early as today. Just hang in there and before you know it you'll be on your way home where you belong, okay? Oh, and Brandon will be coming to see you later today just to explain how everything will work procedurally."

"Great."

They spent another ten minutes making small talk before she had to leave to go meet Brandon. Once she was gone Toby was escorted back to his cell, this time by an overweight guard whose wrinkled and sweat-stained uniform made him look like ten pounds of shit stuffed into a five-pound bag.

"I heard what you and your mommy was talking about back there, asshole, and you're crazy if you think you're going anywhere but up North to the State pen for the rest of your miserable life," the guard said to him. "They just love rapists there, too. Oh yeah, you're gonna get a real hero's welcome. You'll be bending over for twelve inches of black pipe before you've had a chance to say Ku Klux Klan," he said, laughing menacingly like a schoolyard bully.

By this time they were back at his cell and Toby sat on his bed and tried to ignore the obnoxious moron who was still standing in the doorway. "As a matter of fact," the guard continued, "maybe I'll let one of them big bucks come visit you tonight just to give you a little taste of what you have to look forward to for the next forty years or so. Kinda break you in, if you know what I mean."

Toby stood up and walked nonchalantly across the cell until he was face-to-face with him. "Let me tell you something, Hennessey, you fat piece-of-shit," he said in a voice low enough that it could not be heard by anyone else. He'd read his name off the tag pinned crookedly to his filthy uniform. "I don't give a rat's ass what you think, because I *am* getting out of here. And you better hope like hell that nothing happens to me between now and the time I'm released because if anything does, you better grow eyes in the back of that fat melon of yours because one night when you're leaving your shitty little apartment, or leaving this shitty little jail or just leaving the shitty little gay bath house where you hang out with your shitty little fat, gay friends, I'm going to be there, and then maybe it'll be me and you who's acting out a sequel to Deliverance. Now get the hell out of my cell and you better pray I don't get bit by so much as a mosquito tonight."

The guard's cocky smile all but disappeared and had been replaced by one of fear. It wasn't that other inmates hadn't threatened him because they had - many times - but no one had ever looked so goddamned eager to follow through with it. Without saying another word he backed out of the door, locked it and returned to his station. He suddenly needed to take a leak real bad.

CHAPTER 15

"Have you seen this?"

Michael Haas, District Attorney for Marion County, looked up from his paperwork long enough to see his overly excitable Assistant DA, Jay Krump, walking through the door waving some papers. "If that's the emergency petition from the McGrady case, yes, I've seen it. My secretary just brought it in and informed me that McGrady's attorney filed it first thing this morning."

"What do you make of it?" Jay asked, clearly flustered.

"I don't make anything of it; it's saber rattling. Though I have to admit it was a good catch by that rookie lawyer," he said with some admiration. "I'm shocked he picked up on such a small technicality. He isn't going to get anywhere with it but it was a good catch just the same."

"It's legit, though, right?" Jay said. "I mean, about the restriction on when the warrant should have been served? How do we justify serving it at night?"

"Look," Michael said, "thirteen women were raped over nine months, and the last one is still in a coma from the beating she got from this pervert; at least the last one that we know about anyway. We found a ski mask and black leather gloves in his apartment, as well as all the usual accoutrements used by people who make a habit of breaking into homes that don't belong to them. And we have our smoking gun, which is the shirt we found with the last victim's blood all over it, for Christ's sake. Make no mistake about it, Jay, we have our boy, and considering the condition we found that last girl in, justifying what time we served the warrant will be a piece of cake. The court has discretion in something like this and this guy needed to be taken off the street, so there's no way in hell that horny toad is walking out of jail. I'll be surprised if the hearing takes fifteen minutes."

"That's a relief," Jay exhaled. "I thought we were in for it."

Of course you did, Michael thought. *If you were any greener you'd be a shrub.* Jay had less than one year of experience as the Assistant DA as opposed to Michael's four years as an Assistant DA, and now seven years as the DA, and his inexperience made him prone to moments of high excitability. He was very relieved to see that his boss did not appear to be the least bit worried about this newest development.

"As a matter of fact," Michael continued, "we need to get the judge to approve our request to draw a blood sample from this cretin so we can match his DNA to the semen samples we were able to collect from some of the other women. It was frustrating we couldn't get a match from our database, but what odds do you give me on us getting a match this time?" he asked with a confident smile.

"So you're sure it's him?"

"As sure as where a bear shits. And look at the bright side, after we put him away the women in our community will only have ninety-nine demented sex perverts to worry about every time they go out at night instead of the usual one hundred," he said, allowing his cynicism to rear its head.

"The hearing is set for tomorrow morning," Jay informed him.

"Tomorrow morning?" Michael repeated. "I wonder why the judge is so hot and heavy to rule on this?" he wondered aloud. "Well, we'll be there, that's for sure. Have the juror notices gone out yet?" he asked. "We have less than two weeks to sit one so we need to move on it quickly."

"They went out yesterday so we can probably start selection on Monday. Anything special you need me to do to prepare for the hearing tomorrow?"

"No, just have the clerks do the usual as far as pulling the most recent applicable case law, and make sure our request to draw blood from perv-boy is tabled for the hearing as well. Other than that, it'll be a walk in the park. Trust me," he said with a wink.

CHAPTER 16

Rose was already ten minutes late when she arrived at the Carter Hotel so she decided to spend the five bucks and let them valet her car. When she walked in she spotted Brandon sitting on the other side of the atrium talking into his cell phone and by the time she navigated her way over to him he flipped his phone closed, stood up and smiled at her. "Hi, Rose. It's good to see you again." *God, she's beautiful.*

"You too, Brandon," she said, hoping he felt as foolish as she did.

After an awkward moment where neither knew whether to hug, peck each other on the cheek or shake hands, Brandon leaned forward stiffly at the waist and gave her a squeeze that, of course, caused another moment of awkwardness. Finally, he asked her how Toby was doing.

"Oh, he's doing real good," she said, happy the moment was past. "He's very excited about the upcoming hearing." Suddenly a wave of sadness washed over her face. "I didn't mention it to you this morning but my brother passed away yesterday, so I had to break that news to him as well. So I guess all-in-all it was kind of a bittersweet visit," she concluded. He could see that she was managing to keep her emotions in check, but just barely.

"I am so sorry, Rose. Is there anything I can do?"

"I don't think so but thanks."

"Well, in the vein of good news, that was the judge's secretary I was speaking with when you walked in. She informed me that the judge has scheduled the hearing for nine AM tomorrow morning. I'm shocked since I only filed the thing a couple of hours ago."

"That *is* good news," she said, brightening considerably.

"However, as your lawyer I feel compelled to tell you again that I do not share your confidence in winning this."

"Oh ye of little faith," she said, smiling at him. "I keep telling you to trust me and you remain a doubting Thomas."

"What do you have, naked pictures of the judge with a prostitute or something?" he asked her jokingly.

"Something like that," she laughed.

He studied her to see if he could tell whether or not she was kidding. "There's something else, Rose. I received the State's disclosure of evidence yesterday. They claim to have a shirt with bloodstains on it that they say they found in Toby's apartment. Now I'm not sure whether or not you know this, but the last known victim was beaten so badly she's still in a coma."

"I read about that poor girl, but I don't see how that has any relevance. Assuming they didn't plant it, which you'll have a hard time convincing me of, that blood could have been from anywhere. He could have cut his finger or had a bloody nose. He could have even cut himself shaving. It doesn't prove anything."

"Actually it does. The DNA test confirmed that the blood on the shirt belonged to that girl. They also found gloves and a ski mask, which is what all of the victims claim their attacker was wearing."

She just stared at him, trying to comprehend what he had just said, but once again her face quickly became resolute. "Then they planted it," she said firmly. "There's no way Toby is involved with any of this."

Brandon sighed. "I sure hope you're right, Rose, because to be honest with you although I know I lack greatly in the experience department when it comes to matters such as this, something tells me that not everything about this hearing tomorrow is on the up-and-up. I don't know how you're manipulating this case, or even if you are, but from everything I've researched since our last discussion our petition wouldn't normally stand a chance, so before this gets out of hand are you sure there's not something you'd like to tell me?"

"Of course not. Will you stop worrying already," she said reassuringly.

"Alright, but all I can say is I sure hope you know what you're doing, because being wrong means we're turning loose a serial rapist who has now shown a willingness to use physical violence when it suits him."

"How many times do I have to say this, Brandon? Toby – is - innocent." She stated the last slowly and deliberately. "But if it makes you feel better, ask him yourself when you go see him today."

"You know, I might just do that." Suddenly he was struck by a thought. "Have you, Rose?"

"Have I what?" she asked him quizzically.

"Have you asked him point blank if he did it?"

"As a matter of fact I have. He told me he had absolutely nothing to with it and I believe him, and you will too after you speak with him." She reached up and gave him a kiss on the cheek just as she'd done yesterday, lingering for just a moment before pulling away and offering him a shy smile. He in turn responded with a lopsided grin and wouldn't have been a bit surprised if an "aw shucks" had involuntarily slipped out. "I'll see you tomorrow, Brandon."

As he watched her leave it occurred to him that there was more between them than a simple attorney/client relationship and he cautioned himself to proceed slowly. Right now he needed to focus on providing the best defense for her son that he could; which reminded him that he should probably get over there and speak with him.

CHAPTER 17

Anthony sat in his chambers staring blankly at the wall that displayed his law degree, letters of commendation and various appointment certificates. The hearing was to start in five minutes and he was struggling to come to terms with the fact that there was really no way out of this predicament unless he was willing to risk losing his career, his family and probably prison for the rest of his life. He was disappointed that the criminal justice system he had committed his life to had turned out to be so fragile that any average Joe – or Jane, in this case - could coerce a judge into freeing a man who, more than likely, was guilty as hell. He had almost convinced himself to get her on the phone last night and call her bluff, but he knew that the consequences were much too severe if he was wrong.

Skull poked his head in the door. "Everyone's ready and the defendant's in the courtroom, Judge."

"Alright, Joe, I'll be right there," he said.

Skull started to pull back then hesitated. "Everything okay, Judge?"

"Sure, why?"

"You just seem like you have a lot on your mind today. Plus, I can't remember the last time you used my real name. I'm shocked you even remembered it."

Anthony gave him a tired grin. "I'm fine, Skull, but thanks for asking."

"Okay, boss, I'll go make sure the natives don't get too restless."

Anthony stood and watched himself don his robe in the full-length mirror he'd mounted to the back of the door right after his appointment to the bench. He could remember when one of his favorite pastimes had been to stand here and strike judicious poses while experimenting with an assortment of facial expressions that he thought might come in handy as he dealt with each day's eclectic assemblage of defendants and plaintiffs.

He remembered how proud he had been back then; the excitement of finally being in a position where he could help affect positive change in society. And here he was about to bring the greatest dishonor (*How's that for the mother of all oxymorons?*) to what was, in his opinion, the most honorable of professions, and words could not describe how dirty he felt at this moment. He had briefly considered confessing everything to his wife, Francesca, and asking for her opinion on what to do, but imagining the look of disgust and betrayal he would surely see on her face was enough to change his mind. No, he had too much to lose at this juncture of his life. Twenty-three years ago would have been the time to do the right thing; now was not.

May God have mercy on me for the terrible thing I am about to do.

꙰

Once he had commanded everyone to be seated Anthony took a moment to look through the paperwork his clerk handed him, though in actuality he was simply stalling to gather his thoughts. He had already reviewed everything ad nauseum in the past twenty-four hours, searching in vain for something that would provide him a way out of this nightmare; some technicality that would make it legally impossible for him to uphold the defendant's motion. There was nothing.

When he felt he had himself somewhat collected, he looked around the courtroom and noticed, much to his dismay, that there were just as many reporters here today as there had been for the arraignment. Where did these guys get their information so quickly, he wondered? He'd only called this hearing yesterday. Well, one thing was certain, once he'd made his ruling he wouldn't make it back to his chambers before their stories were being drafted for the front page tomorrow. He saw that most of the victims and their families were front and center again, and he found it impossible to meet the confusion and uncertainty in their faces caused by this unexpected development.

He also noticed Rose sitting in the same seat in the corner. Their eyes met briefly and the look of resolve on her face confirmed to him that her position had not changed. Her son was sitting next to his lawyer and he had a smug, relaxed look on his face.

Does he know what's about to happen here today, he wondered? *What about his lawyer? Could he possibly be in on this as well?* He reminded himself to do some digging into Mr. Hill's background when this was over since his appearance on the case never made sense in the first place. He took a deep breath and began.

"In the case of Indiana versus Toby McGrady, two issues have been presented before this court for argument. The first is a motion filed by the defense to suppress evidence." This brought a few gasps from the victims' section and he quickly flashed them a stern look that said, "Don't make me have to remind you about your conduct."

"The second is a request from the State asking this court to order the defendant to provide a blood sample for the purpose of DNA testing. We'll deal with the defense's motion first. Mr. Hill, whenever you are ready."

Brandon stood, spread out his notes in front of him and began delivering the speech he had practiced a hundred times over the past two days.

"Thank you, Your Honor," he began. "We wish to put before this court the issue of the search warrant that was served on Mr. McGrady on February 16th, 2003 at approximately 1:13 a.m. It is our contention that this warrant was improperly served on my client, and therefore anything seized during the subsequent search of his premises is inadmissible as evidence in this case." He paused for a moment to allow that to hang in the air and he could hear restless movement from behind him as the realization of what he had just said began to sink in.

"On what basis was the warrant improperly served, Counsel?" Anthony asked, already knowing full well what he was going to say.

"Your Honor, the search warrant was issued on the basis of reasonable suspicion as opposed to probable cause, and could therefore only be served during daylight hours. In fact, the police served this warrant in the middle of the night, waking my client out of a sound sleep and violating his rights of lawful search and seizure guaranteed under the constitution of the State of Indiana."

Toby sat beside him nodding his head in complete agreement, though he had absolutely no idea whether any of this was even true. It sounded good to him, though.

"Anything else, Counsel?"

"No, Your Honor, I believe that fully and accurately states our position."

"Very well. I assume the State wishes to respond," he said, looking at the District Attorney.

Michael Haas stood and cleared his throat. "Thank you, Your Honor," he began. "If we were talking about a simple breaking and entering, or tax evasion even, then maybe the defense's argument would have a modicum of validity. However, given the heinous nature of the crimes with which the defendant has been charged, once the police obtained information that led them to believe that he was, in fact, the person they had been seeking, they then had a responsibility in the interest of public safety to act as quickly as possible in an effort to remove this threat. Surely the court would agree that this took infinite priority over the expectation that they should worry about a simple clerical oversight. As Your Honor knows, this court has wide discretion with regard to matters such as these, as well as ample case law that would support a ruling denying this groundless motion. Frankly, your Honor, the State can find no scenario that would support an alternate ruling. The State therefore submits that the defense's motion is without merit," he concluded, returning to his seat satisfied that the matter would now be settled favorably.

"Rebuttal?" The Judge asked, looking at the defense table.

Brandon stood up again. "Your Honor, I'm sure we can all appreciate the District Attorney's concern for the safety of the public. However, embracing the State's argument requires this court to ignore the most basic of rights guaranteed to us under the constitution of the United States, and that is the right to be presumed innocent until proven guilty. If we were to subscribe to the D.A.'s logic, then we might as well agree to skip the trial portion of these proceedings and simply throw a rope over a tree branch and hang Mr. McGrady."

"That's a good idea. Let's hang the son of a bitch!" someone said from the gallery seats. This was followed by a cacophony of assent that reverberated around the courtroom. The Judge immediately picked up his gavel and banged it sharply four times in succession. "There will be order in this courtroom," he yelled.

When things did not quiet down immediately he banged his gavel again and looked at the bailiff. "Joe, you will immediately escort out of this courtroom the next person who opens their mouth, and they are to be banned permanently from attending the remainder of these proceedings. Do you understand?" he asked him as he cut his glare sharply around the courtroom.

"Yes, Judge," Skull responded, squaring off with the spectators and daring one of them to give him an excuse to pounce.

This threat of permanent banishment served to finally quiet everyone down as the media scribbled in a frenzied delirium.

"Now continue, Counsel," he said, nodding at Brandon.

"Thank you, Your Honor. We're simply saying that the State would have us believe that they ignored procedure when serving the warrant because they believed in their minds that they were removing a serious threat from the general public. However, agreeing with that argument would require this court to conclude that my client is guilty without so much as a trial. It's absolute nonsense and the D.A. knows it," he concluded, with Toby once again nodding his head vigorously, as if he himself had provided his attorney with this gem of logic.

"There was no clerical typing error as the D.A. submits. The fact is, they requested the warrant under the basis of reasonable suspicion because they knew that a judge would have likely refused to issue it under probable cause given the source of their information."

"Your Honor," the D.A. said, rising, "we're not talking about shoplifting here. This man raped at least thirteen women, beating one of them so severely that she is still in a coma, and . . ."

"Objection, Your Honor!" Brandon said loudly, cutting him off. "My client has only been charged, not convicted, and I would like to remind this court, and the D.A., that he has also pleaded not guilty to those charges. It is both inappropriate and irresponsible for the D.A. to be inferring guilt at this stage of the proceedings and I would ask that the court admonish him against doing so in the future."

"Your Honor . . ." The D.A. started to say.

"Mr. Haas, there's an objection before the court. Please allow me to rule before attempting to proceed."

The D.A., properly chastised, said, "I apologize, Your Honor."

After a pause the judge continued. "The objection is sustained. Mr. Haas, if you were to continue in this vein you would be laying the foundation for a very strong argument in favor of a venue change, not to mention a possible mistrial on appeal. Please stick with only the facts at this time and refrain from playing the role of the jury, please."

It was obvious that this pissed off the D.A.. "I apologize, Your Honor, but what I'm saying is that we're not talking about a petty misdemeanor here. The defendant is *charged* with raping at least thirteen women. Once the police had a viable suspect they had an obligation in the interest of public safety to make an arrest immediately. As I said before, the courts have broad discretion in these matters and this is most certainly an instance where this court should uphold the decision to act sooner rather than later. After all, Your Honor, the police department's motto is to serve and protect, and in this case that's exactly what they did."

Anthony allowed a few seconds to pass to ensure the D.A. was finished, and when Brandon indicated he had concluded his argument as well, he said, "Okay, can we all agree that it doesn't make sense for me to hear arguments on the State's petition until I have ruled on this one?"

"Good," he said, when both sides agreed. "We'll take a fifteen minute recess and when we reconvene I'll have my decision." In the interest of safety he also instructed them to remove the defendant from the courtroom. When he stood to leave Skull again ordered everyone to rise.

When the judge had exited the courtroom Michael Haas looked over at Jay Krump and said, "Can you friggin' believe this? In a million years I wouldn't have believed the judge would entertain this motion for even a second."

Jay just looked at him, at a complete loss for words.

"Look, I need to make a phone call. I'll be back before we reconvene," Michael said. "Do me a favor, call back to the office and have one of the paralegals pull up this judge's track record. I want to know if he's made a habit of bucking precedent in the past. I'm kicking myself for not having done it before but I was so sure this was a slam dunk that . . . well . . . just have them do it and let me know what they find when I get back."

All eyes were riveted on Anthony as he once again assumed his position behind the bench. He noted with some satisfaction that the defendant appeared to be as nervous as the victims and their families, and he hoped that meant that Ms. McGrady at least had had the good sense to keep her extortion scheme between them. He noticed she was staring at him very intently and now that he was about to accede to her blackmail, he stared back at her for just a moment, hoping to convey his disgust for what she was forcing him to do. Finally he took a deep breath and everyone in the courtroom, including the bailiff and clerks, appeared to lean toward the bench as if by some unseen gravitational force.

"I have taken both sides' arguments under serious consideration, and although the State is correct in that this court does have discretion in these matters, there are other aspects of this case that bother me. One in particular is that the warrant was issued based on a tip that, at best, would have to be considered questionable. Now I'm not here to argue the legitimacy of the information obtained by the police, however, I *am* concerned over the way in which the warrant was handled. Reasonable suspicion was, and is, the basis under which the warrant should have been issued simply because the validity of the tip couldn't be confirmed until *after* the warrant was served. On the other hand, had the warrant been issued due to a sequence of events initiated by the police department's own investigative efforts, then the warrant would have more than likely been issued under the premise of probable cause."

At this point Michael Haas had to make a conscious effort to keep his mouth from stupidly dropping open. He'd be damned if it didn't sound like the court was about to rule in favor of the defense. When he'd returned from the recess Jay had told him that this particular judge had no history of bucking legal precedent and that he was, in fact, highly regarded. It was his opinion that they shouldn't have anything to worry about. Well that may be, but he was worried as hell right about now. The Judge continued.

"Now, had that been the case and the warrant had subsequently read *reasonable suspicion* due to a clerical error, then under that circumstance, which I want to point out is vastly different than the actual circumstances in this case, that would most likely have compelled this court to deny the defense's motion."

The Judge paused here for just a moment. He was about to deliver the awful punch line and the courtroom was so still you could practically hear the air moving.

"However, because the warrant *was* issued appropriately, and because the only error here was the manner in which the police department served it . . ."

The D.A. wanted to stand up and scream: "NO! You're about to make a horrible mistake! You can't do this!" But of course he didn't. He sat there and listened like everyone else; helpless to stop what he knew was coming next.

". . . coupled with the fact that the only evidence the State possesses is as a direct result of the search conducted under this warrant, this court agrees with the defense and finds that the warrant was served improperly and therefore, any evidence obtained as a result of that search is inadmissible."

And there it was...

The axe had fallen and it was the State running around the barnyard performing its spastic dance of death as its head flapped grotesquely from side to side. The D.A. just looked at the judge in disbelief. You could have knocked him over with a piece of balsa wood right then. Like the split second between when the warhead finds its target and the cataclysmic eruption that evaporates life for miles, there was just the slightest of pauses as the full implication of the judge's decision registered in everyone's mind.

And then all hell broke loose.

It started with an outraged, "What the fu . . ." that was quickly drowned out by a female's anguished scream of disbelief, which was followed by complete pandemonium. Reporters were simultaneously reaching for their cell phones and climbing over each other to get out of the room so they could call their respective offices. Some, seeing the melee, simply sat where they were and began making calls in the middle of the courtroom.

Most of the victims were somewhere between distraught and completely hysterical, and furious family members looked helpless in their attempts to offer comfort. One girl's dad had to be restrained by three deputies as he attempted to climb over the railing. It was unclear whether his intention was to go after the defendant or the judge.

The fat woman who had accosted Rose in the deli stood up and pointed a sausage-like finger at her, yelling something unintelligible as she lumbered her way across the rows of chairs with a murderous look on her face. Toby saw this and sprang from his chair, shoving the deputy nearest to him as hard as he could. He then hurtled the banister and in two strides caught the enraged woman by the back of her blue-tinted hair just as she was winding up to land another one of her famous haymakers across Rose's face. In spite of her considerable girth Toby easily lifted her off her feet as she squealed like a stuck pig, and flung her two rows away as if she were nothing more than a hollow mannequin. He paused for just a moment to grin at his mom and mouth, "Thank you," a second before two deputies tackled him from behind. He offered no resistance and they quickly had him restrained.

During the ruckus Anthony had been furiously banging his gavel and yelling for order, and though he didn't see the entire episode with Toby and the fat woman, he did see that they had him in handcuffs and were now helping the disheveled woman to her feet. He motioned for Skull to have them remove him from the courtroom, and once things had settled down to a dull roar he ordered the deputies to clear everyone out of the courtroom who didn't have an official reason for being there.

Brandon was speechless as he had listened to the decision. He couldn't believe it - they'd won. He then watched as bedlam broke out and the courtroom became a human zoo. The place was a mad house and all he could think of was how the State now had no evidence against Toby connecting him to any of the crimes. They would have no choice but to drop the charges.

He looked in Rose's direction and when their eyes met, he flashed her a smile which she returned, and gave her a thumbs up. He had then seen the big woman go after her and had witnessed Toby tossing her across the rows of chairs like a rag doll. She must have weighed at least two-fifty and he was awed at how easily he'd lifted her off the ground; partially by her hair no less. He then watched as the deputies escorted everyone but attorneys and court employees out of the courtroom. Most left willingly but some had to be forcibly removed. More than one furious victim or family member screamed an anger-filled epithet at the judge who, to his credit, endured it with quiet dignity. Little did he know that at that moment, there was nothing anyone could have said that would have come even remotely close to matching Anthony's own self-loathing.

☙

Once everyone had been removed Anthony ordered Toby returned to the courtroom. He silently endured the looks of betrayal being directed at him by both the D.A. and his assistant, primarily because he knew he deserved it. He knew that Skull was staring at him as well but avoided making eye contact simply because he didn't want to see the disappointment on his face.

"Okay," he began, "in light of my ruling, is the State in possession of any evidence that was not obtained during the search of the defendant's premises?"

Without standing Michael exhaled audibly, "No, we're not." Toby looked at the D.A. with a cocky smirk and Anthony wanted to step down from the bench and smack it off his face but managed to restrain himself.

"Very well then; in the absence of any evidence linking Mr. McGrady to the crimes with which he's been charged, how does the State wish to proceed with this case?" he continued.

"Well, Judge, as you know, we'd be violating the defendant's rights if we held him with nothing linking him to the crimes. And since you've just seen to it that all of our evidence is worthless, including a shirt with one of the victims blood on it," he said, making sure it was on the record, "then I guess the State has no recourse other than to drop all charges and set this animal free so he can continue terrorizing our community." His eyes never left the judge's, daring him to hold him in contempt.

"Your Honor," Brandon interjected as he jumped to his feet, "we take umbrage with the D.A.'s characterization of . . ."

"Save it, Counsel." The Judge stopped him, holding up his hand. "I've already ruled in your favor and the State has dropped the charges, so stop with the righteous indignation." Brandon returned to his seat without another word.

"If the State is dropping all charges then this case is dismissed and the defendant is ordered released. Before you leave, though, Mr. McGrady," he said, looking at Toby. "I'm going to go on record here and say that I am not convinced of your innocence. As a matter of fact, I believe it's very likely that you are, in fact, guilty of the crimes with which you were charged. However, today you have been the beneficiary of a system designed to protect the rights of every citizen of this country, even in instances where it's likely the individual is guilty, as I believe is true in your case."

"Given this, I think it would be safe for you to assume that your every move will be monitored very closely from this day forward and I would strongly encourage you to reconsider your choice of extracurricular activities, young man."

Toby just looked at him and smiled. "That sounds like the police plan on harassing me, Judge."

Undeterred, the judge said, "Maybe so, Mr. McGrady. You may well be right about that. And maybe the good Lord will see fit to punish where this court has so miserably failed here today." He banged his gavel one last time and said, "This court is adjourned. Please get him out of my sight." He immediately left the courtroom without saying a word to anyone, and returned to his chambers where he locked the door and sat at his desk in the dark.

My God, what have I done?

He didn't know it yet, but that wasn't the last time he would ask himself that question.

CHAPTER 18

Toby had to be processed out of the jail so Brandon told Rose that he would stay, and then bring him straight to her house once he was released. She wanted to get a couple of things done before Toby arrived anyway so she gratefully accepted, thanked him profusely for the *superb* job he had done, and headed home. Just as she was pulling into her garage her phone rang.

"Hello?"

"Ms. McGrady?"

"Yes. Anthony?"

"Yes, it's me. I'm calling because I want to know that this is over now; that I won't have to spend the rest of my life wondering when my phone is going to ring and it's you, or God forbid someone else you've shared our secret with, asking for another favor requiring me to compromise my integrity more than I already have. I need to know it's over."

"I think you've had a bit of practice with the whole *compromising your integrity* thing, so please spare me the pious self-righteousness."

"It was twenty-three years ago, Rose!" he replied, raising his voice slightly. "I was still a kid for Christ's sake! Why are you so intent on punishing me?"

"Because the system was so intent on punishing my son for something *he* didn't do, which is more than we can say about your participation in that girl's death," she responded angrily.

"I hate to be the one to break this to you, Rose, but your son is guilty as hell," he informed her matter-of-factly.

"You're out of your mind."

"See, now that's where you're wrong. You heard what the evidence was just like everyone else in that courtroom." When she didn't answer he said, "How do you feel about that son of yours now?"

"As a matter of fact, I had already been made aware of it," she said. "All I can tell you is that any evidence they claim to have had could only have been there if the police planted it."

"You're wrong, Rose. What you didn't know was that the blood wasn't found on just any shirt, it was found on one of *his* shirts. Are you telling me that the police went to the hospital and talked the doctors into giving them a vial of the girl's blood so they could take it with them when they searched his apartment, and that while they were there they dumped it on his clothes? Because if you believe that then you would have to also believe that more than one police officer would have had to conspire to pull this off. Think about it, if they had planted the blood on the shirt it would have still been wet when they found it. Don't you think that would have raised some eyebrows? No, your son is guilty and I only hope you can live with the consequences of what you made me do today, because to be honest with you, I don't know if I can."

"Oh, I'm sure you'll figure out a way to cope. After all, isn't that what you've been doing ever since you murdered that girl? And don't call me again. As far as I'm concerned this is over, so you don't need to worry about anyone else ever finding out about what you did. It'll be our sordid little secret," she said, hanging up on him.

"The nerve of that guy," she said aloud as she walked into the house and threw her purse on the counter. "What does he know about my son? He's just pissed off that his past finally caught up with him." She looked at her watch. "Toby and Brandon will be here soon, I'd better get something on the stove. They'll be starving."

CHAPTER 19

"So how does it feel?" Brandon asked. After almost two hours of unnecessary and obviously intentional delays, Toby had finally been released and they were now headed to Rose's house.

"How does what feel?"

"You know, being out."

"Beats where I just came from."

"I suppose that would qualify as the understatement of the year."

Toby inspected him. "You were pretty good in there today, Perry Mason. I have to say, I was duly impressed. Your logic was so sound an idiot could have followed it."

"I accept your backhanded compliment, I guess, but I'm still shocked the judge ruled in our favor. Frankly, I didn't think we had a prayer. He could just as easily have ruled against us and no one but you, your mother and I would have cared or even questioned it; he had that much latitude. We should consider ourselves very lucky."

"You're not giving yourself any credit, Brandon. I thought you handled yourself very nicely today. Definitely an improvement from the arraignment hearing, that's for sure."

"I don't know, Toby, we were talking about you potentially going away for life. With those consequences on the line I think I'll stick with being lucky on this one. Maybe the fact that the judge has a daughter your age worked in your favor; a little built-in compassion maybe, who knows?"

"That turdball has a daughter? He doesn't even look capable of procreating."

"Well that *turdball* saved your ass today and yes, he has a daughter. I think her name's Gabriella. I met her a couple of days ago at the courthouse when she stopped by to see her dad. She's a nice girl. I think she's actually planning to follow in her old man's footsteps and go to law school in a couple of years. You know, Toby, Judge Scalini has an impeccable reputation for fairness, and he did rule in your favor today, so I wouldn't look a gift-horse in the mouth if I were you."

"Well you're not me, Brandon, and you weren't the one standing there listening to him accuse you of rape. Mr. Fair Judge can kiss my ass."

They drove in silence for a while, both lost in thought until Brandon finally spoke. "Toby, I want to ask you a question."

"Shoot."

"How do you explain the shirt the police found in your apartment during their search? I mean the one with the blood on it? Your mom is convinced the police planted it there but I can think of about a dozen reasons why that would be next to impossible. Can you think of why it would have been there?"

"Not a single one," Toby replied flatly.

After a moment of uncomfortable silence Toby said, "Why, Brandon, you think he let a guilty man go today?" When Brandon didn't respond right away he continued. "You know, at this point it wouldn't matter even if I was guilty since they can't try me again for the same crime. That's double jeopardy," he stated smugly.

Brandon looked over at him with his eyebrows raised. Had he just heard a confession from this kid?

"Toby, I hate to be the bearer of bad news but double jeopardy only applies to people who have actually been tried and found *not guilty* by either a judge or a jury. You never went to trial so if the police were to find additional evidence linking you to these rapes you would absolutely be arrested again and put on trial."

Toby just stared out his window, seemingly unconcerned with this fairly significant correction to his flawed interpretation of the law. Finally Brandon could no longer ignore the question that had been bothering him the last three days.

"Did you have something to do with those rapes?"

A small grin formed at the corners of Toby's mouth. "Did I have something to do with it? You mean like, did I help the real rapist rape those women?"

"No, Toby, I mean did *you* rape those women?"

Toby sighed heavily. "I think my mom might have grown a little sweet on you in the past few days, Brandon. How do you think she'd feel if I was to tell her that you're accusing her little boy of such a horrible thing? Frankly I'd be surprised if she ever spoke to you again."

"Your mom's not here right now, Toby, it's just you and me and I'm asking you if you raped those women?"

Toby sighed loudly, "Do you have a daughter, Brandon?"

"No, I don't have any children. Why?"

"Then what the hell are you worried about?" he asked, looking intently at him with those eyes that seemed to shimmer and radiate. "Unless the boogeyman's a fag he ain't paying you a visit in the middle of the night so relax and stop worrying about things you can't control, okay?" With that he closed his eyes and leaned back against the headrest, signaling that he was done with the conversation.

Brandon suddenly had a sick feeling in the pit of his stomach. He knew Rose's feelings where her son was concerned, but he couldn't shake his belief that there was a lot more to Toby than she suspected. He watched him for a moment and was deeply troubled at how completely at peace he appeared to be considering all that had just transpired over the past couple of days, and he couldn't help but wonder if he was an unwilling spectator to the sweet, macabre oblivion of sociopathic behavior.

He shivered as a chill ran up his spine and he suddenly couldn't wait to get to Rose's house so he could get Toby out of his car.

∽

"Hi, Sweetheart!" Rose said as she ran to the front door and threw her arms around her son. "Oh, it's just so good to have you home," she said excitedly.

"Mom, please," Toby said as he turned his head to avoid the rapid-fire kisses she was planting on his face. She finally let him go and turned to Brandon. "Brandon, I don't know how I can thank you enough," she said, throwing her arms around his neck and pulling him to her so she could plant a firm kiss on his mouth. "You were just wonderful in that courtroom today – wonderful," she gushed.

Watching her radiate with excitement, Brandon couldn't help but share in it with her to some degree. "Yeah, I was pretty awesome, wasn't I?" he said, feigning complete arrogance and then laughing.

"Awesome? You were brilliant! I could tell the judge was going to rule in our favor as soon as you started talking. Oh, I can't tell you how happy I am that this is all over." She stepped back and beamed at both of them standing just inside the front door, which was all the farther they had made it before she'd pounced on them. "Well come in and take off your coats," she said, waving them further into the house.

"Rose, this is time that you and Toby should spend together. I think I'm going to just head on home from here and let you two get caught up. I'm sure you have a lot to talk about."

"Nonsense," Rose said insistently. "Toby wouldn't even be home tonight if it weren't for you."

"He's right, Mom. You and I need a chance to catch up," Toby chimed in. When she started to object again he said, "I thought you wanted to discuss me moving back in with you for a while?" He knew he'd hit her hot button when a moment later she conceded.

"Well, alright. But you're coming over tomorrow for lunch, okay, Mr. Hill?" she said, grabbing him by the lapels on his jacket and giving him a little tug.

"Sure," Brandon said. "Lunch tomorrow sounds great."

"You know, I don't think I'm going to be able to make that, Mom. I have to go over and inventory the damage those cops inflicted while they were tearing up my apartment.

"Well, we'll figure it out tomorrow," she said, smiling at Brandon. "You take care driving home, okay?"

"I will," he responded. He looked over at Toby and for a moment considered pulling Rose outside and telling her of his suspicions. He was afraid he would alienate her, though, and wasn't prepared to do that at this point in their . . . in their what . . . relationship? Is that what was developing between them? "Okay, well I'll call you in the morning and we can set something up then, okay?"

"Great. I'll wait with bated breath," she said jokingly.

He bent down and kissed her lightly on the mouth only because that had somehow become acceptable without them ever having discussed it. She kissed back and walked the two steps to the door with him as he looked over and saw Toby glaring in their direction. He found it slightly unsettling that he couldn't be sure if it was directed at him, or his mother.

They said goodbye once more, sharing another brief kiss while Toby, who was quickly proving to be quite the emotional chameleon, playfully told them to, "go get a room," which made Rose blush crimson. And then Brandon was in his car and heading home.

He definitely had some questions where Toby was concerned, but right at this moment he let that take a backseat
to the excitement he felt every time he thought of Rose and
the possibility that their flirting could evolve into something more. He hadn't felt this way since he was a teenager
and he had to admit that it was nice. His smile stayed put
the rest of the way home as he forced Toby from his mind
and remembered the softness of Rose's lips against his.

CHAPTER 20

Alleged Serial Rapist Allowed To Walk On Technicality
(D.A. cries abuse of discretion by court and demands investigation)

Anthony threw the paper on the bed and forced himself to breathe slowly and remain calm. After all, what did he expect, congratulations from everyone on such a fine ruling? In one fell swoop he had managed to completely destroy the respect, the trust and the confidence he'd worked so hard to earn from his peers and constituents alike. He may have avoided personal and professional ruination in the immediate, but he didn't stand a chance in hell when he came up for re-election in a little less than three years, at which time he'd have to return to private practice, assuming he even had a license to practice any longer. Well, he'd deal with that when and if the time came, but the bottom line was that he could still take some solace in the fact that he felt he'd done what he had to do to protect his family.

He got up and headed for the shower, deciding he was going into the office after all. It was Friday and he wasn't going to let everyone stew about this over the weekend before making an appearance. Let them throw their stones. He didn't do anything illegal yesterday; he just didn't do what everyone thought he should have. Oh well, you can't please all the people all the time. There's not another person walking this earth who wouldn't have done exactly what I did given the same circumstances, he thought as he shoved his toothbrush in his mouth.

∽

Brett Mitchell had been a man of solid character, always careful to live his life according to the golden rule, and this was reflected in the droves of people who showed up to the viewing to pay their respects to a good friend and colleague, and to offer heartfelt words of comfort to both Sarah and Rose.

It had been a tough day, emotionally draining for both of them, and they were glad it was almost over. Being in the room with him lying so still and silent only a few feet away had been difficult, but finally the last visitor left and it was time to say their own silent good byes. When they were finished the funeral home director walked them out to their cars, where Sarah would be heading home to another sleepless night, and Rose would have the much-needed distraction of Brandon, who was coming to dinner.

Returning inside, the director walked to the casket and took one last admiring look at Brett, appreciating the healthy glow to his skin, the result of using just the right amount of dye and emollient. It was almost a shame that no else was coming to view him, he thought. Finally he sighed and lowered the lid, oblivious to the fact that he was closing the final chapter on the life of a man who, in spite of having lived large and loved large, in the end had been forced to reveal an awful secret about himself. He also couldn't know that Brett hadn't actually divulged everything to Rose, and with his passing there remained only one other person who knew the real truth of that fateful night.

The Internet was an amazing tool if you happened to be one of those people adept at navigating beyond the pedestrian sites listed on most popular search engines. And if you were patient enough to navigate your way through the labyrinth of chat rooms and blogs, one could eventually tap into the underbelly of cyberspace where the moral bottom-feeders congregated, and unimaginable sins were shared between complete strangers. Toby was one of those people. He had honed his skills over the years to the point where there was very little he couldn't find on the Internet when he put his mind to it.

The police had given back to him the items they had taken from his apartment, including his computer, and what he currently studied on the monitor in front of him would have shocked most with its stark, revealing detail. The complete bio and background for Judge Anthony Michael Scalini was displayed in front of him including birth information, banking records, medical history, education, career progression, mortgage company, salary, and even the date and place of his baptism. However, the only thing that interested Toby at the moment was the family history.

Just as Brandon had said, he had a daughter named Gabriella Lynn Scalini, as well as a wife named Francesca. A few more confident keystrokes and Toby was looking at the daughter's personal history. It looked like Gabriella was nineteen years old, currently attending one of the local junior colleges, and judging by her GPA was somewhere near the top of her class. More interesting, though, was the fact that the address listed for her differed from that of her parents. Little Gabriella might not live alone, but she didn't live with her parents. This tidbit of information, with all of its seductively sweet possibilities, caused an execrable grin to form at the corners of his lips.

There was something bothering him, though. He was still confused as to why that judge had let him walk? If he really had the authority to rule either way, why in the hell would he have let him go? It just didn't make sense and this led Toby to the conclusion that there was more to the story than his mother had told him. He decided he was going to see her tomorrow and one way or another he'd convince her to tell him the truth. He was very interested in knowing just exactly what had been discussed between her and Uncle Brett.

And until he did, he would postpone making Gabriella's acquaintance.

∽

As Rose emerged reluctantly from the comfortable embrace of sleep, she was aware of two things. One, that the shrill ringing of the telephone on the night table was the offending culprit that had awoken her and two, Brandon was no longer next to her in bed. She was immediately annoyed at his conspicuous absence as she rolled over to answer the phone, and then immediately sorry when she spotted him sitting in a chair by the sole bedroom window where he apparently had been watching her as she slept. She smiled and favored him with an endearing little wave as she said, "Hello?"

"Hi, Toby. My, aren't you up and around early for a Saturday," she said, throwing a quizzical look toward Brandon.

"This morning? Well, what time were you thinking? No, I don't have any plans that I'm aware of but I'm not even up and showered yet. Okay, well it's nine right now so give me an hour and I'll see you around ten, okay? Alright, I'll see you then."

As she replaced the phone in the cradle she propped herself up on one elbow and looked over at Brandon, "I thought you had left."

"I told you I wouldn't."

"People don't always do what they say you know."

"I do."

"I can see that."

"That was Toby?"

"Yes. He said he wants to talk to me about something *very* important. I have no idea what that might be but it all sounded very Machiavellian," she said with a conspiratorial grin. "Anyway, he's going to be here in an hour so you need to get out of here, Mr. Hill."

"You're kicking me out?" he asked, feigning hurt.

"I don't think Toby seeing you at the breakfast table is the best way to tell him about us, do you," she said, cocking an eyebrow and making him laugh.

"Probably not. Okay, let me get my things and I'll get out of your hair," he said, offering her his best dejected face.

"At least take a shower," she offered.

"That's okay. I'm sure you'd like some time to get ready yourself and I only live ten minutes away, so I'll just take one when I get home."

"Am I going to see you later?" she asked.

"I'm feeling claustrophobic all the sudden," he said.

She stared at him, trying to figure out whether or not he was being serious.

"Kidding! Just kidding," he said, grinning at her. "The only way you're not going to see me tonight is if you join the witness protection program, and even then the odds are fifty-fifty I'll find you."

"Good," she said simply. Then I'll be ready to be picked up at seven sharp! Where are you taking me by the way?" she asked.

"Well, your mind is obviously working better than mine right now because I have no idea. However, I promise I'll know by seven."

When he was dressed she walked him to the door where they kissed deeply, neither wanting to be apart and both already missing the other. "Is it seven yet?" he asked.

"No and I want you to know I'm going to suffer until it is."

"Maybe between now and then I could just call you once or twice . . . or three times even. How does that sound?"

"I think that's a wonderful idea. Now go before Toby shows up early and sees us," she said, pushing him toward the porch. After one more kiss Brandon reluctantly got into his car and headed for home.

He couldn't remember ever feeling this excited about the prospects for his future, and he was still grinning twenty minutes later when he stepped under the steaming spray of the showerhead.

CHAPTER 21

"How did things go last night after I left the showing?" Toby asked his mom.

"Uneventful. The majority of the people who were coming had either already been there and left, or were there when you showed up, so I was back home within an hour of you leaving." An uncomfortable silence settled between them as both remembered how people had stared and talked about him when he'd shown up.

"Toby, I'm sorry for what you've gone through and what you're still going through. And I'm sorry for last night. All I can tell you is that it doesn't matter what other people think or say. They don't know anything about you and they are just as misinformed as the media. If they don't have something horrible to write or talk about they just make it up."

"Doesn't make it any easier to deal with," he said.

"The people who know you believe in you, Toby."

"Like who? You?"

"Yes, like me," she said. "Your Aunt Sarah, too. And if it wasn't for your Uncle Brett you might not even be standing here with me right now so obviously he believed in your innocence. It scares me to death to think how this might have turned out if not for him." The fear of having almost lost her son to a life sentence in a state penitentiary was clearly etched on her face.

"That's actually what I wanted to talk to you about," he said, strumming the flowery vase she had displayed at the entrance to the dining room with the backs of his fingers.

"What's that?" she asked, curious.

"Well, I understand that Uncle Brett was the one who discovered the issue with the warrant, right?"

"Right."

"And that all makes sense to me, what with the incorrect wording and all, but then things get confusing for me. The D.A. prosecuting me, and even my own lawyer, both said that the court had the discretion to rule against me."

"And they were right," she said.

"I mean, even the guards at the jail were telling me there was no way I was going to walk, which means that the judge could have just as easily denied our motion and I'd still be sitting in jail waiting to go on trial."

"But you're not, Toby, and that's all that matters."

"No, there's something else going on here, Mom. I've given this a lot of thought and no matter how you slice it, there's just no good reason why that judge let me go. So I've come up with my own theory."

"Oh you have, have you?" she chided him.

"As matter of fact I have. See, I figure the judge must have been pressured somehow. And since I highly doubt that you would have initiated something like that, and I'm certain it's not that wet-behind-the-ears lawyer you hired for me, that only leaves Uncle Brett."

She didn't appreciate the derogatory comment about Brandon but decided now was not the time to start defending him and let it pass. "Toby, there's nothing more to it than what I already told you," she assured him, hoping that would suffice and he'd drop it. Unfortunately he wasn't ready to.

"No, I'm not buying it. Somehow that judge was pressured to let me go and I want to know how it was done."

"Toby, like I said . . ."

"I heard what you said, Mom, and I told you I don't believe you. Look, why are you keeping this from me? It's my butt that's on the line here and if there's any way at all that this thing – whatever it is - could backfire, then I should know about it so I can be prepared, 'cause I'm not going back to jail. So why don't you stop lying to me and tell me what you and Uncle Brett talked about before he died."

"Isn't it enough that you're free?" she asked him, clearly exasperated. "Why is it so important for you to know all the details?"

"So you admit there's more to it than what you're telling me," he said, a look of triumph on his face.

"There's a little more to it, Toby, but nothing that's really all that important," she said, again hoping to deflect this sudden obsession with knowing all the details.

"I want to know everything, Mom," he said, crossing his arms defiantly.

"Well, I'm not getting into it with you, Toby. Like I said, there's a little more to it than what you know, but I promised Uncle Brett I would keep it between him and I and that's exactly what I intend to do."

"I need to hear it, Mom, and if you won't tell me then I'm going to have to assume there's a good chance that one of these days I could have the police knocking on my door again in the middle of the night. And since I'm not willing to take that chance, I'm leaving."

"Leaving where?" she asked, trying not to show the sudden alarm she felt.

"I'm not going to tell you or anyone else. This way if the police question you, you won't be able to tell them anything."

"You sound like an old Dick Tracy episode, Toby, and a bad one at that," she said, rolling her eyes.

"Say what you want, but I'm serious. I'm out of here tonight." He grabbed his coat off the back of the chair and started for the door.

"Toby!" He turned and looked at her, knowing he had threatened the one thing she couldn't tolerate – losing him.

"I mean it, Mom. I'm not sticking around and waiting for a piano to fall on my head."

"Alright," she conceded, sighing heavily. "Sit down and I'll tell you. But you have to promise me you will never

ever repeat this to anyone, nor use the information to your own advantage."

"You know me better . . ."

"Promise!" she interrupted.

"Okay, okay, I promise." He'd been right; there was more...

"Sit down," she said, pointing to the chair across from her. When he had complied she looked at him and said, "The last thing I ever promised your Uncle was that I would never repeat this, Toby, so I want you to know that I don't appreciate you putting me in a position where I'm forced to break that promise before we've even buried him."

"He's dead, Mom, he doesn't know you're telling me."

"Well *I* know I'm telling you and that's enough." She got up to get herself a glass of tea and to collect her thoughts. When she returned to the table she said, "Do we really have to do this, Toby? I promise it's not as important as you are making it out to be, and I would feel better if you would just trust me rather than have me go back on my word.

"No, Mom, I need to know." And so reluctantly she began to repeat the story her late brother had entrusted her with. . .

∽

Michael Haas had been walking around in a perpetual state of anger for the last three days and it was unmistakable in his voice as he spoke with Judge Leon Fischer, the current chief judge of the United States District Court for the Southern District of Indiana.

"Your Honor, this judge is out of control and there needs to be an investigation."

"Michael, I want you to take a deep breath and relax. It's obvious you don't agree with the ruling Judge Scalini handed down, but we're not going to get anything resolved while your emotions are being fueled by this anger."

"I'm sorry, Your Honor. I know you're right but you didn't have to watch a filthy rapist just waltz right the hell on out of your courtroom when we had evidence that would have put him away forever. Now he's back on the street and no doubt stalking his next victim as we speak."

"I assume we're watching him?"

"Of course we are, but you know how that goes; everyone is vigilant for the first week or so until some uniform lets his guard down and the next thing you know, we don't have a clue where *Ricky Rapist* is anymore. Of course, we'll find out later when some rape center calls to report another victim. I'm beside myself here, Judge. This is absolute bullshit and more women are going to get hurt before this is over. That judge needs to be removed from the bench before he's allowed to wreak any more havoc on our city."

"I certainly hope you've refrained from being too ostentatious where that particular opinion's concerned, Michael. Look, I'm sure this will come as no surprise to you but I'm going to say it anyway. Although there will always be judges who make decisions that do not sit well with others, even other judges, there will also always exist an unspoken loyalty between men and women of the robe; unconditional in most cases. Judges don't always agree with each other, Michael. As a matter of fact, I would submit that if the general public knew how often our opinions actually conflicted, I fear their already-waning confidence in our legal system would vanish completely. Of course, and I'm sure you would agree, once that happens anarchy is just around the corner."

"Point taken, Your Honor. So what do I do?"

"Unfortunately, Michael, there isn't a whole lot you can do other than to file an official complaint which, of course, will be reviewed, but then I'm not telling you anything you don't already know. You also know that as bad as this seems to you – and I'm not implying it's anything other than that – it will most likely withstand scrutiny. He had the discretion to rule either way, and he ruled for the defendant. That doesn't make his decision wrong; it just makes it untenable in your opinion. You may just have to chalk this up to a disagreement between Judge Scalini and the State and move on. Who knows, maybe fate will shine on you, this kid will slip up again soon and you'll get a second crack at him."

"We should all be so lucky, Judge," he said despondently.

"Hang in there, Michael. You've been at this long enough to know you're not going to win them all. I know that was one of the first things I taught you when you came to work for us all those many years ago."

Leon Fischer had been a senior partner at Boyd, Fischer, Harding and Lewis, a highly respected firm that specialized in criminal defense and, at the time, boasted some of the hottest litigators in the state. They had aggressively recruited Michael out of law school and he'd been honored when Leon, twenty years Michael's senior, had taken him under his wing and had shared his tremendous experience and wisdom with him. A few years later Leon was elected to the Monroe County, Indiana Circuit Court and he served the majority of one term before being appointed to the United States District Court where he had served as the chief judge for the past two years. Michael hoped to win a judgeship himself one day, which was why he had originally taken the Assistant D.A. position, and eventually ran for D.A.

"I'll tell you what," the judge continued. "As a favor to you I'll call Judge Scalini myself. We've played in a few golf scrambles together so he'll take the call. I don't expect it to accomplish much but I'll give it a shot. That's all I can promise you."

"I appreciate it, Your Honor. If he gives you any insight into why he ruled the way he did, please share it with me."

"Obviously I'm not making any promises where that's concerned but we'll see, okay?"

"Okay, thanks."

"Michael?"

"Yes, Judge?"

"I've been hearing good things about you so hang in there and keep doing what it is you've been doing. The right people are starting to notice if you know what I mean."

"Thanks again, Your Honor. I appreciate you taking the time to pass that on to me."

"You're welcome, Michael."

As they were hanging up Jay Krump poked his head into the office. "I have an update for you if you have time."

"Absolutely," Michael responded, feeling a little better after speaking with his former mentor.

"Well, as you know, the State boys have assigned a rotating crew of uniforms to keep tabs on McGrady. I just got off the phone with one of their captains and he tells me that so far our boy has been downright boring. He has an Uncle who just passed away from cancer and he showed up for his viewing last night, and right now he's over at his mother's house, but other than that they say he's just been hanging around his apartment. As you know, his apartment's on the second floor so there's really no way for them to see what he's up to in there, and obviously we can't tap his phone since no judge is going to sign off on that warrant right now."

"He's just biding his time," Michael warned. "Once a rapist always a rapist and he'll strike again. I know this as surely as I know it's colder than a witch's tit outside. When the hell is spring going to get here anyway?" He threw the question out expecting no answer, and it dissipated into the stale air that was regurgitated through the building's HVAC system thousands of times a day throughout the numerous offices and common areas. "Stay in contact with them every day, no, twice a day, and make sure they don't forget how dangerous this guy is. He's going to make a move and when he does I don't want to be reading about it in the papers the next day, understand?"

"Got it," Jay said. "By the way, how are your wife and daughters holding up?"

"They're scared shitless, that's how," Michael stated flatly. "Wouldn't you be if you were a woman?"

"Hell, I'm not a woman and that guy still scares me," Jay responded. "Did you see what he did to that lady in the courtroom yesterday? And what's up with those eyes? I couldn't even look at the guy for more than a second or two. It's like looking at the Devil himself."

"Well, whatever he is, let's just make sure he's in a prison cell and not out terrorizing our streets again."

"Okay, I'll update you if they tell me anything's changed," he said, turning to leave.

"Jay?"

"Yeah?" he said, stopping and looking back.

"Update me even if *nothing* changes."

༺༻

"Was she dead?" Toby was leaning forward in his chair, completely fascinated by what his mother was telling him.

"Yes, Toby, she was dead," Rose said.

"So what'd they do?"

"I want you to understand that your Uncle and this judge were both young and they were scared." she told him, hoping to provide some rationale for what she was about to say next.

"I'll bet. I'd be scared too if I was drunk and ran someone over."

Rose let the comment slide. "What they decided to do was hide the girl's body rather than call the police and turn themselves in."

"What? They hid her body?"

"Yes."

"But didn't you say Uncle Brett was driving at the time?"

"Yes."

"So why was the judge worried about the cops? He wasn't going to get in any trouble."

"That wasn't the way they saw it. They figured he'd be held liable just for being in the vehicle. Their biggest concern was going to trial and facing a jury of farmers who already frowned on people they considered *outsiders*. They thought it would ruin their lives and they panicked."

Toby just looked at her, shaking his head in amazement. Finally he said, "Well don't keep me in suspense. What'd they do with her?"

"They put her in the trunk and your uncle first drove the judge back to campus before going on alone to the hide the body."

"Why did he do that?"

"Two reasons: One, apparently the judge was very distraught and your Uncle Brett just wanted to get him back to school and two, they agreed that it would be better if only one of them knew where she was."

"And where is that exactly?" Toby asked.

"I don't know."

"You don't know?" he said, looking at her carefully to determine whether or not she was lying to him.

"No, Toby, I don't know because your Uncle Brett didn't tell me. He knew that once I told the judge I knew everything else, he would never have the guts to call my bluff."

"But why wouldn't he have just told you? You know, on the slight chance he *had* called your bluff?"

"Because he only wanted the information to be used to get you out of jail and that was it. He didn't want anyone to ever be able to find the body and use it as evidence against the judge. He felt bad enough as it was for breaking his promise by telling me."

"Wait a minute, though. If the judge wasn't with Uncle Brett when he got rid of the girl, how could anyone tie him to her even if they did find the body?

"Toby," she said with a heavy sigh. "Does it really matter? I mean, do you have to know every little detail?" she asked him.

"This isn't exactly a little detail, Mom. Are you telling me that the judge didn't challenge you on this?"

"He did," she admitted.

"So what did you tell him?"

She sighed again. "He had left his class ring in your Uncle's car that night after removing it to clean the blood off his hands. Your Uncle Brett told me that he put it in one of the girl's pockets of her blue jeans before he hid her."

"No shit!" Toby exclaimed.

"Toby!" Rose admonished him.

"Sorry, Mom, but that was brilliant on Uncle Brett's part. That ensured that the judge could never try to put the blame off him. I'm impressed."

"There was nothing brilliant about any of it, Toby. It wasn't brilliant that they were drinking and driving. It wasn't brilliant that that poor girl lost her life. And it most certainly wasn't brilliant that they hid her body in God only knows where, instead of taking responsibility for their actions. Can you imagine the pain and anguish this girl's family has suffered all these years?"

Toby ignored this. "Did your opinion of Uncle Brett change after he told you?"

"You know what, I struggled with it at first, but in the end, no, it didn't change my opinion of him, and I'll tell you why. First, I tried to put myself in his shoes at that age and I couldn't honestly say with any conviction that I would have done anything differently. The second thing is that if there's such a thing as redeeming yourself for past mistakes, your uncle did it a thousand times over. He was such a good man who truly loved and cared about people, and I

honestly believe that he punished himself much more severely than any jury ever could have."

"So, was there anything else he told you?"

"No, that's all of it, and I'm reminding you again that you
promised to never repeat any of this, and I expect you to
honor that promise, do you understand?"

"I understand," he said, offering her his most humble and
obedient look. However, his mind was spinning like a
computer hard drive with the interesting possibilities this
newfound information presented - very interesting indeed.

"Does my attorney know about this?"

"No, absolutely not, and he won't know either. If I had told
him he would have had no choice but to stop representing
you, and it's possible he would have had an ethical or even
legal obligation to report what he knew."

"That makes sense. Listen, I really appreciate you leveling
with me, Mom. I feel much better knowing that this thing
can't backfire on us."

"Then I'm glad I was able to put your mind at ease, honey,"
she said. "Do you want to stay and have lunch with me?"

"Maybe tomorrow, but right now I have to go. I've been
checking out some potential jobs in the paper and I need to
e-mail my resume to a few of the interesting ones. I should
probably get that done."

"Okay, but make sure you don't forget about the funeral
tomorrow. We lay Uncle Brett to rest at ten a.m., so why

don't you meet me here at nine and we'll drive over and pick up Aunt Sarah before we go to the funeral home."

"Don't worry, I'll be here on time."

He gave her a quick peck on the cheek, grabbed his jacket and left hurriedly before she could think of another reason to delay him. Driving back to his apartment his mind was in high gear as he considered what he'd just heard. To most, it was just a sad tale of youthful indiscretion and poor judgment, but to Toby it was something else entirely. It was opportunity gift-wrapped.

CHAPTER 22

Anthony set the phone in its cradle and returned to his oatmeal and newspaper. His wife was trying to appear busy at the sink, although if she was actually doing anything Anthony was at a loss as to what it might have been.

"Who was that?" she asked him.

"Another judge I've played golf with a few times in the past," he answered.

"Well it's the middle of February and they're calling for snow tomorrow, so I doubt he was inviting you to join his foursome. What did he want?"

"Do I ask what you talk about every time you conclude a phone call?"

"You rarely ever get calls here at home from other judges, Anthony, and certainly not on the weekends," she shot at him. "So I'm guessing he wanted to discuss that case. Am I right?"

"He was curious about the details of the case, yes," he said.

"And did he agree with your ruling?"

"He didn't really say."

"Sure. Professional courtesy at the expense of public safety and all that, right?" she said sarcastically.

"Why don't you just drop it, Fran," he said, tiring of the assault that had been almost non-stop since yesterday.

"I don't want to *just drop it*, Anthony," she said, mocking him. We have a nineteen year-old daughter who just recently moved out on her own and her father let a serial rapist walk out of his courtroom when it was within his power to do otherwise. You've put our daughter's life in danger and I'm pissed off about it," she fumed.

"First of all, there's no concrete proof that he was the rapist."

"Bullshit!"

"Second," he continued, ignoring her. "I don't appreciate the presumptuousness you employ when you question the manner in which I execute the duties and responsibilities the people of this community have entrusted to me," he fired back. "You know only what you've read in the paper or heard from other just-as-unreliable sources. Are you going to tell me you honestly believe that they have all the facts; or are even accurately reporting the ones they do have for that matter?" he hissed.

Though he knew he had no one to blame but himself for what had happened, the fact that he could never explain it to anyone necessitated that he defend himself as vehemently as if he *had* made the appropriate ruling.

"Okay, I'll concede your point about the press." she said. "So then *you* explain to me why you ruled the way you did. Explain why you let that . . . that filthy animal out of his cage."

"His rights were violated, Fran. It's as simple as that. It would be no different than if it had been you or someone else. The police violated his rights and nothing after that mattered – and I'm referring to any alleged evidence – because it was all obtained illegally. If it was our daughter and her rights had been violated you would have been begging me to rule the way I did, but because the State claimed to have evidence that this kid was the rapist, all of the sudden I'm supposed to ignore the law and treat him differently because everyone wants to play judge, jury and executioner based on the shameless sensationalism of the media, right?"

"I'm thinking of talking to Gabby and seeing if I can convince her to move back home until this guy is back in jail where he belongs," she announced.

"You're wasting your time. She won't move back and all you'll do is make her scared of her own shadow. You know how stubborn she is."

Fran thought about that. "You're probably right."

She turned to look out the window and longed for spring to return when her garden would once again come alive with the blooming brilliance of red and pink roses, yellow buttercups, birds of paradise, white and yellow tulips, baby's breath, primrose, irises and magnolias. Fran adored her garden and seeing it in a state of hibernation through the winter months never failed to sadden her, yet it also served to offer a future promise of something better.

She turned around to look at him. "You've always had a knack for expressing yourself logically, Anthony, and what you're saying makes sense, but there's something about this that isn't right. I can't quite put my finger on it, but it's there nonetheless. I get the feeling you've compromised yourself somehow. I don't know how I know this, but I do. You're lying to me and that isn't like you. I just hope you find that it was worth it in the end."

With that off her chest she walked out of the room and headed upstairs, leaving Anthony with the truth of what she'd said ringing in his ears. He too hoped it was worth it.

CHAPTER 23

Gabriella, or *Gabby* as her friends called her, was nineteen years old, sharp as a tack, as funny as most stand-up comedians, exceedingly loyal to those lucky few she considered friends, and drop-dead gorgeous; the kind of gorgeous that could halt conversation in a room when she walked in. Her thick black hair, a gift from her Italian heritage, reached almost to the small of her back, and on her five foot eight frame it resembled the lush, sultry mane of a regal feline. Her high cheekbones, exquisitely-shaped lips and olive skin all conspired to give her a unique look that bordered on exotic, and she walked with the grace and confidence of someone older and more accomplished.

Her most endearing quality, though, may have been that she knew practically none of this about herself. She rarely noticed the looks men gave her, she assumed her grades were better than average because she studied *harder* than average, and she was never really trying to be funny; she simply saw humor where most others did not. It wasn't that she was lacking in self-esteem, she just didn't believe she was that much different from those around her. She was wrong, though. Gabby was the target of fascination and envy for women, and the object of intense, heated desire for men. Gabriella Scalini was one in a million.

This was her first year at the University of Phoenix in Indianapolis, a junior college based out of Arizona but with campuses spread across the U.S., and she was having a ball. After much convincing, her parents had reluctantly agreed to let her move out of the house and into a small two-bedroom apartment with her best friend Kiley, and although her newfound freedom was exhilarating and came with many temptations, she was determined to show her parents that their trust in her had been well placed.

She hadn't yet declared a major but she'd found herself opting for courses that aligned nicely with a future degree in business. After that she was fairly certain she would apply to law school at her dad's alma mater but, of course, she had a long time to think about it before committing to anything. Right now all she was thinking about as she walked the two blocks from the bus stop to her apartment was what she was going to eat for dinner. It was almost seven-thirty and she had just left her waitressing job at Mulligan's, an Irish-themed sports bar and restaurant that served as a popular hangout with the local college crowd. She'd been employed there for the past six months in spite of the fact that her dad had told her she didn't need to work. He was convinced that she should just concentrate on her studies, but she needed to feel like she was contributing. She was grateful that her parents were paying for her tuition and books, but had announced that she would be buying her own food, clothing and anything else that was not related to academics and although he didn't like it, he also knew how hardheaded she could be so he relented in the end, which was not unusual when it came to his only child.

As she approached the apartment she began digging in her purse for her keys. She knew better than to not have them out already but she couldn't ever seem to remember until she was standing at the door. It took her a minute but she finally found them and as she inserted the right one into the first of two locks, she was unaware of the young, handsome man with the strange eyes watching her from just a few yards away where he sat unnoticed in the gloom of dusk, tucked away behind the steering wheel of his car. An eerie glow shimmered and pulsed from his eyes, appearing to bathe him in a horrible, pestilent halo as he focused intently on her every movement. The thrill of the hunt was intoxicating and he had to check himself. His muscles twitched with anticipation and his breathing became heavy as imagined that final, explosive charge that would climax with his prey gasping and struggling weakly beneath him as he forced his maleficent will upon her and fed his sick, insatiable desire to dominate. And maybe this time . . . just maybe . . . *to kill.*

Had Gabby been privy to the thoughts vomiting forth from the madness of his mind, she would have dropped her keys and started running as she had never run before; as if her very soul depended on it. And she would have never ever stopped.

∽

"Tell me how you're doing with everything that's been going on, Rose." Brandon had picked her up at seven sharp as promised and they had decided on a local restaurant that specialized in Spanish cuisine. Now with their entrees devoured and neither feeling like dessert, they were relaxing in each other's company with a glass of sangria.

"To be very honest with you, Brandon, you've made the difference. If I were going through this alone I wouldn't be fit to be around anyone."

"How's Toby taking his Uncle's death?"

"You know, I wasn't going to say anything but . . . well . . . Toby reacted very strangely when I first broke the news to him about his Uncle's passing."

"Strange how?" he asked her.

"Well, to be completely honest, he didn't act like he even cared. I mean, all he was worried about was how Brett's passing was going to affect him getting out of jail. It was pretty upsetting actually, and I told him as much."

"What did he say when you expressed your feelings to him?"

"Oh, he apologized right away and gave me some excuse about how he was just stressed out about his personal situation, but for some reason his words didn't ring true. I saw no pain or sadness in his eyes where Brett was concerned, and believe me I was looking for it. I didn't know what to make of it then and I still don't."

"Well, maybe it *was* just because of everything that was going on at the time."

"Yeah, maybe," she said, "but I'm not so sure. It was almost like he was . . . *glad*. Isn't that a terrible thing to say about your son?"

Brandon could have left it at that and simply changed the subject, but he didn't. And in a split-second decision he would later regret, he told her the details of the conversation he'd had with Toby in his car as they'd been driving from the jail to her house. Halfway through the telling it became obvious he'd made a gross error in judgment by the look of utter contempt on her face that hardened her normally soft features. And there was no question that it was contempt for him.

CHAPTER 24

"So how was the joint, dude?"

"It was fucking miserable, how do you think it was? And who are you supposed to be, Huggy Bear?"

"Huggy who?"

"Huggy Bear, dipshit. That pimp on Starsky and Hutch who wore the stupid-looking clothes and the big hat with the feather in it."

"Why you askin' if I think I'm him?"

"Because he's probably the last person to ever use the word *joint*."

"Oh, that's real funny."

"So is your vocabulary." Toby had driven out to the Southeastern side of the city to look up a buddy of his, Carl Fuller. He hadn't talked to him since he'd been released but he had no trouble locating him in a shitty little billiard hall called *On Cue* that had always been one of his favorite haunts. This part of town was probably ninety percent black and dangerous, but Carl didn't seem to care even though he was as white as a white boy could get with his unruly thatch of red hair and freckles dotting his entire face. Toby figured he had probably been around the neighborhood for so many years that the *gangstas* had just come to accept him as part of the landscape. Of course, the fact that Carl was also as crazy as a loon and meaner than a cornered rattlesnake might have had something to do with it as well. Someone probably would have tried to take him out by now but the fear of what Carl would do in retaliation if they were unsuccessful was enough to convince most to just ignore him and let him do his thing.

For the most part he stayed to himself anyway. His main job was working as a mechanic for an auto shop over on 13th street, but the owner was a career criminal and Carl spent much more of his time chopping stolen vehicles than he did repairing legitimate ones. Of course, he didn't mind since chopping paid better anyway. Every now and then, though, if things got slow at the shop and he needed some extra cash, he'd either freelance as an enforcer for a couple of the local lone sharks, or he'd sell a few drugs. He normally peddled in a neighborhood that had been claimed by a notorious drug dealer who went by the moniker of Thor due to the beatings he'd been known to mete out with a large sledgehammer he carried in the trunk of his car, but even he never bothered Carl. Whenever one of the young kids he employed to sell for him would come and tell him that that crazy white-boy was in their territory again, he'd just tell them to shut up and go find another corner. Drug dealers were scum but they were also businessmen, and they instinctively knew that life on the street was tough enough without pissing off someone as crazy as Carl. As a matter of fact, there was only one person Toby had ever known Carl to fear – him.

"Whatchoo doin' out in this neck of the woods anyway?" Carl asked him.

"I was bored so I thought I'd drive on out here and see if you were still alive."

"Course I'm alive," he said, bending down to line up on the five ball. "I'm gonna live forever," he announced after drilling it in the side pocket.

"Somehow I don't doubt that," Toby said. "Hey, you remember that business you were into a couple years back?"

"I've been into a lot of things over the years; which thing you talkin' about?"

"The business you ran out of that old warehouse."

"Oh yeah," Carl said. A grin came to his face as he took a brief stroll down memory lane. "Those were the days huh, Toby?" he beamed.

"Yeah, they sure were. Hey, you still have any of your old equipment left?"

"Uh, yeah, I think so. Well, I know I sold a couple of pieces when I was down on my luck but I think I still have most of it. Why?"

"Cause I might wanna borrow it one of these days, that's all. And stop saying shit like *joint* and *down on my luck*. You sound like a goddamn bit actor in a cheap detective movie."

"Fuck you. Are you an English teacher now?" he said, looking up from his shot and grinning. "And you can borrow it anytime. It's collecting dust right now so just let me know and I'll pull it out and clean it up. Think you'll need any help with whatever it is you'd be wantin' to borrow it for?" he asked.

"Maybe. I'll know more in a few days. Want another beer?"

"Does a bear drop trou in the woods?" Carl responded.

Toby walked to the bar and ordered two more beers, catching a few stares from the all-black clientele, but everyone could see he was with Carl so nothing was said to him. When the burly bartender handed him the beers he nodded toward Carl lining up another shot at the pool table. "That white boy's one of the craziest mother fuckers I've ever met. You and him go back a ways?"

"A ways," Toby said, not elaborating.

"Seem like he been around here forever, ya know. Just walkin' around tickin'. Tick, tick, tick . . . like a bomb waitin' to go off," the big man said, shaking his head.

Toby just winked at him then grabbed the beers and headed back to the table. When Carl had taken his he said, "You do what they say you did?"

Toby drained half of his in one swallow, set it on the table and looked at him. "I don't know, what do they say I did?"

"You know what they say you did. They say you're the French Lick Rapist or some shit; that you supposedly raped a bunch of women. You do that?" he asked again, taking a long pull off his beer.

"Do you really give a rat's ass one way or the other?"

Carl appeared to think about that for a moment. "No." he finally decided.

"Then shut the fuck up and let's shoot pool."

"You rack," Carl said as he began chalking his stick.

CHAPTER 25

Jay Krump tapped on his boss's open door. "Got a second?"

"Sure, come on in, Jay. What's up?"

"It's about the McGrady kid."

"What about him?" Michael asked, suddenly attentive.

"Well, it looks like we lost track of him for a couple of hours yesterday toward the early evening."

"What do you mean, *lost track of him*?"

"Apparently they watched him get in his car around six p.m. and he drove away from his house, but then he started driving crazy; whipping down alleys, making illegal u-turns, all kinds of crazy stuff, and then they lost him. They're pretty sure he knows he's being watched."

"Of course he knows he's being watched," Michael said loudly. "The judge told him we'd be watching him for Christ's sake. This isn't some covert CIA operation, we need to keep our thumb on this kid and keep him rattled so he doesn't go after anyone else."

"I know, boss, I know," Jay said. "Do you want me to call the captain over there at the precinct?"

"No, I'll call him. Shit! So do we have any idea where he went?"

"No."

"No calls from any hospitals or rape centers?"

"Not yet."

"Not yet," Michael repeated angrily. "So when did he get home?"

"Around eight. And then later that evening he drove to the East side and hung out at some pool hall for about an hour."

"The East side? He's a little pale to be hanging around that part of town isn't he?"

"You'd think so but apparently the guy he met up with was white as well; some redheaded dude."

"What did he do after that?"

"Went home."

"For the rest of the night?"

"That's what I was told."

"Okay, look, I'm going to call this captain and explain that they need to tighten up their surveillance. Do we know where this joker is now?"

"Yeah, he's attending his Uncle's funeral."

"Too bad it's not his own," Michael mumbled.

"What's that?"

"Nothing. Stay in communication with whomever it is at the precinct that's been giving you the status reports, okay?"

"No problem."

"Listen to me, Jay – this kid is a demented fuck and we simply cannot afford to lose him again and then stand around holding our collective breath while we wait for him to resurface. Ask your point-of-contact to please emphasize this to the officers assigned to watch him, okay? I'll do the same when I get this captain on the phone."

"Will do."

When Jay had left Michael picked up the phone. He and a certain captain were about to have a little heart-to-heart.

∽

Forty-five minutes into the service and two boring eulogies later, Toby was starting to grow restless. He had things to do and they didn't include sitting here listening to every peckerwood who ever knew his Uncle use this as an opportunity for their fifteen minutes of fame. He was a lawyer for crying out loud; how exciting could his life have been?

He began looking around to see if he recognized anyone, and when he cut his eyes to the back of the room he saw a face that looked very familiar. He was sitting off by himself in the last row and as he looked closer his eyes widened. Is that who I think it is? He couldn't believe it but sure enough, Judge Scalini was sitting in the back of the chapel trying his best to look inconspicuous.

Holy shit, Toby thought. He's got a lot of damn nerve I'll give him that. He leaned over to his mom and with as much manufactured emotion as he could muster he whispered, "I need to go get some air, Mom. I'll be back in a couple of minutes, okay?"

She patted his leg sympathetically and said quietly, "Okay, but try not to be gone too long."

As he walked down the center aisle he made a point of not looking at the judge since he didn't want to let on that he'd seen him, and once he made it to the reception area he noticed the only other people out there were a couple of funeral home employees who had been tapped for usher duty. After getting a drink from the fountain he engaged them in some meaningless conversation for a couple of minutes and then announced that he needed to get back in before his mother came looking for him and they had to deal with two funerals that day. They thought that was funny and chuckled noiselessly as one of them held the door open for him to re-enter, but rather than return to where his mother was sitting he walked straight over to the judge and slid quietly into the pew, causing Anthony to involuntarily slide to his right before he had a chance to realize who it was.

In a voice that wouldn't travel to those around them Toby said, "Thought the trial was over, Judge?"

Without looking at him Anthony replied, "I'm here to pay my respects to an old friend, that's all."

"That right? Well I guess I can understand that. After all, from what I hear you and my Uncle went way back; lots of history and all that, right?"

When Anthony didn't respond Toby continued. "That is right, isn't it; about the history? Yeah, my mom told me all about it. About how you and Uncle Brett met at law school and you used to study together and double date together and go drinking together and, of course, run down little girls together."

He saw the judge stiffen but to his credit he still managed to maintain his silence.

"You know, the normal stuff that kids do," Toby finished. Anthony was stunned by what he was hearing but tried not to show it. He had no idea that Ms. McGrady had actually told her son what they had spoken of.

"You got your get out of jail free card, son, what else could you possibly want?"

"Now that's the million dollar question, isn't it?" Toby whispered. "What else could I want? Hmm, well, I suppose it's possible that I'll never want anything from you again. But then again, I guess it just depends on how annoyed I get at those cops who keep following me everywhere I go. They're kind of cramping my style, if you know what I mean. Of course, I'm sure I'm not telling you anything you don't already know seeing as how you're the one who threatened me with harassment in your courtroom. Did you sick them on me?"

"I'm a judge, not the police department. If they have surveillance set up on you that's a decision that's been made by them, not me."

"Maybe so, but you can put a stop to it."

"I cannot just unilaterally tell them to stop *harassing you*, as you put it, Mr. McGrady. There is procedure that must be followed and I could not initiate it even if I wanted to." He had raised his voice slightly and a couple of people turned to give them disapproving looks.

"So how do I get it stopped?"

"Son, I've provided all the help I ever intend to where you're concerned. You're on your own from here on out."

"You know, I kind of like the way that sounds – son," Toby repeated, letting the *s* linger on his tongue as he pronounced it. "We just never know what surprises life has in store for us, do we?"

Sensing a veiled threat, the judge turned and looked at him. "Is there something else you need?"

"Ah, so we're back to that again, are we? Tell you what, Yo Ahnah," Toby said, affecting a southern accent. "I'll have to get back to you on that. I do have one piece of advice for you, though," he said, leaning in even closer. "Whatever you do, don't sell yourself short when it comes to your future participation in my well-being. You may find one day that I've suddenly become a priority in your life again. As a matter of fact, I'm almost sure of it," he said, grinning as if he and a friend had just stumbled upon a fishing hole that no one else knew about.

With that said, Toby stood up, walked around behind the pew and bent down with his mouth close to his ear. "Don't be here when the service is over. You might upset my mom and then I'll have to get upset. Believe me, I'm not nearly this charming when I'm angry." With that he patted him on the shoulder and walked away to rejoin his mother.

The judge stayed for another five minutes and then made his way out to his car where he had to force himself to breathe slowly and evenly. He'd thought this nightmare was over but now it appeared that it quite possibly could just be starting. He was as terrified right now as he had been that night with Brett, the only difference being that unlike when they had run down that girl, the source of his terror this time around was unpredictable - which somehow made it even worse. He now knew how those ducks in the arcades felt when they were being shot repeatedly as they traveled back and forth, exposed and defenseless. He knew he needed to find a way to regain control of his life but barring turning himself in; he couldn't seem to come up with a strategy that made sense. He was going to have to figure out something, though. Today had convinced him that he didn't have any other choice.

CHAPTER 26

Immediately following his Uncle's funeral Toby gathered three of his friends, one being Carl Fuller, and managed to talk them into going with him to Mulligan's. They couldn't understand why he wanted to go hang out with a bunch of preppies and they bitched incessantly until he informed them he'd heard a rumor that all the waitresses were hot. That was all they needed to hear and the mutiny was instantly quelled.

Once they arrived the other three set about the task of verifying the rumor for themselves while he asked the young girl responsible for seating if they could sit in Gabriella Scalini's section. She paused long enough to give him an annoyed look, popped her gum and then told them to follow her as she simultaneously rolled her eyes. Toby was suddenly gripped by an overpowering urge to smash his fist into her face and it took all the willpower he could muster to keep from acting on it. Besides, he had more important things on his mind this night.

Once they were seated Toby spotted Gabriella delivering an order of food to a group of people three tables over. He'd thought she was a knockout as he'd watched her from his car last evening, but she looked even better in the light. After a couple of minutes she hurriedly made her way over to them and stood with pencil poised above order pad.

"What can I get for you, fellas?" she asked. Her long black hair was pulled back in a ponytail and she was wearing the mandatory uniform of white tennis shoes, short black skirt and a white T-shirt with the Mulligan's leprechaun logo on the front and back. It was obvious that the owner only purchased t-shirts in petite sizes as her bust-line stretched hers until the leprechaun on the front grinned distortedly. It was a constant source of irritation to her as she wasn't entirely comfortable with all the stares her chest garnered.

"Wow! I'll take your phone number as an appetizer and some comfort for a weary soul as an entree, please," Carl said, sitting closest to her on the right.

Gabby looked over to see a guy who looked to be in his early twenties with a mop of red, curly hair and a face full of freckles that seemed, to Gabby at least, to be obligatory for people with that hair color. And judging by the smug tone of his voice, he was obviously quite impressed with what he thought to be his considerable wit.

"That's great," she said dryly. "Now why don't you try ordering something that's actually *on* the menu, honey."

Inflected choruses of *"Ooooh's!"*, as well as dramatic simulations of airplanes crashing and burning were immediately bestowed upon Carl by the other two, to which he responded by flipping them the bird and pouring himself another beer from the pitcher. Gabby noticed, however, that the one sitting across the table was not participating. His eyes moved around the table, casually taking it all in with a slightly amused look, but they kept returning to her. The hypnotic intensity and intelligence of that gaze made her feel breathless, dizzy and intensely euphoric all at the same time. He had sandy-blonde hair cut short, strong features, and those eyes . . . those . . . deep . . . emerald . . .

"I'm sorry?" she said, shaking her head slightly is if to shrug free of some horrible embrace. "What did you say?"

"I said you'll have to excuse my friends," Toby repeated. "They tend to become puberty-challenged when in the presence of a beautiful woman." Carl promptly wadded up his napkin and threw it at him, but Toby dodged it easily.

"Oh, that's okay," she responded. "They probably have a promising future with the circus." Toby laughed at that but his friends didn't, although it was anyone's guess as to whether or not their collective attention spans enabled them to actually follow the conversation.

"Now are you all ready to order or should I give you time to compose yourselves and come back later?"

They were hungry so without conferring they unanimously decided they should order while they had the chance. Once that was accomplished, the quiet one motioned for her to come over to his side of the table. She couldn't remember complying but somehow she found herself standing next to him and chewing on her bottom lip like an eighth grader.

Toby leaned back to look at her. "In order to reassure you that I was not, in fact, born with the same "*stuck in adolescence for life*" gene that appears to afflict my friends here," he said with an encompassing wave of his hand. "I'm going to do something unorthodox and ask you now, rather than at the end of the evening, if you would consider going out with me. This way you'll have an opportunity to get to know me a little before you have to actually decide."

Gabby's mouth started to move – though she had no idea what it was she was going to say – when he abruptly held up his hand.

"Don't answer me now. Only after you've assured yourself that I'm an alright guy, then you can give me an answer before we leave – okay?" he said, smiling warmly.

She nodded her head and began walking slowly toward the kitchen with their orders, pissed at herself for feeling awkward and not knowing how to respond. Suddenly she stopped and turned around . . . "Do you have a name?"

"Toby. And you don't need to reciprocate, Gabriella, as your name tag has already betrayed you." She involuntarily glanced down, then looked back up and flashed him a shy grin as she left to put their orders in.

"Damn, that bitch is smokin'!" Carl proclaimed. "And I think she likes you, dude."

"Of course she likes me," Toby responded jokingly. "What's not to like?"

That prompted two more wadded napkins and a spoon to be launched at him, which made them all laugh. Other tables noticed the shenanigans but no one said a word. Most people can inherently sense trouble when it's near and one didn't have to look too hard to find it lurking amongst these four.

The next hour consisted of Gabby bringing them their food, refilling their drinks, and checking on them more often than was really necessary. On the one hand she felt silly and obvious, but on the other hand she couldn't get enough of the brief snatches of conversation and flirtatious looks that were passing between the two of them. Later, when they had demolished their plates, Toby asked his three buddies if they minded going over to the bar area so he could talk to her alone. At first he got nothing but grief but when he offered to pay for the first round he was suddenly alone at the table.

"Where are your friends?" Gabby asked when she returned to check on them for the umpteenth time.

"I sent them to the bar. Can you take a break?" he asked, motioning to the chair next to him.

She looked at her watch nervously. "Sure, but only for a couple of minutes."

"Good, so why don't you tell me about yourself."

Gabby started to blush. "What do you want to know?"

"Everything, but you can start with why you work here."

"Oh, well I attend college at the University of Phoenix and I work here so I have money for all the important things in life like fast food and clothes," she said, only half joking.

"How long have you been attending college?"

"This is my first year."

"What's your major?"

"Technically I don't have one yet, but somehow I managed to pick all the prerequisites for a business degree without really trying, so I'm thinking that maybe my folks did some subliminal brainwashing when I was growing up."

Toby laughed at that. He was aware that a number of other men in the restaurant were watching him with unabashed jealousy and he basked in every envious look.

"Are you close with your folks?"

"Oh yeah, my folks are great," she said, her face lighting up. "I'm really close with them. My dad is actually a judge if you can believe that."

"No kidding. Well they sound like nice people. And I suppose if I ever hope to be able to meet these amazing parents I'm going to have to get in tight with their daughter which, of course, is going to require at least three or four dates. Am I correct?" he asked her.

"I suppose you're right," she said, blushing again.

"And as they say, a journey of a thousand miles begins with a single date."

"That's not exactly what they say," she corrected him, grinning.

"Okay, well maybe my adages are a little skewed, but that doesn't change my question. So will you go out with me?"

"I don't know. You haven't told me anything about yourself yet."

"Well then, that will be our main topic of conversation over dinner." He could see she was thinking about it. "Better hurry," he encouraged her, "my buddies will be back any minute and we both know we don't want to be having this conversation when they're here."

She recognized the wisdom in this and said, "Okay, I'll go out with you. Is tomorrow night good for you? I don't have to work."

"You mean the college-girl doesn't have to study on her night off?" he teased her.

"Look, do you want to go out or not?" she asked him, feigning impatience.

"Okay, you talked me into it. Where do I pick you up and what time?" he asked, knowing exactly where he would be picking her up.

"I'll write my address on this napkin for you and you can pick me up at seven-thirty. How does that sound?"

"That sounds fantastic, Gabriella. Did I tell you that you have a beautiful name by the way?"

"You just did," she said, standing up and straightening her skirt.

"I'm really looking forward to our date and getting to know you better," Toby said.

"I am too, Toby. I'll see you tomorrow." She favored him with one more smile before going back to work.

Toby met his buddies over at the bar, had one beer with them and left. He had accomplished what he came here to do and he still had one other important thing he needed to get done this evening. The anticipation of that made him smile.

CHAPTER 27

Anthony was sitting in his office at home, turning over and over in his mind the run-in he'd had with Toby McGrady earlier that day. Truth be told, he'd been able to think of little else since. Rose had obviously told her son everything and that fact now put an entirely different spin on things. He'd thought it was over but her son had left little doubt that it was far from that. He had no idea what he was going to do but he knew he had better do something before his world came crashing down around him. The problem, though, was that there was really no simple solution. Every scenario he came up with required that he confess what he'd done to someone who didn't already know about it, and then there was the risk of that person taking it to the police.

He considered his priest but decided that although it would serve to purge his conscience in the short term, he doubted he would be able to help him with the Toby McGrady problem. He'd finally decided that he needed to know how many people Ms. McGrady had told so that he would at least know what he was up against, and the first person he intended to call was Brandon Spencer Hill, Jr. He obtained his contact information through directory services, correctly assuming he was too new to this game to have pissed off enough of his loser clients to have it unlisted yet, and punched in the numbers. He waited while it rang.

Brandon was standing in his kitchen trying to decide what to eat when his phone rang. He shouldn't have been here to answer it since he and Rose had made plans a day earlier to eat at her place, but his decision to tell her about his conversation with Toby had gone over like a lead balloon and so, here he was fending for himself. Luckily she hadn't gone as far as telling him they were through, but she had made it abundantly clear that any relationship to be salvaged would be played out on her terms.

"Hello?"

"Yes, is this Brandon Hill?"

"This is he. Who's calling, please?"

"Mr. Hill, this is, uh . . . this is Judge Anthony Scalini."

"Yes, Your Honor, what can I do for you?" To say that Brandon was shocked and not a little unnerved to hear the judge's voice on the other end would be an understatement. His curiosity was instantly piqued.

"Mr. Hill . . . "

"Please, call me Brandon, Your Honor."

"I'm sorry to bother you," he continued, "but I was wondering if you had a couple of minutes for me."

"Of course, what can I do for you?"

"Fine, well, Brandon, to start with I was hoping that we could keep this call confidential if that's alright with you."

"Sure," Brandon replied, having no idea where this was going.

"I wanted to talk to you about Ms. McGrady, Toby McGrady's mother."

Alarms instantly began to go off for Brandon. "What about her, Your Honor?" he said tentatively.

"She was the one who hired you to represent her son, correct?"

"Yes, that's correct."

"Just out of curiosity, who was it that caught the fact that the search warrant had been improperly served?"

"As much as I'd love to take credit for it, Judge, it was actually her brother who caught it. Apparently he was an attorney. Unfortunately he passed away recently."

"I'm sorry to hear that," he said, ensuring he betrayed nothing of his past relationship with Brett Mitchell. "So he was the one who pointed it out to you and recommended you file the motion for inadmissibility of evidence?"

"Specifically it was Ms. McGrady. I never actually met her brother. But yes, technically it was on his advice that we filed the motion."

"I see. Did she happen to offer you any additional advice regarding the issue of evidence?"

"I'm not sure what you mean, Your Honor."

"I mean did she tell you that her brother may have had any additional advice on how you should proceed?"

"No, that was pretty much it. I verified what I'd been told regarding the wording on the warrant and then went ahead and filed the motion. To be quite honest, Your Honor, I was a little shocked when you ruled in our favor since I seriously doubted that we had any chance at all of prevailing."

"No?" Anthony said, trying to decide whether or not he was telling the truth.

"Don't get me wrong, I was ecstatic that we won, but I know the court had the latitude to rule either way."

"So that was it? Ms. McGrady's brother caught the mistake with the warrant, she told you about it and you went ahead and filed the petition and hoped for the best?"

"That about sums it up. Is there something that's happened I should be made aware of, Judge?" he asked him, fishing now.

There was a short pause as he concluded in his mind that Mr. Hill was likely telling the truth. In one way it was a small measure of relief, but this only added an additional layer of complexity to an already convoluted situation. "No, Brandon, nothing has happened so please don't worry yourself needlessly. Listen, I appreciate you taking the time to speak with me and I also appreciate you maintaining the confidentiality of this call."

"Sure, no problem, Your Honor," Brandon replied, but the confusion was apparent in his voice. First there were his doubts about being able to win on the motion, and then there was his suspicion that there had been something else that had contributed to the favorable ruling. And, of course, there was Toby. If he was a betting man he'd lay odds that Toby was guilty as sin. He may not be guilty of raping all those women necessarily, though Brandon suspected he was, but he was definitely guilty of something. That kid was bad news and something was going on that even Rose didn't know about, regardless of how well she claimed she knew her son. Brandon decided to take a shot in the dark.

"Your Honor, is there something you want to tell me? I want you to know that I meant it when I said I would keep this conversation confidential."

He could here the judge breathing, as if he had started to say something and then changed his mind, but finally all he said was, "I'm not sure what you're getting at?"

"To be completely honest neither am I, Your Honor. I just have the feeling that there's something more you'd like to say to me but something's causing you to hold back."

"I believe I've taken up enough of your time already, Brandon." He was starting to regret making this call in the first place, and if Rose found out, there was no telling what she or her son would do.

"Your Honor," Brandon said hurriedly, "one question, please, if I may."

"Of course, you've certainly been kind enough to accommodate me."

"Did you rule in our favor because you believed it was the right thing to do, or was there another reason?"

Anthony considered the question carefully before answering. "Brandon, sometimes the belief in a person's right to a fair trial and the belief in their innocence goes hand-in-hand. Then again, sometimes they are separated by a distance too great to measure. Between you and I, if you have fulfilled the obligations of your representation of Mr. McGrady, and do not yet feel you have desecrated your soul, then my advice would be to move on with your life, never look back for even a second, and consider yourself to be a very lucky man. Enjoy the rest of your evening, Brandon, and thank you again for keeping this between us."

"You're welcome, Your Honor," he responded absently, still trying to get his arms around what the judge had just said. When he heard a short, quick beeping in his ear he realized that the judge had hung up and he did likewise.

CHAPTER 28

"The natives are all tucked in for the night," Corporal Brian Hennessey announced as Sergeant Landler came on post. The Sergeant was there to relieve him and would now stand guard over the prisoners of Monroe County for the remainder of the night. "No issues?" Landler asked him.

Hennessey was in his late twenties, overweight, took no pride in how he looked in his uniform, apparently wasn't a fan of soap and water, had a perpetually bad attitude, and was constantly going out of his way to antagonize the prisoners in spite of being warned repeatedly by both his peers and superiors alike that this last practice was a very bad idea. Landler, as well as a majority of the other guards, held to the collective opinion that Hennessey was to the jail system what a perforated condom was to birth control as far as effectiveness was concerned.

"You know there're never any issues when I'm on duty," Hennessey responded cockily, "I keep these shit birds in line."

"Is that right?" Landler said. "Well one of these days one of these shit birds is going to stick a homemade shank through your spleen."

"When hell freezes over," he shot back defiantly.

"Okay, but don't say I didn't warn you," he said. "You can take off now, I've got it."

"Good enough. I'll see ya."

"Yeah, I'll see you," he said, shaking his head in disgust as he watched him waddle down the hall toward the changing room. Guards couldn't wear their uniforms outside of the jail so they had to arrive and leave in civvies. When Hennessey had changed he wadded up his uniform and stuffed it into a gym bag - he'd more than likely put the same one on tomorrow without ironing it - and proceeded to the last hard-line before the exit. He had to push a button to get Landler's attention to buzz him through, and when the sergeant looked at one of the dozen or so monitors in front of him to verify who it was, he saw Hennessey flipping off the camera with a shit-eating grin on his fat face. He shook his head again and pushed the button that cut the power to the magnetic lock and watched him go through. He then waited for him to secure the door behind him before buzzing him through the exit that led out into the dark parking lot. Here he disappeared from the camera's unblinking eye since there was no surveillance in the parking lot. *Good riddance, dipshit.*

Damn, it's colder than an Eskimo's pecker out here Hennessey thought to himself as he made his way to the beat-up Toyota pick-up truck that was his pride and joy. He fancied himself a macho guy and any moron could tell you that macho guys drove pick-ups. Of course, the fact that he hadn't been on a date in over two years and had only a couple of friends who could stand to be around him for more than ten minutes seemed to be lost on him. When he arrived at the driver's door he began fumbling in his jeans for his keys.

"Hey, Homie? Fancy meeting you here."

Hennessey froze and his breath lodged in his diaphragm like a painful mass as something fluttered at the fringes of his mind . . . something familiar . . . he knew he recognized the voice . . . he . . . and then it came to him. His eyes grew wide and his sphincter convulsed as he began to turn around.

There was a violent explosion of pain accompanied by a brilliant burst of white light, and then blackness as he crumpled to the icy asphalt. "Oops, too late, mother fucker."

∽

Carl and the other two guys were having a ball messing with the cops. Before leaving Mulligan's he had switched jackets with Toby and all four of them had walked through the parking lot to their cars with their hoods up. Carl and the other two got into Toby's car with instructions to take the cops on a little joy ride for a couple of hours, which would give Toby time to take care of some pressing business. Later he would meet them at his apartment and they would switch back. Carl was amused at how easy it was to fool these idiots. This was almost too much fun.

∽

When Corporal Hennessey began to regain consciousness he realized two things almost simultaneously. The first was that his head felt as though it had been trampled by an entire herd of buffalo. The second was that he was freezing his ass off. As a matter of fact, he couldn't remember ever being so cold in his life. The pain in his head caused him to cry out but he was surprised to find that he was able to emit only a faint muffled sound. That surprise quickly turned to panic, though, as he realized that his mouth had been stuffed full of dirt and taped closed. He tried to raise his hands to remove the tape but discovered he couldn't move them from behind his back. As a matter of fact he couldn't move anything, and as the intense cold forced the cobwebs from his mind, just how dire his situation was started to become clear.

He could tell that he was tied to a tree, but it was so much worse than that. For starters, he appeared to be completely naked. His body was facing toward the tree, which was approximately two feet in circumference, but he was probably three or four feet off the ground with his legs wrapped around the trunk and bound tightly together on the other side, which was causing his unprotected groin to press painfully into the rough bark. His upper body was being held against the tree by a rope that was wrapped around the back of his neck and also secured on the opposite side of the tree. It was holding his head immobile and he could feel the bark cutting into the left side of his face. In this vulnerable position his body weight was being primarily supporting by his neck and groin, and the pain was quickly becoming unbearable. He needed to figure out a way to free himself – and fast – or he would freeze to death.

"It's a funny thing about people, Hennessey. They never take you seriously until you show them just how seriously they really should have taken you."

His body tensed at the sound of the voice behind him. He'd assumed that he had just been tied up and left here to die, and though that would have been bad enough, knowing someone was still here not only struck unimaginable terror in him, but forced him to consider that things could potentially get a lot worse before they got better.

Toby walked around and stood on Hennessey's right side where he could see him. "Know what I mean?" The recognition on Hennessey's face was immediate. His eyes were wide and the whites dominated the pupils like a cow being herded down the slaughter chute, terrified by the smell of death in the air. He tried to say something but could only make muted, choking sounds.

"I wouldn't try to talk if I were you, fat-boy. You've got a couple of handfuls of Mother Nature's finest stuffed in your soup-cooler and I'd sure hate to have you croak before I'm done with you. Besides, I humped your fat ass more than half a mile out into these woods so there's no one around to hear you anyway. By the way, you really should think about going on a diet." He was holding a stick that looked to be about three feet long and maybe two inches thick, and he continued to talk as he absently whittled one end to a point.

"See, I have this theory. Interested in hearing it?" When he didn't receive the eager response he was expecting he stopped and raised the pointed end of the stick to within an inch of Hennessey's right eye. "I asked you a question, chubby," he said, cocking an eyebrow expectantly.

Hennessey could feel the bark tear at his face as he nodded his head. He was shivering uncontrollably from the cold and was probably in the beginning stages of hypothermia.

"Good," Toby said, going back to his whittling. "Okay, so the theory goes like this: There're leaders in the world and there're those who are destined to be dominated by those leaders. Think of it as life's natural caste system, if you will. Now most people seem to have an inherent understanding as to which category they fall into, but every once in awhile you come across some dipshit who's suffering from an identity crisis. You see, he *wants* to be the man." Toby raked the air with the index and middle fingers of both hands to simulate quotation marks when he said *the man.* "He *wants* to dominate others, but in reality all he's doing is perpetrating a fraud. You've heard that saying, haven't you? Perpetrating a fraud? The brothers in the ghetto like to use it. Makes 'em feel smart. So anyway, think of a little Chihuahua that wants to be a Great Dane. It does a lot of posturing but at the end of the day it's still just a piece-of-shit little dog with no ass to back up its bark. Kind of like you, Hennessey," he said, looking up.

"See, you fancy yourself a tough guy, and you run your mouth like you're a tough guy, but when it's time to put up or shut up, you're really just a big fat Chihuahua, aren't you?" Hennessey didn't respond and with absolutely no hesitation, Toby stepped forward and viciously jabbed the stick through the right side of his cheek until the point struck teeth and gums. The pain caused him to squeal deep within his throat and his eyes grew wide again as he sucked in and exhaled rapidly through his nose, trying desperately to draw oxygen into his lungs.

"Better relax, hombre, or you're going to choke to death," Toby advised him as he extracted the bloody point of the stick from his face. "I assume you're starting to see a pattern develop here, correct? See, I ask you a question, and you..." He pointed the stick at his eye again. "...well you provide an immediate answer. I think even *you* can handle that, can't you?" Hennessey immediately nodded his head, further tearing the skin on his face against the bark.

"Good for you," Toby said, patting him on his head. "And just to be fair, I'm telling you right now that there is no such thing as a rhetorical question in this conversation, okay?" Again he nodded, having no clue as to what a rhetorical question actually was but agreeing just the same. He was starting to get his breathing under control and the fear of suffocation began to pass for the time being. However, he was beginning to shiver uncontrollably.

"So the question then becomes one of behavioral conditioning; how do you get a Chihuahua to act like a Chihuahua, and not a Great Dane?" he said, resuming his sharpening of the bloodied stick. "Actually it's quite simple. See, it's a little thing I like to refer to as *shock therapy.* Have you heard of it?"

Hennessey did his best to shake his head no, though the rope around his neck had his head pulled so tightly against the tree that it was difficult. His scrotum and penis felt like they were on fire in spite of the sub-freezing temperature, and he was pretty sure he was bleeding down there.

"Well let me explain it to you," Toby continued. "Let's say a Chihuahua comes running up to you and starts in with its goddamned yipping and nipping at your pant leg, right?" Toby wasn't looking for a response but Hennessey was nodding vigorously anyway. "You're annoyed so you point your finger at it and tell it to shut the hell up, but does that work? Hell no, it doesn't work," he said, providing his own answer. "You go through all that and the Chihuahua still thinks it's a Great Dane. So what should you have done differently?"

Hennessey shrugged his shoulders since yes or no wasn't an appropriate response, and this caused Toby to laugh. "See, this just showcases the difference between you and me. *I know*."

The next time this little fur-biscuit comes running up on you like that, you just haul back and kick the little bastard as hard as you can and send him squealing into the nearest wall. Now if you did that, do you think it would come back for more?" Hennessey shook his head no.

"No, of course not. And you know why too, don't you?" He nodded this time, though he was thankful he didn't have to actually provide an answer.

"Because with one swift kick you've dispelled any illusion about him being something he's not. He finally gets it, and he'll understand his place the next time he sees you. That's why it's called shock therapy."

Hennessey nodded. He understood now and he was terrified at how this might relate to his situation. He tried to say something but the dirt had sucked all the moisture from his mouth and it was all he could do to keep from gagging.

"You sound like you have something to say, fat-boy. The problem is I think you said all I wanted to hear that day you were walking me back to my cell. You remember don't you? You said, and I quote, ""*They just love rapists there. You'll be bending over for twelve inches of black pipe before you've had a chance to say Ku Klux Klan.*"" Does that sound about right? Does that sound like something you might have said to me?"

Hennessey knew he'd said it but the fear of what would happen if he agreed caused him to hesitate. Unfortunately that proved to be a huge mistake.

Toby gave him a disappointed look as he raised the stick again, and with the calm precision of a maniacal surgeon, he pressed the sharp point against Hennessey's right eye. After the slightest of hesitations during which Hennessey saw with his other eye that Toby was grinning crazily, he rammed the stick deep into his socket. He heard as much as felt a sickening, wet pop, and the pain that erupted was unlike anything he had ever experienced or could have possibly imagined. It was as if someone had placed a white phosphorous grenade inside his eye socket and then stood back and watched as it seared through layer after layer of flesh, bone, and brain matter. Thankfully he passed out.

When he came to he had no idea how long he'd been out, but he awoke to the sensation of liquid washing over his face and body. The place where his ruined eye had formerly resided felt like it was on fire. When he opened his other eye he saw that Toby was pouring bottle after bottle of beer over him which at first had a warming effect against the near zero degree temperature, but it wasn't long before his upper body and head were encased in a frozen layer of barley and hops.

"I thought that might wake you up," Toby said, looking at his work with the critical eye of an artist. "So where were we? Ah, now I remember, I was waiting for you to confirm whether I had remembered your threat correctly."

Hennessey began to nod immediately, accompanied by a low moan from deep in his throat. "Good! Now we're getting somewhere," Toby said jubilantly. "So you see, you're just like that Chihuahua. You yip and you yip but no matter how many times you stand your fat, disgusting ass in front of that mirror and flex like a Great Dane, you're still just a Chihuahua. This creates a dilemma for me, though, because obviously I can't kick you across the room, can I?" Hennessey shook his head.

"No, of course not. You're too damn fat. However, I think you'd agree with me that the need for shock treatment still exists." Hennessey's moaning became louder and he began shaking his head back and forth as much as his position would allow.

"What, you don't think so? Well, if I recall correctly, in response to your rude assertion that I was destined for an assault on my nether regions, I believe I responded by telling you that it just may be you who ends up in a compromising position over a fallen log. I assume you remember that part of the movie, right?"

He nodded again as he desperately sucked and pushed air through his nostrils in an attempt to deliver oxygen to his ravaged body.

"Well here's some good news for you, fat-boy . . . I'm not a faggot."

Hennessey felt a modicum of relief that was short-lived as he watched Toby drop the stick and reach up over his head, pulling down a rope that he had slung over a tree branch earlier. Hennessey hadn't noticed it before but panic set in when he saw that it was tied into a noose. He struggled to free himself but it was useless and at this point he didn't think he had any feeling in his arms and legs anyway. The shivering had gotten so bad that the bark was tearing his skin off in layers as Toby stepped forward and placed the noose over his head, forcing it between his face and the tree trunk. He then slid the knot down until it was tight against the back of his neck.

"See, when I cut the rope that's around your fat neck," he said, pulling a knife from his waistband, "your upper body will fall backwards. But since your legs are still tied around the tree you'll just hang that way until you slowly asphyxiate. Do you know what that means, Hennessey? Asphyxiate?"

He nodded again. "Good. So as you might imagine it'll hurt some, but luckily it's not as bad as a poke in the eye with a sharp stick, right?" This caused a deep bellowing laugh to erupt from Toby, which ended as abruptly as it began and then he was serious again.

"Guys like you, Hennessey – you're not even a challenge. You're a mere distraction. Most of those women put up more of a fight than you did." Hennessey's one eye looked at him as he realized somewhere through the intense fog of pain that he was hearing a confession from a serial rapist.

"Oh, don't look so shocked. I never told you I *didn't* do it, did I? Anyhow, I hope you don't think I've hurt you up to this point, Corporal. No, sir, I surely hope you don't, because thus far it's been child's play compared to what's coming next. Did you honestly think you could talk to me like that and that I'd just let it go?"

Hennessey began moaning in rhythm with his shivering as it became more and more apparent that he wasn't getting out of this alive, and he now prayed that the end would be quick. Unfortunately God's grace was reserved for someone else that night and unbeknownst to him, the only blessing he'd be receiving had already been delivered. It lay hidden in the fact that Toby had not bothered to tell him up front how all this was going to end for him for had he known, he probably would have gone stark raving mad which, all things considered, might have been the best thing that could have happened.

Toby retrieved the stick from where he had dropped it on the ground earlier and stood where Hennessey could see him clearly with his one good eye. "If you've never believed anything in your life, Hennessey, believe this: In a few seconds you're going to wish like hell it *was* me back there gruntin' and howlin' like a toothless hillbilly, you miserable piece-of-shit." With that he walked around behind him, dropped down on one knee and placed the point of the stick against the opening of his anus, inserting the tip about half an inch.

Hennessey screamed with every ounce of energy remaining in his abused body, but all he accomplished was swallowing a good portion of the dirt in his mouth and with no saliva left, it lodged in his throat and he began to choke. At the same time, Toby grabbed the bottom of the stick with both hands and shoved upward. Later, when he had time to reflect on the evening's festivities, he'd find it remarkable that other than some slight resistance during the initial penetration, the rest was similar to impaling thick, wet toilet paper as the stick tore through the small and large intestine, the stomach and liver and reached midway through the lungs before stopping.

An inhuman, guttural sound escaped in spite of the dirt stuffed into his mouth and when Toby walked quickly around to the side again, eager to look into his face before the life drained from him, Hennessey began convulsing as his one remaining eye rolled back into his head. Toby then took out the knife and placed the edge against the rope securing his head against the tree. "Adios, mother fucker," he said as he sliced it in two and watched Hennessey's upper body fall away from the tree and jerk to a stop. He stood directly over him and watched him suffer for a full five minutes without a trace of emotion on his face before finally gathering his things and beginning the lengthy walk out of the woods and back to his car. It was a relaxing stroll without the extra two hundred and fifty pounds draped over his shoulders, and he whistled a new song he'd heard recently by a group called *Godsmack*. The name of the song was *Serenity*.

It would take Corporal Hennessey thirty more minutes to die.

⁘

Toby parked Carl's car behind his own, flipped up the hood on his jacket, and walked into the house with a shit-eating grin on his face. He had given Carl his house key when they were at the restaurant so the three of them were already waiting for him inside and as far as the police were concerned, he was just one more friend who happened to be stopping by. No one asked him what he'd been up to and that suited him just fine since he kept his personal business to himself.

Before long someone mentioned poker, and after a quick beer run down to the corner 7-11 that had the cops practically tripping over each other, they settled in for a long night of Texas hold 'em and drinking. Every once in awhile someone would fold early and amuse themselves by walking to the window and either flipping the bird to the cops, or dropping their pants and pressing their butt cheeks against the window. The latter never failed to have the entire group laughing so hard that at least one of them would fall out of his chair.

Toby was in an especially good mood. Taking care of that pig Hennessey was partially responsible, but his pending date with Gabriella tomorrow evening was the kicker. He was really looking forward to getting to know her better. Actually, he was looking forward to getting to know the whole family better. The thought fairly warmed his soul.

"C'mon, deal 'em up," he said.

CHAPTER 29

"You fucking believe this?" Detective David Bronsky had finally found his way out from the road to this remote spot in the woods, and was busy picking leaves and other various hitchhikers off his clothes while he listened to a very agitated uniformed cop who had been assigned to maintain a perimeter around the crime scene.

"I mean, who does something like that to another person?" Without waiting for a response he stuck out his hand and introduced himself. "Sergeant Weisenberger, Willow Grove PD. You with State homicide?"

"Yeah," Bronsky answered, looking past him to where four plainclothes were searching the area around a body that appeared to be tied to a tree. "It's bad, huh?"

"Sickest thing I've ever seen."

"Do we have an ID on the body yet?"

"Yeah, his clothes were thrown over in the brush about twenty yards away. Name's Brian Hennessey. He's a guard at the Monroe County jail."

"No shit? Any leads on who might have done it?"

"Who the hell knows? All I know is that looking at that stick hanging out of his backside makes my friggin' sack shrivel. Can you even imagine? That ain't all he did to him either. One of his eyes is gouged out and stuck to his cheek like a piece of frozen egg white. We're assuming it was done with the same stick."

"Okay, well, I don't guess he's going to get up and dust himself off so I suppose I should get at it."

"Good luck," the Sergeant said. "By the way, you gonna get sex crimes involved seein' as how he's got that stick hanging outta his ass?"

"Yeah, as a matter of fact, can you get one of your boys to call them in for me? Ask for Detective Ray Johnson. Oh, and verify that the coroner's on his way."

"Will do."

"Thanks, I appreciate it. Oh, by the way, who found him?"

"Couple of hunters. I'm guessing they won't be sleeping too good for awhile."

"No doubt. Okay, thanks." And with that he pulled on a pair of gloves and walked over to examine the body. By the time he was finished Detective Johnson was on the scene.

"How you doing, Ray?" David asked as they shook hands.

"Another day at Disneyland. So what do we have?"

"Someone had a real bad night," he said, gesturing toward Hennessey.

"Holy moly! Is that a stick?"

"It would seem so. It also looks as though our killer gouged out his right eye, tried to give him a root canal through his cheek, and then poured beer on him of all things."

"Do we know who he is?"

"Yeah, he's one of the guards over at the Monroe County jail. Name's Hennessey. My guess is that a former prisoner had a beef with him."

"I don't know, David. Prisoners and guards talk smack to each other all the time but I've never heard of it escalating to something like this. Seriously, I mean what kind of rage would it take to cause a man to do something like this to another person?"

"Maybe it isn't rage" Bronsky said thoughtfully. "Maybe the guy who did it was having fun."

Johnson looked at him for a moment and considered what he'd said. "That's just what we need, a damn psycho on the prowl, as if I don't have enough on my plate with this serial fucking rapist on the loose."

Bronsky looked confused. "I thought you guys caught him?"

"We did. And then some shithead judge let him walk on a technicality; said the warrant was supposed be served during daylight hours and we served it at night. You fucking believe that?"

"Yeah, I believe it. Half the time these incompetent judges are the criminals' best friend. Are you pretty sure you had the right guy?"

"Hell yes we had the right guy. We found a shirt in his apartment with one of the victim's blood all over it. That girl is still in a coma and it doesn't look she's ever coming out of it. The judge let him walk before we could make him give blood so we never did match his DNA to the semen samples we have, but I know he's the one. All we can do now is wait until he goes after another victim and hope we're around to stop him before he rapes her - or worse. Personally I think we've got a guy on our hands who's ready to start killing."

"Think so?"

"Yeah, I do. I don't think the raping is enough for him any longer. He beat the holy bejeezus out of his last victim and it didn't appear as though she had even struggled with him, so you have to wonder what it was that set him off."

"The whole world's going to hell in a hand basket, Ray," Bronsky offered, shaking his head.

"You won't get any argument from me there. Let me snap some pictures and then we can cut him down. But for crying out loud, whatever you do don't let him fall on his ass. If that stick disappears I won't be able hold my food down for a week."

ᗣ

"Did you hear about that body they found this morning?" Jay asked. He and the D.A. were in a conference room poring over the details of a case they were taking to trial the following week.

"I heard somebody talking about it but I don't know any of the details," Michael responded, flipping through a number of motions that needed to be filed for other cases.

"Apparently it was some guy who workcd at the jail as a guard. They found him tied naked to a tree. One of his eyes had been gouged out and something like two and half feet of a three foot stick had been shoved in his ass."

Michael stopped what he was doing and looked up at him. "You're joking, right?"

"I wish I were. There are some sick sons of bitches out there, that's for sure."

Suddenly something occurred to Michael. "Where was our boy last night, Jay?"

"I already thought about that and called my contact at the PD. He told me that McGrady was home all night and had friends over. There's no doubt they were there because the officers assigned to watch him reported that they had been mooned out the window at least a dozen times."

"Are we sure *McGrady* was there?"

"They say he was, boss. I can only go by what they tell me unless I stake him out myself."

"It just might come to that, Jay," Michael said, suddenly feeling sick to his stomach.

CHAPTER 30

"Hey, Beautiful," Toby said when Gabriella answered the door. She was wearing a knee-length skirt with tall, black leather boots and a pearl-white turtle neck sweater that contrasted nicely with her long, black hair. *Damn, she is a piece of ass,* Toby thought to himself.

"Hey yourself, Handsome. Come on in," she said, moving aside.

Her roommate, Kiley, was sitting on the couch and trying her best to act disinterested, though in reality she had been anxiously awaiting this opportunity to meet her roommate's newest romantic interest; especially considering that she hadn't shut up about him since she'd woken up this morning. Gabby was known to be a little excitable and she had taken her description of him with a grain of salt, but when he walked in she had to admit that she was impressed by what she saw. Without a doubt his most striking feature was his eyes. They were an emerald-green color of such brilliance that they almost appeared to be backlighted.

"Hi," Toby said, smiling warmly at her.

"Hello," Kiley returned.

"Toby, this is Kiley and Kiley, this is Toby," Gabby said, getting the introductions out of the way.

"Nice to meet you, Kiley," Toby said.

"Likewise," Kiley said. "Where are you taking her tonight?"

"Kiley!" Gabby exclaimed. "Don't be rude!" But she was grinning.

"Yeah, where are you taking me 'cause I'm starving," she said, laughing and rubbing her stomach at the same time.

"It's a surprise. I could tell you but then . . . well, you know how it would have to end," he said, smiling mischievously.

"You wouldn't really kill me on our first date, would you?"

"Perish the thought. I normally don't even consider it until at least the fourth or fifth date," he replied, grinning at her easily.

"Well let's go before I pass out. I feel like I've been fasting for a week."

"Oh, stop exaggerating, Gabby," Kiley said. "Be careful, Toby, she can eat her body weight in pasta."

"Then I guess it's a good thing I'm taking her to Denny's," he said. Both girls looked at him to see if he was serious. "I'm just joking," he laughed.

"I'm going to get my coat," Gabby said, disappearing down a short hallway and through a door he assumed led to her bedroom.

"And how about you, Kiley? Surely you're not staying home all alone tonight, are you? No boyfriend?"

"Nope, no boyfriend at the moment and I have a lot of studying to do tonight. Why, do you have a good-looking friend who's desperate?"

"Oh, I don't think a guy would have to be desperate to want to get to know you better," he stated matter-of-factly.

This embarrassed her and she didn't know how to respond, so she was relieved when Gabby reappeared carrying a knee-length leather coat. Toby took it from her and held it as she slipped it on.

"All ready to go," she announced, turning around to face him.

"Fantastic. It was nice meeting you," he said to Kiley. "Remember, though, all work and no play made Jack a dull boy and it'll do the same to Kiley, so don't study too hard."

"I'll try to keep that in mind," she said, winking at Gabby. "You guys have fun and don't get her home too late, Toby."

"Thanks for the concern, Mom, but don't bother waiting up," Gabby responded with a wink as she closed the door.

Later when Kiley had time to think back on it, she would remember that when he had looked directly at her it was almost as if she could feel him inside her head. She knew it was crazy but she remembered feeling both exhilarated and terrified at the same time, as if she had glimpsed pure, unadulterated evil beckoning seductively to her. An involuntary shiver went through her.

∽

"So where *are* you taking me?" Gabby asked when they were in the car.

"Well, coincidentally I made us reservations at Ravioli's."

"Oh, I love that place," she gushed.

"Good, so I have one brownie point to start off the evening?"

"Sure, but you should know that I hand out demerits like they're going out of style so you'd better watch your step," she warned him. He just looked at her and laughed.

Once they were in the restaurant and seated at their table Toby ordered a bottle of cabernet. The waiter looked as though he were about to ask them for some ID but a hard look from Toby seemed to make him reconsider and he left to retrieve it.

"You're brave," Gabby said. "Weren't you afraid he'd card us?"

"Not really."

"Are you saying I look older than my tender age of nineteen," she teased him.

"No, I'm saying that I look older than *my* tender age of twenty and besides, I gave him a scary look so he wouldn't ask." She laughed at that.

After the waiter had returned with the wine and they'd both ordered, she laced her fingers together under her chin and looked at him across the table. "You promised that if I went to dinner with you you'd tell me all about yourself."

"That I did," he agreed. "So where do I start? Hmm, well, I was born and raised right here locally, went to school at Ben-Davis, and right now I'm working construction with a buddy of mine until I figure out what it is I want to be when I grow up. See how utterly uninteresting it all is," he concluded.

Gabby smiled. "How about your parents?"

"My mom actually lives here locally as well. My dad left us a few years ago and we haven't seen or heard from him since, so it's anyone's guess as to whether or not he's even still alive," he said.

"I'm so sorry, Toby," Gabby said, reaching across the table to take his hands in hers. "That must have been difficult for you and your mother." He noticed she had beautiful, manicured nails that were painted a deep shade of red. "We all make choices in life. My parents didn't get along very well and I guess my dad decided he didn't want to be a part of our lives any longer. What are you gonna do?" he said, offering her a smile, though she noticed it stopped short of his eyes.

"Are you considering going to school?" she asked him, sensing she should change the subject.

"Why, are you concerned what your parents will think about you dating a derelict?" he teased her.

"Of course not, don't be silly. I was just curious."

"I don't know, I haven't ruled it out, but I think I might try to make a go of it as a private contractor. You know, remodeling, add-ons, that sort of thing; see if I can't get something going through a little bit of advertising and word-of-mouth. There's money to be made but your work has to be stellar because you live or die by your reputation."

"That sounds great, Toby. I hope it works out for you if that's what you ultimately decide to do."

"And if it doesn't work out I can always rob banks," he said mischievously.

"I think you might want to work real hard at the construction thing before you consider that."

"Yeah, you're probably right."

Their dinners finally arrived and true to her roommate's warning, Gabriella commenced putting away her spaghetti Bolognese like a champ, while at the same time still managing to look cute and demure. She couldn't have weighed more than a hundred and twenty pounds and he wondered where she was putting it all.

When they were finished the waiter filled their glasses with the last of the wine and asked if they wanted to order dessert, which they both declined. Finally, when their glasses were empty and they had pushed the envelope of their comfort level for a first date, Toby drove her back home. He was relieved to see that she appeared to be unaware of the dark sedan that had been following them throughout the evening.

"I had a really great time tonight," he said as they approached her front door.

"I did too, Toby."

"I hope I can I see you again."

"Oh, I think that could be arranged," she responded. "You have my number so don't be shy about using it. As a matter of fact, if I don't hear from you in the next twenty-four hours I'm going to have to assume you find me hideous and disgusting and start looking for another boyfriend," she said, offering him the most serious look she could muster.

"Is that what I am; your boyfriend?"

She blushed at that. "Well, maybe not just yet, but you're walking away from our first date with more brownie points than demerits so your chances are looking pretty good right about now."

"I'll call you tomorrow," he said, kissing her softly on the forehead. She was still nodding in assent as she watched him get into his car and drive away.

As expected, Kiley was waiting up for her. "Well, don't keep me in suspense – how did it go?" she asked her, clearly excited to hear all the details.

Gabby took a deep breath and looking positively radiant announced, "I think he could be the one, Kiley. I really think he could."

Somewhere deep within Kiley's mind a warning sounded and for the briefest of moments she was overwhelmed with a sense of dread – and then just as quickly it passed. The only lingering effects were the hairs standing straight up on her arms as if an electric current had passed through her body.

෯

Toby was ecstatic as he drove home. In such a good mood, in fact, that he didn't even mind the unmarked cop car behind him. Everything had gone perfectly and he was certain she was falling for him. *The ol' McGrady charm - it works every time,* he thought humorlessly.

When he had parked he started toward the stairs leading up to his apartment, but abruptly changed his mind and instead began walking down the sidewalk until he reached the dark-brown Buick sedan that had parked half a block away. He walked up and rapped on the driver's side window with his knuckles, and after a moment's hesitation the window retracted and the faces of two nervous cops peered out at him.

"Not bad, huh boys?"

"What are you talking about?" the one on the passenger side responded hotly.

"Oh come on now, fellas, you know what I'm talking about. The girl. Not bad for a guy who's supposed to be a rapist, huh?" he said, grinning widely.

"Take a hike, pervert." This came from the one behind the wheel.

"A hike?" Toby appeared to consider it.

"Well, I suppose it's an idea. But the problem is you guys would just follow me, so I think I'll pass."

"That cockiness is going to be your undoing, McGrady." This from the passenger again. "You think you're untouchable but trust me, sooner or later you'll screw up, and when you do we're going to be right there waiting to bust your ass."

"See, now that hurts," Toby said, placing his hand over his heart and appearing to be insulted. He made as if he was going to leave and then snapped his fingers as if he had forgotten something and leaned down to their level. He was amused to see them both flinch.

"I promise you that by the end of the week, you won't be camping out on my doorstep any longer. Bank on it, assholes." He flashed them a huge grin, slapped the car door as he stood up, and walked casually back to his apartment whistling loudly as he went. Yes sir, things were definitely looking up.

CHAPTER 31

"I want those morons to leave me the hell alone."

"Are you sure it's the police?" Brandon asked him.

Toby had gone to his office first thing this morning to see what could be done about the constant harassment. It was getting old and he wanted it to stop.

"Hell yes I'm sure. They've been following me since the day I was released and I'm tired of it. I even walked up to their car last night and had a little chat with them."

"What do you mean you had a *chat* with them?"

"You know - a chat. I knocked on their window, they rolled it down and we chatted," he said, grinning.

"Assuming you're right and they *are* the police, I don't think antagonizing them is the best course of action."

"Then it's a good thing I didn't come here to ask for your opinion, isn't it?"

"Toby, as your attorney, part of my job is to provide you with an objective point of view. Obviously you don't have to act on my advice, but that doesn't relieve me of my obligations. Do you understand what I'm saying?"

"So how's my mom doing, Brandon?" The question came out of left field and he had to collect himself before he could respond.

"Why would you ask me that?"

"Well seeing as how you're the one sleeping with her, who else do you suggest I ask?" Brandon started to say something and changed his mind.

"Now, Brandon, you're not going to insult my intelligence by denying it, are you? After all, I've seen your car parked in her driveway."

"Do you make it a habit to spy on your own mother?"

"I think spy is a harsh word. After all, she is my mother and I believe I have a responsibility to look out for her well-being. Surely you can understand that."

Brandon said nothing for most of thirty seconds as he toyed with a paperclip on his desk. Finally he looked up. "Who are you, Toby? I mean, I've seen your little act when your mother's around, but you and I both know it's just that – an act. So I'm wondering who you really are?"

Toby was inspecting a paperweight he had picked up off of the desk. "So are you going to get the police off my ass, or not?" It was obvious he wasn't going to allow himself to be baited.

"Sure, I'll file the paperwork today, but first let's you and I come to an understanding. You start treating me with some respect and mind your own business where your mother and I are concerned and as a favor to her, I'll continue to represent you for the time being. But the next time you come in here trying to intimidate me with your inappropriate comments and questions about things that don't concern you, then I'm washing my hands of you and you can go find yourself another attorney who'll put up with your bullshit. Fair enough?"

Toby put the paperweight down, leaned back in his chair and began clapping. "Bravo, Brandon, bravo. I'll be damned; you actually do have a pair of balls under that jellyfish exterior. Well good for you," he said as he stood up and walked slowly around the desk until he was standing next to him. Brandon started to stand but Toby put a hand on his shoulder and held him in his chair with what appeared to be frightening little effort. He then leaned down until their faces were less than a foot apart. "Brandon, my man, I can appreciate a display of bravado just like the next guy. Really, I can. But sometimes a man just needs to recognize when he's about to bite off more than he can chew. Do you understand what I'm saying to you, 'cause I surely hope you do?"

Brandon didn't respond. He was ashamed to admit that he was scared and his breath was coming in shallow, ragged pulls. He could feel Toby's eyes boring into him, and if he'd ever doubted just how dangerous this kid was, those doubts had just been erased forever.

"Given that this little talk is most likely going to set a precedent for all future interaction between you and I, I'm afraid I'm going to have to insist on some kind of a response from you," he said, giving his shoulder a firm squeeze. "A simple nod will suffice."

"I understand," he finally managed to choke out.

Toby stood up abruptly; a broad smile adorning his face. "Good! Well I'm glad we were able to get past that. So you'll file the paperwork today?"

Brandon nodded again and was relieved to see him start for the door. He put his hand on the knob but stopped short of opening it, instead turning back toward him.

"By the way, did you happen to read in the paper this morning about those hunters who found some guy tied to a tree out in the woods? It said that whoever it was killed him had gouged out one of his eyes and impaled him with a stick where the sun don't shine. Can you imagine, Brandon – having a stick shoved up the ol' derriere? Who do you suppose would do something like that, anyway?" He paused as if to consider his own question, then shrugged and moved to open the door.

"The paper didn't say anything about a stick, Toby. It also didn't specify where he'd been impaled."

Toby stopped but didn't turn around. "Didn't it? Hmm, well maybe I read a different paper. Or maybe I've just watched *Deliverance* one too many times and can't get that scene out of my mind where them hillbillies put that fat city boy over the fallen tree and make him squeal like a pig." He started laughing at this. "I swear that's one of my all-time favorite movies."

"No, Toby, before you arrived I was talking to someone I know at the police station and he gave me some of the details that haven't been reported yet. There *was* a stick, and he *was* impaled where you say. Now how could you know that?" he asked him pointedly.

Toby turned and smiled broadly. "Well how do you like that, I may actually be clairvoyant. Maybe I could go on the talk show circuit or something. Well, anyway, don't forget to file that paperwork for me? Oh, and make sure you request that Judge Scalini hear it." And with that he was gone.

Brandon sat at his desk for most of ten minutes, not trusting his legs to stand. He knew that most people would probably go straight to the police if they'd heard what he'd just heard. Unfortunately, there were two reasons why he wasn't going to do that. The first was that his relationship with Rose was already tenuous and he wasn't prepared to completely throw it away over her loser son. The second was a simple truth he could no longer deny; he was terrified of Toby and of what he might do to him if he found out. No, for now he was just going to have to cross his fingers and hope the police were able to put him back in prison where he belonged.

CHAPTER 32

"Your Honor, this guy is a rapist; a *serial* rapist. We're not talking one victim here; we're talking many - more than ten that we know of. And with all due respect, now that this court has put him back on the street there *will* be more; especially if he knows we're not watching him any longer." The D.A. was beside himself. Not only had this judge let McGrady waltz out the door, but now he was calling to inform him that he was issuing a court order that would prevent the police department from continuing their surveillance.

"Michael, I understand this is difficult for you to accept but I'm sure I don't need to remind you that it wasn't the court who set McGrady free, it was the police department's disregard for procedure."

"We have a t-shirt covered with the blood of one of his victims who's probably going to be a vegetable for the rest of her life," he practically screamed.

"What the State has is a t-shirt that's been ruled inadmissible as evidence so your point is moot."

"Judge, what do you think is going to happen when we give him free reign again?"

"Mr. Haas, you cannot harass someone who hasn't been either charged with or found guilty of a crime, regardless of how strongly you believe in their guilt. You know this."

"We need to make an exception, Your Honor. I'm telling you, all hell is going to break loose if you issue this injunction."

"I'm sorry but my hands are tied. The police department simply cannot continue with its surveillance."

"Okay, but I want to go on record with you right now in saying that there's only one way this thing can end, and that's badly. Now if you'll excuse me, I have a wife and two daughters I need to warn. Good day, Judge."

"Good day, Mr. Haas, and good luck."

The next call Anthony made was to Brandon Hill.

"Hello?" Brandon answered.

"Mr. Hill, this is Judge Scalini."

"Yes, Judge, what can I do for you?" Brandon asked, once again wondering why the judge was calling him directly.

"I'm calling to inform you that I have issued the injunction, so you may inform your client that there will be no more surveillance or harassment of any kind by the police department."

"That's great news, Your Honor," Brandon said, the sentiment ringing hollow.

"Is it?" Anthony asked him.

"What do you mean, Judge?"

"I mean is it great news that the only people who can stop this guy have just been told that they can no longer keep tabs on him?"

"What choice did you have? The police can't harass people who haven't even been charged with a crime."

"I agree, but it doesn't make this one any easier."

"Judge, no doubt this will come as quite a shock to you, but I'm actually seeing his mother; romantically, that is. It started shortly after the arraignment hearing. Anyway, my point is that I'm in a position to have at least some idea as to McGrady's whereabouts. Should he disappear for too long, or do or say anything out of the ordinary, rest assured I'll inform the appropriate people."

"Thank you, Brandon."

After they had hung up Anthony stood from behind the desk and walked to his door. *You're a spineless son of a bitch!* he spat at the reflection in the mirror. He then put on his robe and headed back to his courtroom for another day of handing down jail sentences to people who, in most cases, warranted less jail time than he himself deserved. Hypocrisy is like quitting, he thought ruefully. Both are indicative of a flaw in one's character, but each gets easier with repetition. For the first time he began to seriously consider resigning from the bench.

∽

Brandon managed to track down Toby on his cell phone and give him the news.

"You don't say?" was his initial response. "See, I knew you were good, Brandon."

"It was a no-brainer, Toby. The police couldn't justify putting you under surveillance. Any judge would have ruled in our favor."

"Whatever. I'll leave the legalese to you. So when should I see the ubiquitous shadows disappear?"

"I suppose they'll get the word today and I suspect by tonight they'll be gone."

"Good, that works for me. Listen, you keep up the good work, Brandon. I think I'm starting to see a little of what my mom sees in you. Scary, huh?"

"You have no idea," Brandon responded. "Oh, and, Toby, try to stay out of trouble, okay?"

"Me? In trouble? Perish the thought. I'm a model citizen – you know that. I'll see ya, Brandon. You take care of my mom now, ya here?"

CHAPTER 33

"Is she there?" Toby asked Carl.

"Yeah, she's here. I just followed her over."

"What's the name of the church?"

"St. Mathew over here off of Blaylock."

"Playing bingo, huh?" Toby asked, shaking his head.

"Yeah, you know how these blue hairs are; they got nothing better to do. So this fat bitch attacked your mother in the courtroom, huh?"

"Like an enraged buffalo. Listen, I assume she'll be there for awhile but you just hang tight and call me if you see her leaving, alright?"

"I think I can handle that."

"Okay, I'll let you know as soon as I'm done."

"Have fun, brother."

"You just know I will," Toby responded.

❧

Twenty-one year old Jeanine Brandt had just gotten into her nightgown and was curled up on the couch preparing to watch one of her favorite reality TV shows. She used to love these shows but they now served less as entertainment and more as a distraction from the constant horror she lived with since that night seven months ago.

She would never be able to erase the memory of waking up in her apartment to see a shadow move swiftly across the room toward her bed, covering her mouth with a rough hand before she could scream and warning that he'd kill her if she made a sound. He had then ripped off a piece of her nightgown and stuffed it into her mouth before tearing off two more strips and tying her hands to the bedposts.

For the next three hours she had endured the pain and humiliation of being brutally violated in almost every sick and perverted way imaginable, and since that night her only goal when she awoke each morning was to maintain her tenuous grasp on the fragile thread connecting her to her sanity. There was no doubt that the urge to simply let go and fall into the oblivion of madness was stronger on some days than others, but so far she had managed to resist its maniacal seduction.

When the knock came at the door, she jumped as almost every muscle in her body spasmed. She wasn't expecting anyone other than her mother, and not only was she not due back from bingo for at least another hour, but she wouldn't have needed to knock on the front door since she always came in through the garage after parking the car.

Walking quietly up to the door she put her eye to the peephole and her breath caught in her throat as she saw a man wearing a baseball hat, jeans and a leather jacket standing on the porch. While she was still looking, he stepped forward and knocked again, causing her to back away as she realized that no more than an inch of hollow door separated her from his hand. There was no way she could have known this, but if she had simply returned to her TV show and ignored him, her life would have just continued as it had for the past seven months. Unfortunately, that isn't what she did.

"No solicitors, please," she said through the door with a quivering voice.

"I'm not a solicitor, ma'am, I'm a policeman. There's been an accident and I need to speak with you, please."

"An accident involving whom?" she asked.

"Ma'am, if you'll open the door it would be easier for us to talk."

"Who was involved in the accident?" she demanded.

Toby exhaled impatiently. "Your mother, ma'am. I'm afraid it's bad."

Suddenly it felt like she had a golf ball lodged in her throat. "Do you have a badge? Show me your badge, please."

"Yes ma'am. If you'll open the door I'll be happy to show it to you," he said.

"Just hold it up to the peephole so I can see it, please."

From the inside pocket of his jacket he pulled out a badge he had purchased at a military surplus store and held it up to the eyehole. "Can you open the door now, ma'am?"

Jeanine could think of a couple of hundred other things she'd rather do than open the door to a strange man, even if he was a policeman, but the thought of her mother being hurt in an accident overrode her caution and she disengaged the dead bolt to let him in. She realized her mistake an instant too late as Toby threw his weight against the door, knocking her backward as he stepped inside. He grabbed her around the waist and lifted her off the ground with one arm while he covered her mouth with the other and kicked the door closed. She tried to struggle but was no match for his strength and he held her easily. "Hello, Jeanine, remember me?"

Her fear was immediate and debilitating as she recognized the voice that spoke to her each night in her dreams – nightmares actually; horrible, un-Godly nightmares. And suddenly she knew the meaning of stark raving terror.

"You *do* remember me, don't you?" he said. "I'm flattered." He carried her down the hall searching for a bedroom since his first visit had been at her own apartment. "You're a lucky girl, Jeanine. I don't normally date women more than once, but I'm making an exception in your case and you have that fat-ass mother of yours and her temper to thank for it. However, I feel it's only fair that I should warn you; I'm not going to be nearly as nice as I was last time."

Luckily for Jeanine, before this night would end the load-bearing walls of her sanity would come crumbling down and, mercifully, she would become oblivious to the abuse being inflicted on her body. In about three hours her mother would find her wandering the house naked, mumbling both rhythmically and incoherently. Two weeks later she would launch herself through a sixth floor window of the hospital's psychiatric wing when a young, male doctor enters her room unaccompanied. Had he bothered to read her chart, as dictated by protocol, he would have known that the very sight of a man – any man - would send her into a frenzied, psychotic episode. The doctor received a reprimand for his oversight, but for Jeanine . . . well, her nightmare would finally end.

Toby had parked his car two blocks away and as he made his way back to it he dialed Carl's cell phone.

"Yeah?"

"Is she still in there?" Toby asked him.

"Oh yeah. Probably bellowing *"Bingo!"* as we speak." This made both of them laugh. "Okay, well I'm finished here so you can go ahead and take off. I'll give you a call sometime tomorrow. Maybe we'll shoot some pool."

"Sounds good," Carl said.

"Thanks for your help."

"Anytime, man, anytime."

CHAPTER 34

"Come on in, Toby, it's great to see you," Gabby said, planting a firm kiss on his mouth. "My Dad's running late but Mom's in the kitchen stressing over dinner. Come on, I'll introduce you. Oh, and I hope you like lasagna." She had talked him into coming over to her parent's house for dinner this evening, and was obviously very excited that he would finally get to meet them, though only he knew that her excitement would pale in comparison to her father's when he saw who was joining them for dinner. He could hardly wait.

"I love lasagna," he said, as he stepped into the living room. As he was shrugging out of his jacket he was surprised to see Kiley sitting on the couch with a textbook laid out in front of her and a notepad on either side.

"Wow, you even study at other people's houses, huh?" he remarked.

"Always," she responded. "Nice to see you again."

"Likewise."

"Come on, Toby, come meet my mom," Gabby said impatiently, tugging on his arm.

When they walked into the kitchen Toby saw a nice-looking woman of about fifty wearing an apron and bending over to pull a steaming pan of lasagna out of the oven. "Well, this must be the amazing Mrs. Scalini that Gabby has told me so much about. Nice to finally meet you," he said pleasantly. He walked directly up to her and gave her a big hug. "At least now I finally have the answer to the mystery."

"Oh? What mystery's that?" she asked him, smiling expectantly.

"Where Gabriella gets her knockout looks, of course."

Fran smiled broadly and winked at Gabby. "Well it's nice to finally meet you too, Toby. Gabriella has been talking about you non-stop and we figured the only way we'd get her to shut up would be to meet you for ourselves."

"I hope I'm not imposing. Gabby kind of sprung this on me at the last minute."

"We're not imposing, silly," Gabby said, punching him playfully in the arm. "Mom thinks I don't like her anymore if I don't come over for dinner at least once a week. So why don't you go talk to Kiley for a few minutes and I'll help her finish up in here, okay?"

"I'm game if she is," he responded, heading back the way he'd come. Nice to meet you again, Mrs. Scalini," he said over his shoulder. When he reached the living room he planted himself at the other end of the couch from where Kiley was sitting. "They told me I had to come and bother you while they finish getting dinner ready," he said.

"Oh, no problem," she said, closing her textbook. "So what do you do for a living, Toby?"

"I'm in construction."

"And how long have you been doing that?"

"Since I was seventeen, so about three years I guess."

"Any plans to go to college?"

"Doubtful. I think I got my fill of studying in high school."

"Do your folks live around here?"

"Actually it's just my mom and I. She lives here locally about ten miles from my apartment.

"Were you raised in this area?"

"Yeah, how about you?"

"Yeah, I went to Ben-Davis."

"So did I," he said, surprised.

"Really? What class?"

"Class of 2000."

"How about that, I was only a year behind you – oh one. You know, I thought you looked familiar the first time I met you. What's your last name?"

"McGrady," he said. In an instant her face changed and she became silent. "What's wrong?" Toby asked her.

"You . . . you're Toby . . . McGrady?"

"All my life," he said cheerily. He immediately recognized the change in her demeanor. "Why?"

"Does Gabriella know your last name?" she asked. Her hands had become very fidgety and he noticed she was no longer making eye contact with him.

"You know, I don't believe it's ever come up to tell you the truth. Why, what's wrong, Kiley? You look like you've just seen a ghost."

"I'm s-sorry, but I just have to ask . . . are you the Toby McGrady who has been in the news lately?"

"Are you talking about the guy who was charged with committing all those rapes?"

"Yes," she said, trying unsuccessfully to make herself look at him.

"Well now that you mention it, I guess I am. Huh! Go figure. When you least expect it you find out that you're sitting right next to a real live celebrity. Isn't life funny like that?"

"I - I need to go take care of something," she said, offering him a quick, nervous smile.

"You know, you haven't looked at me since I told you my name. I don't know whether or not I should feel insulted. Should I?"

"I really need to go take care of something," she responded.

"Kiley, you don't really think I'm guilty of the horrible things they said I did, do you? They were just looking for a scapegoat and I happened to be in the wrong place at the wrong time."

"That isn't what the news has been saying," she said hesitantly. "They said they had conclusive evidence against you and that some judge let you go on a technicality."

"Do you believe everything you hear in the news?"

"No, not everything," she said nervously. "Look, Toby, I really need to go."

He reached over and put his hand on her forearm, making it clear he wasn't finished talking to her. "You aren't thinking of doing something stupid like worrying Gabby with your groundless paranoia, are you?" Kiley didn't respond and he could see that she was growing more and more frightened. "You're a sexy girl, Kiley, and I'm sure you have your hands full beating off the guys without worrying about your roommate's love life, am I right?" he said, slightly increasing the pressure on her arm. She nodded slightly, keeping her eyes glued to the ground.

"That's good, because if I remember correctly from what I've read about this rapist, you fit the victim profile to a "T"; petite little blonde, nice tight body, a little too outspoken. Of course, that's only if you believe everything you read, right?" Again she didn't respond and he could see that her breathing was coming in short gasps.

"Look, it's obvious to me that you're going to be a little uncomfortable this evening so what I want you to do is go tell Gabby that you just remembered you have an exam tomorrow that slipped your mind, and that you need to go to the library to cram. Regrettably, you'll have to beg off dinner but you'll be sure and make it up to her. Sound good?" he asked her.

She nodded.

"Good. Well, off you go. Musn't keep the books waiting."

"W-Wasn't Gabby's father the judge assigned to your case?" she asked, looking at him for the first time since he had told her his name.

"You know what . . . I believe he just might have been. Now how's that for a coincidence?"

"He'll kill you when he finds out about you and Gabby."

"Oh contraire, I don't agree with your assessment of the situation at all. I am supremely confident that her father and I will find that we actually have quite a bit in common. I wouldn't be a bit surprised if we're discussing the prospects for the Colts getting back to the Super Bowl well before the second course of dinner is ever served. You see, I believe in happy endings," he said, offering her a broad smile. "Don't you?" She continued to stare at the floor, not responding. "Listen, Kiley, I really like Gabby and our relationship has been progressing nicely the past few days. It would really upset me if something were to change that, so what do you say you and I just keep this between the two of us?"

She nodded her head as if in a daze. "I have to go now."

"Of course you do. Well, best of luck on that test tomorrow and don't study too hard, okay?" he said, removing his hand from her arm.

The instant she felt his arm move she stood up and stepped quickly away from him, leaving her study material where it lay, and walked hurriedly to retrieve her coat from the closet. He then followed her into the kitchen and stood by silently as he listened to her tell Gabby the lie he had concocted for her. At first Gabby wouldn't hear of it but to Kiley's credit she was very convincing and in the end Gabby conceded, telling her they would do it again when she could be there as well.

As Kiley grabbed her books from the table he said, "I'm sorry you won't be joining us for dinner. I was really looking forward to getting to know you better."

She stopped at the front door and looked from him to Gabby and then nodded. "Bye, Gabby," she said as she closed the door behind her.

"Wow. That was all kind of sudden, wasn't it? She's never forgotten about an exam before," Gabby said.

"Well, you're the one who told me that she always has some kind of drama going on. Maybe she's just been distracted lately."

"Maybe, but I don't think she's seeing anyone right now. Oh well, it's her loss since she's the one who'll be missing out on my mom's world-famous lasagna," she laughed.

"That's okay, I'll eat her portion too," Toby promised her.

❧

"It's cold out there," Anthony remarked. "I thought 'ol Punxsutawney Phil failed to see his shadow this year? I can't understand it, I don't feel a hint of spring in the air."

"Who's Puckasawney whatever?" Gabby asked as she came from the kitchen to greet her dad.

"Punxsutawney Phil," he corrected her. "He's that ground-hog who comes out of his hole every February to look for his shadow. You know, *"Today because my shadow I see, six more weeks of winter there will be!"* Or something like that," he laughed.

Gabby just shook her head and looked at her mother who had joined them. "I don't know what to tell you, sweet-heart," she said, shrugging her shoulders. "I have to put up with him every day."

"Poor mommy," she said giving her a sympathetic hug.

"Hey, I'm standing right here," Anthony said good-na-turedly and they all started laughing.

Her dad then leaned forward and in a whisper said, "Well . . ?"

Gabby just grinned and played along, "Well what?"

"I thought I was meeting the newest love of your life?" he said. "That *is* why I had to come straight home after work, right?"

"Oh, him . . ." she said. "I think he left already. He got tired of waiting."

"Blame that on your mother, Sweetie. She spends the mon-ey faster than I can make it so I have to work my fingers practically to the bone."

"Don't you believe that for a second, honey," her mother said, giving her a conspiratorial wink. About that time the bathroom door opened and Toby came down the hallway, wiping water from his hands onto his jeans.

"Hello, Mr. Scalini," he said, reaching out and taking Anthony's hand. He gave a subtle but unmistakable shake of his head as a clear warning that he would be well advised to keep his mouth shut.

Anthony just stared at him dumbly, saying nothing. He felt as though an elephant was sitting on his chest and breathing had suddenly become difficult. "F-Fine," he said.

"What's that, honey?" Fran asked him.

"I, I said I'm fine is all," he repeated.

"He didn't ask you how you were doing, Anthony. He just said hello. Are you okay? You look like you're sweating all of the sudden. Why don't you come over here and sit down on the couch for a few minutes, dear. Come on," she said, taking him by the arm. He pulled his hand away from Toby's and followed her into the living room with Toby and Gabby following.

"Are you okay, Daddy? Can I get you something to drink?"

"Bring him some water, honey," her mother said.

"No, I'm fine," Anthony finally said. "I'm fine. It's just a little hot in here is all."

"Are you sure, Daddy?" Gabby asked him, worry dominating her pretty features.

"Yes, I'm fine, sweetheart. Why don't you and your mother finish up whatever you were doing in the kitchen and give Toby and I a chance to get to know each other."

"Okay," she said. "But if you need anything . . ."

"You'll be the first person I'll call," he interrupted, still looking at Toby. She continued to watch him until she was convinced there wasn't a crisis, then finally looked at her mother, "Come on, we're being banished to the kitchen. And I hope you realize that we're setting the women's movement back at least thirty years by complying."

"Path of least resistance, sweetie. Remember that and your relationships will be smooth sailing," her mom confided to her loud enough for both Anthony and Toby to overhear, though neither of them took the bait. Once the women disappeared and they were alone, Anthony took his glasses off and began cleaning them on his sweater, not speaking to Toby or looking in his direction. The sight of him walking down the hallway and the sudden, sickening realization that *he* was the new boyfriend Gabby had been wanting them to meet was like getting kicked in the gut by a Clydesdale. He had a hundred questions but he was trying to collect his thoughts. Toby wasn't saying anything either and when at last he returned his glasses to their perch atop his nose, he looked over to find him staring at him with an amused grin on his face.

"Why are you here?"

"I'm here for the same reason you are – your daughter."

"I'm not a believer in coincidences and I don't believe for a second that you met Gabby by chance. You're a calculating son of a bitch and I want to know what you want with her?" he demanded.

"Relax, Judge. I actually kind of like her if you want to know the truth. And believe you me, I definitely can't say that about all the women I've humped."

"You son of a bitch!" Anthony hissed.

"You already called me that," he pointed out calmly. "Oh come on, Judge, relax. You're not mad at me because I slept with her, are you? Hell, can you blame me? I mean, Jesus Christ on a jumped-up Popsicle stick, she is one sweet little piece of ass, ain't she? And she's a hellion in the sack too, let me just go on record with that headliner right now." He leaned toward Anthony and lowered his voice to a whisper. "You're not seriously going to tell me that you've never thought about hitting that yourself, are you?"

"You're sick! Sick!" Anthony said, looking away in disgust.

"So I've been told, Judge," he stated flatly, sitting up straight again.

"You and your mother got what you wanted, didn't you? So why are you doing this?"

"Now that's a damn appropriate question, Judge, and I'll be happy to answer it for you. You see, there's a certain judge I know who was in a car that ran down a little girl twenty-some odd years ago, and rather than taking his punishment like a man, he just helped hide her body. Now this same judge, he has the incredible audacity to walk into his courtroom every day and sentence others to a fate that he wasn't man enough to face himself. Are you with me so far?

Anthony didn't answer so he continued. "Now don't ask me why he's a hypocrite, I just know that he is. And I also know that all I would have to do is send an anonymous letter to the police directing them to her body, and they'd find that judge's college class ring in one of her pockets. At that point I think it would be safe to say that life as this judge knows it would more than likely cease to exist. He would lose his career, the love and respect of his family, and most likely spend his golden years rotting away in a prison cell right alongside all those poor bastards he was responsible for sending there. And I don't think they'd be real appreciative, do you?"

He paused and looked at him. "So do I have your attention yet?" When Anthony nodded pitifully he continued. "Good, because it's very important to me that you understand this last part, 'cause it's a real eye-opener. Now I think we can both agree that all those other reasons are important and significant, right? But, unfortunately, none of them gets top billing. Because you see, the real reason I'm doing this is for exactly the same reason a dog licks his balls."

When he saw confusion cloud Anthony's face he said, "Don't you know why that is, Judge? Don't you know why a dog licks his balls?" Anthony shook his head miserably.

"Because he can!" Toby concluded with a flourishing sweep of his hand. "Do you get it, Judge? Do you get the bitter fucking pill I'm forcing you to swallow? I'm banging your daughter right in front of you because you didn't have the huevos to take your punishment like a man when you had the chance, and I happen to be one of only two people on this earth who can take you to task for it if I should happen to wake up on the wrong side of the bed one morning. Now the good news is that that's highly unlikely, seeing as how all I have to do is roll over and I have

Gabby's gravity-defying D-cups staring at me to ensure that I always start the day off in a good mood. So you see, Judge, every cloud really does have a silver lining. Ain't that cool?"

Anthony swallowed hard. "I don't understand why you're continuing to punish me like this. I did everything you and your mother asked. Why can't you just leave me and my family alone?"

"Did you not hear a word I just said, Judge?" he asked him, shaking his head as if he were speaking to a child with attention deficit disorder.

"Yes, I heard you, but I don't accept it. There's has to be something more."

"I wish there were, Judge - I surely do – but honest to God there's not. I understand it'll be difficult for you for a few days while you get used to the idea of me sleeping with your daughter, but trust me it'll grow on you. However, be warned: If I find out you told anyone else about any of this . . . well damn, Judge, I just don't know what would happen. I can only tell you that I wouldn't want to chance it if I were you."

"Are my two favorite guys hungry?" Gabby asked them as she came in from the kitchen.

"I don't know about your dad here but I'm starving," Toby announced, offering her a big smile.

"How about you, Dad?"

"I'm looking forward to a helping of your mom's lasagna, honey," Anthony smiled thinly.

"Are you sure you're okay, Dad? You look awfully pale to me."

"I'm fine. Why don't you give us a few more seconds and we'll be right in."

"Okay, but don't be too long. By the way, it's great to see you both getting along so well," she observed, smiling at each of them.

When she had left again Anthony looked at Toby and said, "I don't believe a damn thing you just told me, but unfortunately I'm not in a position to do anything about it right now. However, I'm telling you right now that if I have the slightest premonition that my daughter is in danger, I'll kill you myself you arrogant bastard. Now do *you* understand *that?*"

Toby appeared to think about this. "You know, if you had shown some of that intestinal fortitude all those years ago you wouldn't be in the position you're in now, would you?"

Anthony just looked at him; hating him with a depth and passion of which he had previously believed himself incapable.

"Let's go eat, Judge, and remember – not a word."

"You were awfully quiet tonight," Francesca said to Anthony when they finally had the house to themselves again. "You hardly said a word at dinner. Are you sure you're feeling alright?"

"I'm fine," he answered. "Just a little tired is all."

"Maybe you need to take a few days off to recharge your batteries. It's been ages since you've had a vacation."

"The dockets are so full, Fran, it's hard to find the time."

"Well you're not going to be any good to anyone if you collapse from exhaustion," she scolded him.

"Don't be melodramatic."

"Suit yourself, but I think you need some rest."

When it was obvious he was finished with that particular subject she said, "What did you think about Gabby's new boyfriend?"

"He's just another boyfriend. Like most girls her age she'll probably be introducing us to someone new within a couple of weeks," he predicted. Inside he was praying that that would be the case.

"Well aren't you just a pillar of optimism," she shot at him. "I thought he was a nice guy, and Gabby's obviously crazy about him."

"Do you think so?" he said, looking at her for the first time.

"What? That he's a nice guy or that our daughter is crazy about him?"

"Do you really think she's crazy about him?"

"Would that be so terrible if she was?"

"I don't know, there's just something about him that seemed a little strange to me."

"Your problem is that you deal with the dregs of society day-in and day-out and you've become much too cynical in your old age."

"Maybe so," he said, "but there was something about him that just didn't sit well with me."

"Then Gabby should be thankful that her father doesn't get to choose her boyfriends because she'd be one lonely girl if that was the case." She laughed but Anthony didn't join her. He was scared to death for Gabby and had no idea what to do about it. His past imprisoned him like an iron maiden and he feared things would get worse before they got better – *if* they got better. He knew he needed to speak with someone about this; someone with whom he could confide his ugly past without jeopardizing his family's future, but he didn't know who. Maybe Brandon Hill. Their last conversation left him with the distinct impression that he wasn't a huge fan of this kid's either. It certainly warranted consideration because one thing was certain – he couldn't just stand by while Toby McGrady waltzed in and destroyed his family. He was not going to let that happen. If it came to it he'd turn himself in first.

"Just do me a favor and call her often to ensure she's doing okay? Will you do that for me?"

"Well, she'll probably get annoyed with me but if it'll make you sleep better then okay, I'll call her more often."

"Thank you."

CHAPTER 35

"Hi, sleepy head." Gabby greeted Kiley when she finally emerged from her bedroom around ten o'clock. "There's an extra bagel on the counter if you're hungry."

"I'm not, but thanks," she said, grabbing one of the over-sized throw pillows and plopping down next to her on the couch with her legs tucked under her. She hugged the pillow to her chest as she watched Gabby rifle through a pile of crib notes. "How did it go last night?"

"It went great," she exclaimed. "Toby was a perfect gentle-man and I think my parents loved him."

"Really?" Kiley replied, hoping she didn't sound as sur-prised as she was.

"Of course really. Why wouldn't they?" Gabby asked, looking at her like she'd lost her mind.

Kiley ignored the question. "How was your dad last night?"

"Well, he *was* a little quiet but I don't think he was feeling well. He started sweating as soon as he walked in and his face became very flushed. Come to think of it I need to check on him. I hope he didn't go into work today."

Kiley had returned home after leaving Gabby's parent's house, but in spite of going to bed early she hadn't slept more than an hour all night. She couldn't get the disturbing conversation with Toby out of her mind and she'd spent the last few hours debating with herself on whether or not she should tell Gabby about it. His vague threats scared the hell out of her, but in the end she'd decided she had an obligation to tell her what she knew. If she didn't and something was to happen she'd never forgive herself.

She took a deep breath. "Your dad wasn't sick last night, Gabby."

"What?" Gabby responded absently as she continued to look through her papers.

"I said your dad wasn't sick last night."

Gabby stopped what she was doing and looked at her. "What are you talking about, Kiley? You weren't even there when he came home."

"Your dad was sweating because he recognized Toby, not because he was sick."

"What do you mean *recognized him*? My dad and Toby don't even know each other," she said, her confusion obvious.

"Believe me, they do," Kiley assured her. "Has Toby ever told you his last name?"

"Come to think of it I don't believe I've ever asked him what it was. Why?"

"It's McGrady. Toby McGrady," she said. "Does that name ring a bell?"

"That rapist who's been in the news?"

"One and the same," Kiley said.

"My father was the judge on that case."

"Exactly."

"There's no way Toby is that guy, Kiley. What would make you think something ridiculous like that?"

"How about the fact that he told me so himself last night."

"You left, Kiley, remember? You told me you had to go cram for an exam. Which reminds me, what time do you have to be there?"

"There is no exam, Gabby."

Gabby looked at her in disbelief. "You mean you lied to me?"

"I had no choice. Your boyfriend was threatening me." She could see that Gabby was about to explode so she quickly held up her hands and said, "Look, let me back up and explain what happened before you start hating on me, okay?"

At first it appeared to be touch and go as to whether or not Gabby was going to listen to anything further, but then curiosity got the better of her and she relented. She put the papers down and turned toward her. "Okay, I'm waiting."

Kiley took another deep breath then and began recounting the conversation she'd had with Toby the previous evening, ensuring she didn't leave out a single disturbing detail. Gabby said nothing, listening stoically as her best friend described a scene from a horror movie that starred her boyfriend. She flinched noticeably, however, when she told her how Toby had basically threatened her with rape or worse if she were to repeat any of this to her. When at last she finished she had tears streaming down her face and was hugging the pillow tightly for comfort, and although Gabby wasn't ready to believe that her boyfriend was a serial rapist – she had slept with him for Christ's sake – it was obvious that Kiley believed what she was saying because she'd never seen her like this.

"I'm not saying you're lying, Kiley, because it's obvious that something upset you, but if my dad knew who he was why wouldn't he have said something to me. He's not going to let his daughter go out with a rapist so how do you explain that?"

"I don't know, Gabby. Maybe he threatened him as well. Were they ever alone together?"

"Yeah, come to think of it they were in the living room talking for almost twenty minutes while my mom and I got dinner on the table."

"There you go then. He probably threatened your dad just like he threatened me."

"Well we're going to find out because I'm calling him right now to find out."

"Who?" Kiley asked, becoming alarmed.

"My dad. Relax, I'm not calling Toby - yet."

"You can't tell him you know, Gabby," she pleaded. "I'm afraid of what he'll do to me...and you!"

"Let's take this one step at a time. First let me talk to my dad and we'll worry about what to do next after that, okay?" she said, getting up to retrieve the phone. Kiley nodded in agreement.

She tried him at his office first, assuming that even if he were sick he would be too stubborn to stay home and rest. His secretary answered on the second ring and informed her that her father was in court at the moment but that she would have him return her call on his next break if that was okay with her. She said it was and hung up after thanking her.

"He'll call me back within the hour so just try to relax until then, okay?"

∽

Jay answered the phone at his desk. "Can you come in here, please?" It was Michael.

"Sure, I'll be right there."

"What's up?" he asked, walking into his boss's office.

"Does the name Jeanine Brandt ring a bell to you?"

Jay thought about it for a second. "It does, but I can't place it right now."

"She's one of the women who was raped by our boy about seven months ago. Ring a bell now?"

"Yeah, now it does. Why, what's up?

"While her mother was at church playing bingo last night someone broke into their house and assaulted her – again."

"You're shitting me," Jay said with a mixture of disgust and disbelief on his face.

"I wish like hell I was. Let me ask you something, Jay, do you believe in coincidences?"

"Yeah, and Santa Claus and the Easter Bunny and that little naked abomination they call Cupid," he responded in a voice devoid of amusement.

"I'm glad to hear you say that, because I sure as hell don't either. As incomprehensible as it sounds, I know it was McGrady. If you recall, it was this girl's mother who went after McGrady's mom in the court room."

"Was she able to identify him this time?"

"Hell no. She's so messed up they doubt whether she'll ever be able to form a coherent sentence again. This is that damned judge's fault! I warned him this would happen."

"But why would he do it? I mean, what kind of balls does someone have to have to rape the same woman twice?"

"I'm telling you, Jay, that boy is evil personified."

"So what are we going to do?"

"For starters I'm going to talk to that captain down at the precinct and see if I can convince him to put McGrady under surveillance again."

"I guess I don't need to remind you about the court injunction," Jay said, reminding him anyway.

"Screw the injunction. We'll just have to make sure we're not as obvious about it this time. By the way, see if you can get me the name of the detective who handled the Hennessey murder. You know, the guard they found murdered in the woods? I've been thinking about it and I'll bet my pension that McGrady had something to do with that as well.

"Will do, boss, anything else?"

"No, but I need that detective's name ASAP."

"I'm on it."

∽

As promised, on his next break Anthony's secretary informed him his daughter had called and he immediately went into his chambers and dialed her number. When she answered he said, "Hi, Gabby, it's Dad. I received a message to call you?"

"Oh, hi, Daddy," she said, looking toward Kiley to ensure she knew who it was.

"Daddy, I need to ask you something."

"What is it, sweetheart?"

"Well, Kiley tells me that she had kind of a strange conversation with Toby last night right before you guys arrived."

"Really?" he said, suddenly very concerned. "What kind of conversation?"

"Well . . . Daddy did you know that Toby's last name was McGrady?"

After a noticeable hesitation he said, "Actually, I did. At least I did after I saw him last night."

"And this is the same Toby McGrady who was just sitting in your courtroom a few days ago on trial for rape?"

"Yes." He said quietly. He could hear in her voice that she was starting to get upset.

"So you're telling me that when Toby came out of the bathroom last night you recognized who he was right away?"

Kiley looked at her and mouthed, *"Told you so."*

"Yes."

"So let me get this straight . . . my dad finds out that his only daughter is seeing a guy who was accused of raping multiple women, and he didn't think it was important enough to bother telling her?" she asked, incredulous.

This was the last thing Anthony had expected to hear when he'd called and he was racking his brain trying to come up with a logical response. "Gabby, I knew who he was but there are a couple of reason why I didn't tell you.

"Pray tell," she said.

He let her sarcasm pass since he knew he deserved it. "To begin with, he was never convicted of any crime and in this country you're supposed to be treated as if you are innocent until proven otherwise. The second reason is because you seemed so happy and I didn't want to spoil your evening."

Gabby thought about that for a second. "Does mom know?"

"No, she doesn't know and I'm not going to be the one to tell her either. Look, Gabby, you have to be the one to decide whether or not you and Toby are right for each other. I would suggest that you discuss it with him and see where it goes from there. If he's treating you right, then that's the main thing. If he's not, or you find his behavior odd, then maybe you should consider going your separate ways." He so wanted to tell his daughter the truth but was terrified of what would happen if Toby thought he'd counseled Gabby to leave him.

"Oh, you can bet he and I are going to be talking; tonight as a matter of fact."

"Just remember, you are a strong woman and you don't have to stay in any relationship you don't feel comfortable with, understand?"

"Yes, I understand. And thanks for being honest with me, Dad."

"Okay. Well I have to get back in my courtroom – lots of criminals and all that, you know. Take care, Sweetheart, and listen, you may want to hold off mentioning this to your mother. You know how she can get. Speak with Toby first and see what happens. She agreed that that was probably best and they said goodbye. When Kiley saw her hang up she looked at her expectantly.

"Well?"

"He said that he knew who Toby was."

"Then why didn't he say something to you about it?"

"He said that because Toby hadn't been convicted of a crime he was willing to give him the benefit of the doubt and that I should be the one to speak with him about it." When she saw Kiley shaking her head she said, "Are you sure you didn't just misinterpret your conversation with him, Kiley. I mean, is it possible that he felt he had to defend himself because of the way you reacted when you found out who he was?"

"No, that's not the way it happened at all. When I asked him if you knew who he was he got this crazy look in his eyes and started threatening me. And like I told you, there was no test I had to go cram for. He was the one who told me to lie about it, probably because he was afraid I would say something to you last night."

"Would you have?"

"I don't know – probably."

"Well, then I guess he was right."

"It wasn't like that, Gabby. There's something wrong with him and you can't see it. He's . . . evil."

"Look, did he say anything bad about me? Did he give you the impression that he was going to hurt me?"

"No," she conceded. "He actually said that he was happy with the way your relationship was going. But that doesn't mean anything!" she blurted when she saw that Gabby was about to jump on that.

"I'm telling you, he was acting scary and he was threatening me."

"Did he actually tell you he was going to do something to you, Kiley?" Gabby asked, starting to get annoyed with her now.

"He didn't say anything specific, but he told me that I fit the profile of some of the rape victims and that I should be careful when I'm out at night."

"Well that doesn't really sound like a threat to me. It sounds like he was just watching out for you."

"Gabby, you have to believe me. There's something very wrong with him and I'm afraid you're the one who's going to wind up getting hurt."

"Okay, look, I'm going to speak with him about it and you can bet I'll be asking him why he neglected to tell me who he really was. But if afterwards I feel everything is on the up and up, then you need to promise me that you'll let this go, okay?"

Kiley nodded her head reluctantly. "Okay."

CHAPTER 36

"Detective Bronsky?"

"Speaking," came the gruff reply through the phone.

"This is Michael Haas, District Attorney for Monroe County, how are you?"

"I've had better days. What can I do for you?"

"Haven't we all. Listen, I was wondering if you're investigating the Hennessey murder?"

"Yeah, I'm actually the lead on that one. Why, you wanna confess?" he asked hopefully.

"I haven't always been the poster-boy for piety but I'm afraid I wasn't involved in this one."

"Too bad," he said, and Michael thought he heard actual disappointment. "That was some of the sickest shit I've ever seen."

"Do you have any leads?" Michael asked him.

"No, not a one," he said, sounding as frustrated as he felt.

"Listen, we had a girl raped last night . . ."

"What does that have to do with me?" Bronsky interrupted. "Sounds like you should be talking to sex crimes."

"That girl is one of the French Lick rapist's victims and now this is the second time she's been raped in the last seven months."

"You gotta be kidding me," he said in disbelief. "Do you think it's a coincidence?"

"Not even close."

"I still don't know why you're calling me."

"Do you remember a few days ago when that judge let Toby McGrady walk on a technicality?"

"Toby McGrady?"

"Yeah, he was the guy we had arrested for all those rapes. We served a warrant on him and found a shirt with blood on it that matched the one of the victims."

"Okay, I'm with you now. I assume we've been watching him like a hawk, though, right?"

"I wish. McGrady filed a harassment charge against the police for following him and that same judge issued an injunction. We haven't had surveillance on him for the past two days."

"Holy shit. So you think he went to this girl's house for round two?"

"That's exactly what I believe."

"Well, I don't want to be redundant here, but so far you haven't told me anyone's died, so how is this relevant to homicide?"

"I think McGrady murdered Hennessey," he stated flatly.

"Yeah, and what makes you think that?"

"Call it a hunch. But I know it was McGrady who raped that girl last night, and the fact that that guard was murdered not more than a couple of days after he was released from jail just seems too coincidental. If I were you I'd get a hold of the logbooks and find out if Hennessey ever had any contact with McGrady while he was locked up. I'm willing to bet that he did."

"That's an awful lot of speculation, Michael."

"You don't know this kid. He is bad through and through and there's no doubt in my mind that he's capable of committing murder. The scary thing is that Hennessey might have just been a warm-up."

"Okay, I'll tell you what. I'll track down Mr. McGrady and ask him a few questions; see if he can come up with an alibi for that evening. I'll also talk to my counterpart in sex crimes and ask him if they were able to get any usable forensic evidence from the house."

"Thanks, detective, I really appreciate it."

"Don't thank me, Michael. If you're right I want this creep off the street as badly as you do."

"Do me a favor and keep me posted if you come up with anything, will you?"

"Count on it," he said.

After they had hung up Bronsky placed a call to his buddy Ray Johnson in sex crimes.

"Ray this is David. You got a second? Yeah, I know you're on the other side of the building. Just do me favor and walk your lazy ass over here. You're not going to believe the phone call I just received."

CHAPTER 37

"Hey, Gabby, it's me."

"Hi," she said irritably.

Toby pulled the phone away and looked at it for a second before returning it to his ear. "Is something wrong?"

"No." Gabby was standing in the kitchen fixing herself a sandwich and wasn't prepared to have this conversation with him over the phone.

"Okay, so is this a game to see who can use the least number of words and still make a complete sentence?" he asked.

"No, I'm fixing lunch. I have classes this afternoon and then I have to work until midnight so I'm kind of in a hurry."

"Interested in some company for lunch?" he asked her.

She thought about it. "Sure. How long will it take you to get here?"

"I'll be there in fifteen minutes. Are you sure everything's okay?"

"Everything's fine, Toby, I'll see you in a little bit."

As they hung up he turned around and looked at his reflection in the mirror that hung by his front door. The face he saw had an amused grin that never seemed to quite reach his eyes, which at this moment flashed cold and deadly.

"Well, well, well . . . Somebody's been telling secrets," he said in a disturbing singsong.

∽

He arrived in just under the promised fifteen minutes, and as soon as she answered the door he could see that this was going to be anything other than a relaxed lunch date.

"Hi, Toby. Come on in," she said, moving out of the way to let him pass.

"You sounded like you were upset about something on the phone earlier," he said, watching her face closely.

"There's something you and I need to discuss and I think you know what it is."

He shrugged his shoulders. "I wish I did, but I wracked my brain on the way over here trying to figure out why you might be upset at me and I couldn't come up with anything. Did I do something wrong?" he asked, following her into the kitchen.

"It's not what you did, Toby. It's what you didn't do. Why didn't you tell me who you really were?"

"I don't know what you mean. Last time I checked I was really me," he said, smiling.

"This isn't funny," she deadpanned. "Why didn't you tell me your last name was McGrady?"

"Well I think maybe I did, but if I didn't it would probably be because you never asked what my last name was. Besides, why is this so important all the sudden?"

"Oh, I don't know," she said sarcastically. "Maybe because you were sitting in jail a few days ago charged with rape? Maybe because my father was the judge assigned to your case? Is any of this starting to ring a bell?" She had her hands on her hips and her anger was palpable. "I defy you to tell me you didn't know who my father was when you saw him," she challenged.

He knew further denial would be futile so at last he allowed his face to reveal what she already knew to be true. "Gabby, let me explain."

"Oh, I'm all ears," she shot at him.

"The truth is that I didn't know who your dad was until *after* you and I started seeing each other. It was only when you told me he was a judge and I learned your last name that I put two and two together."

"Then why didn't you tell me once you knew?" she demanded.

"Try to put yourself in my shoes. First of all, I certainly didn't do what they said I did, and that should be obvious due to the fact that I'm here with you right now and not in a courtroom fighting for my freedom. And second, by the time I figured all this out I was already falling for you. I didn't want to take a chance on screwing things up so I just kept my mouth shut. I'm really sorry if you think I misled you but I thought I was doing the right thing."

"I read that the police had evidence linking you to one of the women. How do you explain that?" she demanded.

"That was nothing but a bunch of lies. They didn't find anything in my apartment. That would have been impossible because I didn't have anything to do with those women being raped. Any evidence they claimed to have had was planted, and that's assuming they really had anything, which I doubt. They were just looking for a scapegoat and I happened to be in the wrong place at the wrong time. Do you know how they even came to suspect me?" he asked her.

She shook her head.

"On the same night that one of the women was attacked, I was coming back from hanging out with one of my buddies and I got a flat tire on my car. While I was changing it on the side of the road the tire iron slipped off of a lug nut and I cut my hand. It was bleeding pretty badly and I didn't have any rags so I kept wiping it on an old t-shirt I was wearing. Later, when I got home, one of my paranoid neighbors must have seen me with blood all over my shirt. Of course, the next morning they hear on the news that another woman was attacked and decide to call the police, who show up later that night practically knocking down my door screaming something about a search warrant. Believe me, I had no idea what was going on and I was scared to death. Well, you know the rest of the story," he said, watching her face closely to see if she was buying what he was trying to sell her.

Gabby just looked at him, comparing what he'd said to what she had learned from the news and her father. "What about your conversation with Kiley while I was in the kitchen helping my mom?"

"What about it?"

"She told me she asked you your last name because you guys discovered that you had both gone to the same school."

"Yeah, that's right."

"And that when you told her, she recognized you from the news and got scared. She says that you starting threatening her to not say anything to me."

"That's completely out of context, Gabby. It's true that she looked concerned when she found out who I was, but I certainly didn't threaten her. When she asked me if you knew who I was I told her no and that I would appreciate it if she wouldn't say anything to you; that I planned on having the discussion with you soon. She was skeptical and when it became apparent that she was going to have a difficult time acting normal at dinner, I suggested that maybe she could find an excuse to bow out. I told her it was very important to me that I be the one to explain things to you and finally she agreed, which is when she came up with the story about having to go study for an exam. That was her idea – not mine."

"Well, that actually makes sense based on what she told me. You scared the hell out of her, though, Toby. Are you aware of that?"

"I'm sure I probably did. You can't believe how difficult it's been for me. When people find out who I am they treat me like I'm some kind of serial killer. You know, I always thought you were supposed to be presumed innocent until

proven guilty in this country, but apparently that isn't reality because I sure as hell haven't seen it."

"It's funny you say that, because that's exactly what my
dad said."

"You talked to him about this?"

"Of course I did. I called him right after Kiley told me
about your conversation. He told me that he had recognized you right away but because he was willing to give
you the benefit of the doubt, and the fact that he knew I
was happy with you, he decided not to say anything."

"Is that all he said?"

"No, he also told me that I was a big girl and that it was
up to me to decide whether or not I wanted to be in this
relationship, and that I shouldn't listen to what others say."

"Your dad's a wise man," he said, offering her a smile.

"I repeat that what you've said all makes sense, Toby, but I
would be lying to you if I told you I don't have some misgivings. You have to admit that this is a lot to digest when
it's dropped on you all at once."

"No, you're right, I understand perfectly. I just hope this
doesn't drive a wedge between us, Gabby. I'm crazy about
you and I hope you know that."

"Just give me some time to sort out everything. I'll speak
to Kiley again and hopefully she'll see how things were
misinterpreted. Call me tomorrow and we'll talk again,
okay?" she offered.

"Right now I'll take what I can get," he said, grinning at her. "As a matter of fact, I'm going to maintain an optimistic attitude and make dinner reservations for us for tomorrow evening. I can always cancel them, but hopefully we can get past all of this by then. Sound good?"

"Yeah, that sounds good," she agreed, offering him a smile.

When he was back in his car he headed over to visit Carl. It wasn't long before he noticed a green sedan in his rearview mirror that had been following at a considerable distance for the past few miles. He decided to make a few random turns, making sure he adhered to the posted speed limits so as to not tip them off just in case his hunch was right. Sure enough, after seven turns the car was still back there.

"Son of a bitch," he said angrily, making an abrupt right-hand turn onto the next side street and accelerating quickly before turning left into a blind alley. He got out and waited.

The two officers who had been assigned to keep tabs on Toby had been cautioned against letting him see them. They were well aware that they were violating a court order and this knowledge required them to follow at a much greater distance than was normal. Because of this extra cushion, by the time they turned right on the street they'd seen Toby turn onto, his car was nowhere to be seen. They gave each other a puzzled look and decreased their speed.

Toby stood just out of sight, listening for the car's approach, and when he heard the sound of rubber crunching over gravel-strewn asphalt just a few yards away, he stepped out from the alley into the street and began walking purposefully toward the car. When the cops saw him emerge it took them a second to realize who he was, but once they did the driver slammed on the brakes.

"What do you want to do?" he asked his partner as he watched Toby bend down and pick up a large object.

"Put it in reverse and let's get out of here," he said. "There's going to be hell to pay if he reports this."

Toby increased his pace as he closed with the car, his mouth stretching into a venomous smile as he saw the look of confusion on their faces. He could see the driver fumbling to shift the car into reverse – find it – and then suddenly the car was backing away. He immediately launched the rock he was holding, striking the windshield dead center and leaving behind a satisfying six-inch crack as the car continued to roar in reverse until they hit the main road where they changed direction and were gone. Satisfied, he turned and began whistling as he made his way back to his car.

He doubted anyone would be following him the rest of this day.

CHAPTER 38

When Toby arrived back home he noticed an unfamiliar car parked in front of his apartment building and when he reached the front stairwell, two men emerged from it and began walking in his direction.

"You guys just don't learn, do you?" he spat over his shoulder as they drew near. "I've got a court order that says you can't harass me anymore."

"Relax, Toby. My name's Detective Bronsky and this is Detective Johnson. We're with homicide and sex crimes," he said as both of them flashed their badges. "We just need to ask you a couple of questions."

"And I don't need to answer them without my attorney present," he shot back.

"Why so defiant, Toby? Do you have something to hide?" Bronsky asked him. Toby just looked at him calmly but said nothing.

"Well, it's like this, if you don't answer our questions now we're just going to leave and come back with a warrant to bring you downtown. Of course, then you'll be in our custody, so you decide how you want to do this?"

He didn't know whether or not they could do what they were threatening but he'd seen enough of the inside of a jail. "Alright, shoot," he said, turning to face them.

"That's more like it. We just need to know where you were two nights ago between six p.m. and midnight."

Toby thought about this for a second. Finally he said, "I was at a friend's house drinking beer and watching movies."

"What movies?"

"I don't remember."

"You don't remember what movies you watched two nights ago?"

"I don't believe I stuttered."

"Okay, so what's the name of your friend?"

"Carl."

"And does Carl have a last name?"

"Fuller."

"So this Carl Fuller, he'll corroborate your story?"

"I don't know, I guess you'll have to go ask him."

"Do you know a Jeanine Brandt?" Detective Johnson asked him.

"Doesn't ring a bell, why?"

"We think you know why, Toby. What's the matter? Was she so good the first time that you had to go back for seconds? And how about Brian Hennessey? Did you and he have a problem while you were locked up?"

"Are we done yet?" he asked, looking disinterested.

"I'm just curious," Bronsky jumped in. "What kind of hate motivates a man to shove a three-foot stick up someone's ass?"

"Like I said, are we done yet?"

Bronsky looked at Johnson then back at Toby. "Yeah, we're done," he said. "We need to go find this friend of yours and see what he has to say. No doubt he'll back your story, but don't think for a second that that means squat to us. You're a rapist, McGrady, and now you're a murderer, and it's only a matter of time until you make a mistake. The best part, though, is that once we nail you we're both going to be there in the front row to watch you die when they stick that needle in your arm."

"Well, it's been real, boys, but I have things to do and you have your tails to chase so good luck to you and I hope you find your killer," he said, disappearing up the stairs and leaving them standing on the sidewalk. He watched them through the curtains of his front window as they got back into their car and drove off.

"Assholes," he said aloud.

∽

"So how did he act?" Detectives Bronsky and Johnson had both stopped by the D.A.'s office to fill him in.

"He was belligerent as hell, that's how," Bronsky fumed. "The kid's nothing but bad attitude."

"I'll say," Johnson seconded.

"Did he have an alibi?"

"Yeah, said he was at a friend's house, one Carl Fuller, watching movies and drinking beer."

"I assumed you followed up on it. Did it pan out?"

"Oh yeah. This Fuller guy's a piece of work too. Both of them have the disposition of a badger with a toothache."

"But he backed up McGrady's story?"

"Yeah. Of course *he* couldn't remember what they had watched either."

"They're both lying their asses off," Johnson said. "There wasn't even a VCR or DVD player in his living room, so unless they were giving each other a puppet show, I don't know what they would have been watching."

"So where does that leave us?" Michael asked them.

"It leaves us with nothing for the time being. Hopefully the forensic boys will find something but we'll just have to wait and see. It's all we can really do at this point."

"Damn!" Michael said. "As if that isn't bad enough, he picked up on the car we had tailing him earlier today. Suckered them into pulling down a side street where he was waiting with a handful of rocks."

Bronsky looked at him in disbelief. "What?"

"Yeah, this kid is crazy. I don't know if I'll be able to convince them to put another tail on him. They're all running scared because they know they're violating a court order."

"Well, cross your fingers," Johnson said. "We'll keep plugging away on our end and hopefully we'll either get a break or he'll get careless and make a mistake."

"We can only hope," Michael said.

CHAPTER 39

"Are we good to go for tonight?"

Toby was talking into his cell phone as he drove toward Gabby's apartment. He had spoken with her about an hour ago and was encouraged when she had agreed to go to dinner with him.

"All set," Carl responded evenly. It was early but he already had his game-face on.

"Beautiful. Listen, after I drop Gabby off this evening I'll come over and you can tell me all about it."

"Sounds like a plan." They hung up as he parked in front of her complex. Gabby acted happy to see him when she opened the door and he took that as a good sign. As usual she was dressed to the nines and looked gorgeous.

"Hi," she said, standing on her tiptoes to give him a kiss. He pulled her firmly against him, feeling the soft swell of her breasts. "Thank you for believing in me," he said.

She looked up at him and said simply, "You're welcome." He then noticed they were alone. "Kiley's not here? I was hoping I would see her so I could apologize for the misunderstanding," he said, looking disappointed.

"She's actually in her room but I'd leave her alone for now. We just need to give her some time, Toby, she'll come around eventually."

"I'm sure you're right. So are you ready to go eat?" he asked as he helped her with her jacket.

"Always." she responded, turning around and offering him a sweet smile. When they exited the apartment Gabby watched him turn the knob back and forth to ensure it was locked. Satisfied, she got in the car as he held the door for her.

"Chivalry lives," she commented pleasantly.

As he walked to his side of the car he glanced back at the apartment and spotted Kiley peeking out from around the curtain that covered her bedroom window. Their eyes met for a brief moment and then she disappeared, but not before she had seen the dangerous smile playing at the corners of his mouth.

Carl walked quickly down the sidewalk with his hands stuffed in his pockets and his head pulled as far into his jacket as possible like a turtle in an attempt to escape the cold. His breath puffed rhythmic clouds that floated lazily ahead of him for a brief moment only to dissipate into the night just as the next one appeared. It was approximately ten o'clock on a weeknight and the roads were typically devoid of any appreciable traffic as he walked the remaining four blocks to his destination from where he had parked. The last thing he needed was someone casually looking out their window and remembering his car if the police happened to question them.

When he arrived he tried the door and was relieved to find it unlocked. He eased it open just a crack, listening for any sign that someone was occupying what he had been told would be the living room. When he didn't hear anything he slowly pushed it open further and held his breath as he waited for the hinges to voice their displeasure. There was a faint creak but it was negligible and he slowly exhaled as he looked quickly down the sidewalk in both directions to make sure there wasn't anyone approaching. Confident he hadn't been seen, he stepped inside and closed the door behind him, locking it.

He stood silently while he waited for his eyes to adjust to the darkness. When finally he felt he could safely navigate without tripping or knocking over anything he moved forward through the living room toward the hallway to his left. When he reached it he peered through the darkness and could make out an amber glow escaping under the last door on the left, and in the absence of light his heightened sense of hearing detected the rustle of papers.

He grinned crazily and felt his breath quicken as he donned his ski mask. She was home.

∽

"It must have been horrible for you."

"Which part?"

"Well, all of it I suppose, but especially the being in jail part. What was that like?" Toby and Gabriella had finished eating their dinner and had even tackled dessert this time. Stuffed, they decided to retire to the lounge and, as usual, Toby had worked his magic on the bartender and managed to get two margaritas delivered to their table. It was obvious to him that the revelation of who he was and what he had been through had been on Gabby's mind all evening, but to her credit she had avoided the subject over dinner. Now that they were relaxing in the dim light with half a drink consumed, she wanted to talk about it.

"I guess the best way to summarize it is to say simply that all of the rumors you've ever heard about jail are true. The place is a pigsty, the food is horrible, the other prisoners are dangerous, the guards are all assholes and most of them probably belong in jail themselves. I don't know what else I can tell you about it."

"Wow," she said. "You know it's scary to think that my dad sends people there every day."

"You would think that would be a lot of pressure on someone."

"What do you mean?" she asked him.

"You know, when you're in a position to take away someone's freedom or give it back to them, and you do it every day, it's probably a lot of pressure to live up to the expectations people must place on you. I mean, if you make one mistake in your own life you'd look like the biggest hypocrite in the world."

"I never really thought about it like that but yeah, I guess you're right. It's no problem for my dad, though. He's like a modern day Dudley Do-Right."

"Really, you think so?"

"Of course, are you kidding? I don't think my dad's ever done anything wrong in his life. He's one of those people who return the money when someone gives him back too much change. Or one time when a soda machine dispensed two cokes instead of one, he called the vendor to tell him his machine was malfunctioning. Who does that anyway?" she laughed.

"Did it ever occur to you that maybe all of your dad's good deeds are just acts of contrition for something he did wrong in the past?"

Gabby looked at him funny. "Why, do you know something I don't?"

Toby just laughed. "No, of course not. I just always wonder when I see people going out of their way to do nice things for others if maybe they did something really bad in their past and they're trying to make up for it. I know that sounds terribly cynical but as you know, we don't live in a utopian society and everyone has skeletons in their closet. You, me, and I'm sure even your dad has a couple; it's just part of life. It doesn't make you a bad person. It makes you . . . normal, I suppose."

"You're crazy," she said, smiling sweetly at him. "And maybe you're right. Maybe my dad is actually a mass murderer and he figured that lawyers were already so sleazy that he'd fit right in unnoticed."

"Well, here's to our skeletons and keeping them locked in the closet where they belong," he said, holding up his glass. *You'll find out soon enough the dirty little secret your old man's been keeping all these years, Gabriella. And then we'll see how much you think he resembles ol' Dudley Do-Right.*

∽

He stood silently outside her door, listening to the occasional turning of a page and what he presumed were the sounds of thoughts being transcribed to paper. He could picture her concentrating on the words in front of her, oblivious to his presence.

He listened for a while longer and then reached out with a steady hand and began slowly turning the doorknob. When he was sure the latch had cleared the faceplate he quickly pushed it open and stepped into her room.

"Hello, Kiley, nice to finally meet you."

CHAPTER 40

When Detective David Bronsky walked into the apartment two things registered immediately. The first was the sight of a beautiful, young brunette sitting on the couch sobbing uncontrollably as a female officer knelt before her and spoke in a soft, soothing voice. The second was seeing Toby McGrady, without handcuffs on, standing off to the side speaking quietly with a uniformed officer who David knew. The whole scene seemed surreal and he had to fight the sudden urge to charge across the room and beat McGrady to the ground before he could get away. He managed to get the officer's attention and motioned him over.

"How you doing, David?" the officer greeted him, extending his hand.

Bronsky took it and said, "I don't know, J.P., why don't you tell me. What the hell is he doing here anyhow?" he said, nodding to where Toby stood watching them. When Toby saw him look over he nodded to him like they were old friends.

"He's the brunette's boyfriend and apparently she's the dead girl's roommate. They're the ones who found her when they came home this evening."

"You mean he's not a suspect?"

"Couldn't be. He was with her all night," he said, pointing toward Gabby.

David shook his head in bewilderment.

"Do you know who that scumbag is?"

"Yeah, said his name was McGrady. Why?"

"Toby McGrady," he informed him. "That doesn't ring a bell?"

"Huh uh, should it?"

"The French Lick rapist?

"No shit!" he said. "The guy they just allowed to walk on a technicality?"

"One and the same."

"Then you're not going to believe this. Do you know who that brunette is?"

When David shook his head he said, "That's Gabriella Scalini – Judge Scalini's daughter."

Bronsky looked up at the ceiling and did a half pirouette, throwing his hands up. "Am I the one who's crazy here or has the whole world lost it's friggin' mind?" When the officer didn't respond he said, "Okay, look, is the coroner on his way?"

"Yeah, should be here any minute."

"Where's the body?"

"Down the hall in her bedroom."

"Was she sexually assaulted?"

"No, whoever it was tied her hands behind her back and then put duct tape over her mouth and nose and watched her suffocate to death. Can you imagine? Oh, and there's no sign of any forced entry either so it's possible the victim knew her killer."

"Interesting. Do me a favor and bring Ms. Scalini over here. She and I need to have a little chat."

It took some coaxing but eventually Gabby got up from the couch and came over to where Ray was waiting.

"Hi, Ms. Scalini, I'm Detective Bronsky. Mind telling me your version of what happened here tonight?"

"I – I don't know. We came home from having dinner and I just . . . found her like that," she stammered around her sobs.

"So you were out to dinner with your boyfriend over there?"

"Yes. He p-picked me up around eight."

"What time did you arrive back home?"

"I think it was right around midnight."

"That was kind of a long dinner, wasn't it?"

"It wasn't all dinner. We sat in the lounge and talked for quite a while after we ate."

"Okay, so then you guys left and came straight home?"

"Yes."

"And what did you see when you walked in the apartment?"

"Nothing - which was strange. Normally Kiley would have been waiting up for me. We always wait up for each other if one of us is on a date, but the apartment was dark."

"So what did you do?"

"I turned on the lights in the living room and then went down the hall and knocked on her door. There was no answer and at first I thought she had fallen asleep studying. When I went in I . . . ." At this point Gabby broke down again and buried her face in her hands.

"I know this must be difficult for you but it's important we get through the details while they're still fresh in your mind, okay?"

Gabby nodded, took a deep breath and swiped at her eyes before continuing. "I found her lying on the floor and I immediately ran over and shook her to see if she was alright but, she . . . didn't respond. She wasn't moving and that's when I saw that her mouth and her n-nose had been taped closed. Oh my God, I just can't believe she's dead," she cried.

"Ms. Scalini, was your boyfriend with you the entire evening?"

Gabby stopped crying and looked at him. "Of course he was with me. I already told you that."

"You do know who your boyfriend is, correct?" When she didn't answer he continued. "I mean, I'm assuming you're aware that he was sitting in jail just a little over a week ago charged with thirteen counts of rape, right, and that your father was the judge assigned to the case?"

"What's your point, Detective?"

"My point, young lady, is that I find it odd that a man is arrested and charged with multiple counts of rape and violent assault, a judge lets him walk for reasons known only to him, then that same judge's daughter starts dating the scumbag, and now your roommate is dead. Now I don't know many people who would chalk all that up to mere coincidence, do you? As a matter of fact, I'm quite sure I don't know a *single* person who would. And whether you want to admit it or not, I can see by your face that you're not really buying into it either. So I'm going to ask you again . . . was Mr. McGrady ever out of your sight for more than a couple of minutes this evening?"

"I already told you no." By this time the coroner had arrived and they watched him walk back to the bedroom to begin his examination.

"Okay, that's all I have for now, Ms. Scalini." As she started to turn away he said, "Umm, I don't know if anyone told you yet, but whoever killed your roommate waltzed right through the front door, so either they had a key or it was unlocked. What do you think?"

"I have no idea," she answered, but he could tell this declaration troubled her. "Can I go now?"

"Sure, just make sure you give the officers a number where they can contact the girl's parents." She nodded and walked back to the couch and the comfort of the female officer.

Ray then walked over to where Toby was still standing, casually watching the goings on. "I can't even imagine the terror that must have been in that poor girl's eyes as whoever killed her stood there watching her slowly suffocate. But what am I thinking? You've witnessed this firsthand at least a dozen times, haven't you?" If he was hoping to read something in Toby's face he was disappointed. He could just as well have been watching The Simpsons at home in his living room.

"Kiss my ass, Detective," was all he said.

"You going to tell me you didn't have anything to do with this?"

"How could I? I spent all evening with my girlfriend. But I'm sure she already told you that."

Bronsky studied him for a moment. "I gotta give you props, kid. Not only do you happen to find the only judge in the country that would have ruled on that warrant the way he did, but a week later you're banging his daughter. You are sleeping with her, right?"

"Every chance I get," he said without looking at him.

"I think I'm gonna go have a little chat with this judge tomorrow. Just kinda feel him out and see what's what."

"Knock yourself out."

"Toby, I know you think you're slick and that you have us all chasing our tails, but I'm here to tell you that you're just fooling yourself. There ain't a lot of sure things in life but you can bet your ass that that's one of them. Before this is over you're gonna know what it's like to rot on death row, waiting for your last appeal to be denied before they haul your ass into that fishbowl where all your victims and their families get to watch you die with a needle stuck in your arm."

"Do tell." Toby said, still refusing to look at him.

"You die by suffocation, you know." Bronsky continued. "Oh yeah, they say it's so inhumane that they're trying to pass a law right now to prevent veterinarians from using it on animals. You see, as you lay there, your lungs start slowing down and over the course of about ten minutes your oxygen intake becomes less and less until you start to feel like you're drowning. And when your body is screaming for air like a banshee, and your lungs aren't cooperating any longer, they just collapse and this white mucus-looking shit comes shooting up through your trachea and oozing out of your nose and mouth. So I guess the reality is that you are actually drowning now that I think about it," he said almost to himself. "Kind of like what your girlfriend's roommate went through tonight. But the funny thing is that everyone watching thinks you're unconscious and just passing peacefully into la la land, when in actuality the first drug they inject into you paralyzes your entire body so you can't even open your eyes. You can still hear and feel every single thing that's happening to you, it's just that your body can't thrash around in agony like a normal person's. Ain't that a hoot?"

"Get away from me," Toby said flatly.

"Sure thing, Toby. I'm finished with you for now. But I *am* going to find the answer to this incestuous little riddle, you can believe that," he said as he turned and walked away.

Toby walked over and sat next to Gabby on the couch, indicating to the officer that he would take over now. "Do you want to stay at my place tonight?" he asked her.

She looked over at him and he could see the red puffiness in her face. "I don't think so, Toby. I'm going to call my parents and have them come and get me. I think I just need to be with my family right now."

"I understand," was all he said.

Gabby looked down at her feet and chewed on her lower lip as she considered what she wanted to say next. Finally she decided to just say it. "Toby, I need you to tell me that you had nothing to do with this," she said, searching his eyes for reassurance. Instead, what she saw was disappointment.

"I can't believe you just asked me that. I was with you all night, Gabby. How could I have possibly been involved?" When she didn't answer he said, "Is this the way our relationship is going to be; filled with suspicion and doubt every time life throws a curve ball at us?"

"No, that's not what I meant."

"Then what did you mean?"

"Nothing," she said. "Look, I'm sorry I said anything – I didn't mean it. I'm just upset right now and after listening to some of the things that detective was saying . . ."

"That detective is an idiot. I didn't tell you this but they've been following me ever since I was released. And when I'm home they just sit out there in the street, watching my apartment. I finally had to have my attorney file to get a court order against them for harassment. See, this is the problem with being falsely accused of something so horrible; no one will let you resume your life. You're forever branded a criminal regardless of whether or not you were convicted. It just sucks."

"Toby . . ." Gabby began, reaching for his hands. "I'm sorry. I had no right to ask you that. Let's just forget about it, okay?"

"Fine. Look, call me tomorrow from your folks' house as soon as you get up. If you don't I'm going to start worrying," he said, pulling her close and enfolding her with his arms. "And give my condolences to Kiley's parents, will you?"

"Thank you for being so understanding, Toby."

"There's nothing to understand, Gabby. It's horrible what happened and I know you're going through a lot. Just don't hesitate to call if you need to talk, okay?" He stood up and bent down to kiss her on the forehead. When he reached the door he paused to look around the room and saw Detective Bronsky and another cop looking at him and he stared back for just a moment before raising his right thumb and forefinger to his hairline and simulated tipping his hat like the greeter at a speakeasy. When neither of them responded he turned and left. He still had another date this evening with an ugly redhead named Carl, and this one promised to be much more interesting.

CHAPTER 41

The next morning after breakfast Gabby had called Toby as promised and he came over to pick her up. When they were back at her apartment the emptiness was a stark contrast to the events of last night. The forensics people had finished up this morning and there were only subtle signs they had ever been there; a lampshade askew, a couple of cabinets standing open, but other than that the place looked pretty much as it had before Kiley's life had been taken.

"You were awfully quiet on the way over here," he said as they sat down at the kitchen table.

"I know, I'm sorry. I've just been in such a mood since I woke up this morning and I didn't want to burden you with it. I just can't believe Kiley's gone. It scares me to death to think that a stranger was in here last night. It scares my parents, too, and they are begging me to move back home with them. To tell you the truth, I'm seriously considering it."

"How are your parents taking this?"

"My mother is obviously terrified of me staying here alone. My dad, though, his mood was hard to explain. I can't really put my finger on it but . . . well . . . I know this is going to sound silly but it was almost as though he wasn't surprised; like he'd been expecting something bad to happen and now that it had he was upset that he hadn't been able to prevent it. Does that make any sense?"

"Everyone handles tragedy differently, Gabby. I'm not sure there's such a thing as a *normal* reaction. People just react the way they react and there's really no use trying to rationalize it at the time."

"You're probably right," she agreed.

"Listen, it's understandable that you're scared after last night, but I don't believe you want to give up your freedom, do you?"

"Not really, but I don't know if I can stay here alone either. Plus, now I have to come up with all the rent myself and I can't afford it." Toby pushed a crumb around with his finger, appearing to consider something. Suddenly he looked up at her and said, "What if I moved in with you?"

"You?" she asked.

"Do you have another boyfriend you'd rather live with?" he teased.

"No, of course not, but . . ."

"But what? I'm crazy about you, I believe you feel the same way about me, and I would be here to protect you so your parents wouldn't have anything to worry about," he reasoned.

"You don't think it's too soon?"

"It's probably sooner than we would have wanted under normal circumstances, but we also didn't anticipate what happened last night, did we?"

"No, of course not," she said. "What would you do with your apartment?"

"Give it up. I'm on a month-to-month so it's no big deal."

He watched the wheels turning as she considered his proposition.

"Soooo . . . what do you think?" he asked her, reaching over and covering her hands with his own.

She was silent for a while, but when she looked up she was smiling. "Okay, I'm game if you are," she blurted happily.

"Oh, I'm definitely game," he said, returning her smile.

"I'm going to call my parents right now and let them know so they can stop worrying, okay?"

"There's no time like the present," he agreed. *God, what I'd do to be a fly on the wall when she breaks this news to them.*

∽

"She's what?" Anthony blurted.

"I said Toby's moving in with her," Francesca repeated.

"The hell he is."

"Oh, don't be a prude, Anthony. Do you really believe they aren't sleeping together already? What's the difference? Besides, this is the perfect solution since Gabby wasn't very receptive to the idea of moving back home anyway."

"Gabby needs to be concentrating on school, not playing house with some guy she barely knows. Her roommate was just murdered for crying out loud."

"I know, Anthony, and it scares the hell out me too, but we can't force her to move home. And if it doesn't work out, then Gabby's strong enough to do the right thing and break it off with him – so stop worrying."

"I have to go," Anthony announced suddenly.

"Where are you going?" Fran asked him, surprised.

"I have something I need to take care of, that's all. I'll be back in a little while," he told her, kissing her on the cheek as he headed for the door.

Once he was in his car he had to force himself to breathe deeply in an effort to calm down. This had already gone too far and now it was out of control. He would not let a rapist move into his daughter's life under any circumstances – even if it meant he had to do the unthinkable. However, before he made that decision there was someone he needed to go see first.

∽

"Mr. Hill, you have an Anthony Scalini here to see you," Brandon's secretary informed him over the office intercom.

"Okay, send him in, please." *I wonder what this is about?*

When Anthony walked in Brandon came out from behind his desk and extended his hand. "Good to see you, Judge.

I have to admit that this is a bit of a surprise. What can I do for you?"

"Hello, Mr. Hill. Thanks for seeing me on short notice. Would it be okay if we closed the door?"

"Sure." He walked over and informed his secretary to hold his calls as he closed the door and then returned to his desk, motioning Anthony to sit as well. He could see that the judge was deeply troubled by something. "I'm assuming you didn't just drop by to say hello."

"I wish that's all it was, Mr. Hill. I'm here because I believe my family is in danger; specifically my daughter, Gabriella, and I don't know what to do about it."

"What are we talking about here, Judge?"

"I'm talking about Toby McGrady." Brandon should have been shocked but for some reason he wasn't. "Do you want to give me anymore detail than that?"

"He's been seeing my daughter."

Brandon was shocked but he didn't show it.

Anthony continued. "Gabriella asked if she could bring her new boyfriend over for dinner a couple of days ago, and when they showed up it turned out to be none other than Toby McGrady."

This time Brandon responded. "Did you tell your daughter who he was?"

"Sort of. It's a long story."

"Do you want to tell me about it?"

"I think I do. I need to tell someone about it, and given your relationship with his mother, I was hoping that maybe you could ask her to intervene."

"Did you speak with Toby?"

"Yes."

"Well, what did he have to say? Surely this is more than just a coincidence."

"He told me that he was doing it for the same reason a dog licks his balls – because he could."

"Why didn't you just kick him out of the house?"

Anthony lowered his face into his hands and rubbed nervously at his temples, as if he were debating what he should say next. When he looked up, Brandon saw an interesting mix of shame and resignation on his face. "Because he knows something about me that could destroy my family, end my career and potentially land me in prison for the rest of my life."

Brandon wasn't expecting this at all. "Are you sure I'm the one you should be talking to, Judge?"

"Right now you're the only one I trust. I don't believe you would use any of this against me and you could possibly help my situation through your relationship with his mother."

"Okay, I'm listening," he said, leaning back in his chair and folding his arms across his chest. He had a feeling this was going to take a while.

Anthony took a deep breath and began. "You probably don't know this but Brett Mitchell and I were best of friends in law school."

Brandon thought it better to just listen and not respond so Anthony continued. "Anyway, one night during our last year of law school we attended a party thrown by one of the senior partners of a law firm Brett was joining right after graduation. We both had quite a bit to drink and we should have had a taxi pick us up and take us back to the campus. Instead, we made a bad decision and got into Brett's mustang and drove ourselves. This turned out to be the second biggest mistake of our lives." His voice faltered at this point so he took a deep breath and cleared his throat before resuming. "She just seemed to materialize out of nowhere."

"Who?" Brandon asked.

"The sad thing is that I don't even know. She was just a young girl; maybe a runaway or maybe one of the locals' daughters. All I know is that she was walking on the road and we hit her." He paused again as the awful details of that night returned in a nauseous wave.

"It was horrible, Brandon. We were going way over the speed limit when we hit her and it was only by a miracle that we didn't skid into a tree and kill ourselves as well. Sometimes I wish we had," he added softly.

Brandon wanted to ask a hundred questions but he forced himself to remain silent.

"We walked back to where she was lying in the road and Brett checked for a pulse, but she was already dead." He paused here for a moment to collect himself. "Now I told you a moment ago that driving back to campus that night was the second biggest mistake of our lives. The biggest mistake was what we did next." Brandon leaned forward in his chair slightly.

"Instead of calling the police and taking responsibility for what we'd done, we decided to hide her body. I didn't want to do it," he said, looking directly at Brandon, his eyes pleading for understanding. "But while I was distraught and not thinking clearly, Brett was incredibly calm and convinced me that it was the best thing to do since turning ourselves in wouldn't bring her back, and it would most likely ruin our lives. So we put her body in the trunk of his car and he dropped me off at campus before going on alone to hide the body. He said that it would be best if only one of us knew where she was."

Brandon had a hundred questions he wanted to ask but decided they could wait for another time. "So how does all of this relate to Toby?"

"Apparently when Toby was arrested Rose went to her brother for help. As you know, he was the one who picked up on the procedural mistake with the warrant, but he had to also know that no judge was going to let the kid walk on something like that. And although it was purely coincidence that I happened to be the judge assigned to the case, apparently when he found out he told Rose the story I just told you and had her blackmail me with it. I have to believe that the only reason he did it was because he knew he was dying. Otherwise I don't think he would have ever told her because he would have been implicated as well. It was a chicken shit thing for him to do but, then again, if I had acted like a man all those years ago I wouldn't be sitting here spilling my guts to you right now, would I?"

Brandon's brain was working overtime. "So how did all this play out? I mean, how did Rose go about blackmailing you?"

"She passes a note to me through the bailiff asking me to call her."

"Did you?" Brandon asked, aware of the impropriety of such a request.

Obviously I wouldn't have under normal circumstances, but the note also indicated that she may know something about the girl that we hit so I didn't feel as though I had a choice. We met later that night in a parking lot and that was when she confirmed that she knew everything and said that if I didn't rule in her son's favor she would tell the police what I had done and take them to the body."

Brett considered this for a second then asked, "But how would that have implicated you even if she'd followed through with her threat? Without Brett there's no one who could even place you at the scene."

"When I was cleaning the blood off of my hands in the car that night, I took off my class ring. Apparently I forgot it when Brett dropped me off and he told Rose that he had placed it in one of the girl's pockets. He told her that originally he did it just for insurance in case I came down with a bout of guilty conscience and decided to tell someone."

"Wow," Brett exclaimed, shaking his head. "That must have been a lot to have to live with all these years."

"Believe me, Brandon, it's been like a cancer slowly eating away at my soul."

"I believe it. I also have to say that I'm a little embarrassed myself since it would now appear that I was nothing more than a pawn in this whole thing. It makes sense, though, because I never could figure out why Rose would hire someone like me who had no experience in a case of this magnitude. Now I see that she didn't need an experienced lawyer; it was already a done deal."

He looked at the judge. "I appreciate you taking me into your confidence by telling me all this, but what are you looking for from me?"

"Apparently Rose told her son everything."

Brandon's heart skipped a beat. "You have got to be kidding me," he said in disbelief.

"I wish I were. He's been holding it over my head where my daughter Gabriella is concerned and I fear he's prepared to take it to another level. And last night Gabriella's roommate was murdered in their apartment while they were out to dinner."

"What!"

"I'm afraid so. Whoever murdered her suffocated her to death by taping her mouth and nose closed."

"But obviously it couldn't have been Toby if he was with your daughter, right?"

"That's right, but I don't believe for a second that he wasn't involved somehow. Also, I just found out today that he's moving in with her. We tried to get her to move back home but apparently he's very persuasive where she's concerned."

"I don't know what to say, Judge."

"My hands are tied, Brandon. If I go against him he says he'll go to the police and take them to the girl's remains. However, I'm not going to stand by idly and watch my daughter get hurt either. I will turn myself in before I let that happen. Before I do that, though, I was hoping that maybe you would confront Ms. McGrady about this and see if she can call him off."

"You can bet that's exactly what I'm going to do. She is completely oblivious to just what a cretin that son of hers really is, so maybe this will serve as a wake-up call for her. Out of curiosity, does your wife know about any of this?"

"Heavens no, she would lose her mind and probably go after McGrady herself if she knew who he really was. This kid is a loose cannon and there's no telling what he might do if he feels threatened. No, I can't chance that so I've kept her completely in the dark."

"Okay, give me a number where I can reach you after I've spoken to Rose. I'm heading over there as soon as you leave so cross your fingers and I'll let you know what happens."

"I can't tell you how much I appreciate this, Brandon."

"I want Toby's ass back behind bars just as badly as you, Judge. If I can help make that happen it'll be my pleasure, I assure you."

When Anthony had left and he was alone again, Brandon sat at his desk turning over in his mind everything the judge had told him. He felt like he had unwittingly walked into a Stephen King novel and was suddenly one of the main characters. He shook his head in bewilderment and dialed Rose at home.

"Hi, Rose, it's me. Can I come over? I have something important I need to speak with you about."

CHAPTER 42

As soon as Rose opened the door she could see that something was wrong. "Are you okay, Brandon?" she asked him worriedly.

"No, I'm not okay. I just had an unexpected visit at my office from someone I think you know pretty well."

"Who?" she said cautiously.

"Judge Scalini." As soon as the name left his mouth her expression changed and he knew instantly that everything the judge had told him was true. He could have left right then and never had another doubt, but that wasn't the entire reason he was here.

"What does that have to do with me?" she said, recovering quickly and trying to appear disinterested.

"Don't do that, Rose," Brandon said quietly. "If our relationship means anything to you at all, please don't stand right there in front of me and lie."

"What do you want, Brandon?" she asked him defiantly.

"Oh, I don't know. How about we start with why you've been lying to me since the day we met or maybe you could tell me all about blackmailing a criminal court judge; how about that?"

"So he told you everything. That bastard," she hissed.

He was taken aback by the venom in her voice. "He didn't have any choice, Rose," he fired back. "What's the matter, blackmailing him wasn't enough for you? You had to go and tell Toby too? Do you have any idea what your boy's been up to since you handed him the keys to the kingdom? Do you?" He shook his head disgustedly. "I really thought you were smarter than that."

"None of this is any of your business, Brandon," she warned him.

"Bullshit." he shot back. "You made it my business when you hired me to be a pawn in this idiotic scheme of yours. Let me ask you something, Rose. Did you know that Toby has been seeing that judge's daughter since he got out of jail?"

"That's not true." Rose countered. "Toby would have told me if he were seeing someone, and he hasn't mentioned it."

Brandon laughed harshly. "Would you just listen to yourself? You're completely blind when it comes to that psycho son of yours, aren't you?"

"Stop it!" Rose screamed at him. "Just stop it. Do not come into my home and speak like that about my only child."

"That's your problem, Rose. You're so consumed with the fact that he's the only family you have left now, that you're willing to turn a blind eye to what's so obvious to everyone else."

"I'm not listening to this," she said, turning to walk away.

"Do you know what Toby told the judge when he asked him why he was seeing his daughter?" Rose continued to walk away. "He told him he was seeing his daughter for the same reason a dog licks its balls. Do you know why that is, Rose?" She stopped but still had her back to him.

"Well don't feel bad, because neither did I. He told the judge he's seeing his daughter because he can. And that there wasn't a damn thing he could do about it because he has a secret that would ruin him and his family if he ever decides to go to the police with it. Is that why you told him, Rose, so he could waltz into this judge's life and destroy him and his family? Your son is sick, do you understand that? He needs to be removed from society, not given a free pass to continue hurting people."

"I'm not having this discussion with you," she said, turning to face him.

"He's moving in with her, you know." He could tell that this declaration surprised her so he pressed on. "Yeah, her roommate was murdered last night and she's scared to death, so now Toby's moving in. I suppose you think that's just a coincidence, huh?"

He could tell she had questions but her anger and stubbornness prevailed.

"Oh, don't worry, he has an airtight alibi but I still think he had something to do with it."

"I said I'm not having this conversation with you," she practically screamed.

"You can't blackmail a judge, Rose. Do you realize that you could go to prison if this ever came out?"

Rose began walking toward him; her eyes never wavering from his, until she stopped an arm's distance away. "You and I are done, Brandon, and I will not stand here and listen to these lies any longer. Please leave," she said, pointing toward the door.

"That isn't why I came here, Rose. I came here to make you aware of what Toby's been doing; to see if you would talk to him and make him leave this judge's family alone?"

"Well it might not be what you came for, Brandon, but it's what you're leaving with. I don't ever want to see you again. Now get out." She turned and without another word left the room.

Brandon stood where he was for a while longer, trying to figure out what had just happened. If he'd followed that exchange correctly it sounded as if he had accomplished absolutely nothing where Toby was concerned and had lost his girlfriend in the process. Finally he turned and walked out the door, shaking his head in frustration.

As Anthony was pulling into the courthouse parking lot the next morning, he was still thinking about the conversation he'd had with Brandon. He had called him immediately after speaking with Rose and informed him that the conversation had not gone well at all. Apparently she was not interested in anything anyone had to say regarding her son and had finally kicked him out of the house, telling him she didn't want to see him any longer. Anthony told him he was sorry but Brandon assured him it wasn't his fault. He had also warned him that there was a good possibility Rose would go straight to Toby and tell him what had happened, and that he should be prepared for anything at that point. This was definitely not what Anthony wanted to hear and he was more frightened for his daughter now than he'd been *before* he had come clean.

As soon as he got out of his car, though, he realized that Brandon had been wrong. Rose wasn't going to talk to Toby after all; she was going to talk to him. He could see her standing in the courtyard waiting for him, and for a brief moment he considered getting back in his car and driving away, but he knew if she didn't catch him today she'd be back tomorrow. Besides, it was possible he could calm her down and maybe then she wouldn't alert her son to what had happened. He grabbed his briefcase and started toward her. "Hello, Rose," he said as he drew near.

"You've got a lot of nerve, you know that?" she snarled at him.

"Your son is endangering my family."

"Yeah, I know that's the lie you told Brandon."

"It's not a lie. He moved in with my daughter yesterday. Do you really believe it's just a coincidence that he's seeing her?"

"I don't believe any of this, but you can bet that I'll be going to see him today and find out for myself. But I'm telling you, Anthony, even if he is seeing your daughter – which I doubt – that doesn't mean anything. Are you telling me that he isn't good enough for her? Is that what you're implying?"

"Rose, I know you don't want to hear this but your son is sick, and he's already destroyed a lot of lives. I'd prefer my daughter's not be next on his list."

"Do you mean sick like a judge who runs an innocent girl down in the middle of the night and then throws her away like a bag of garbage? Is that what you mean by sick?

"I acknowledge the mistake I made, but let's not forget that your brother was with me that night and, in fact, was the one driving the car."

"My brother was a great man and he was sincerely sorry for what he'd done."

"Rose, I knew Brett very well and I know he would have never told you about that night if he'd known how this was going to turn out. I can't for the life of me understand why you would have told your son about it, but the fact is he knows, and now he's using it to get at my family. He told me he would turn me in to the police if I interfered with his and Gabriella's relationship."

"You and Brandon," she said, as if she were expelling a piece of rotted flesh. "I'm sick of your accusations. And I'm warning you right now, that if I find out you've told a single other person about this, I will go straight to the nearest police station and write out a sworn statement regarding what Brett told me you two did, and then I'll take them to her body and they'll find *your* ring in her pocket. How do you suppose you'll explain that? Huh?" she challenged him.

Anthony took a deep breath and exhaled slowly. His situation was impossible and it was obvious that he couldn't expect any sympathy from this woman as long as she refused to accept the truth about her son.

"Please just ask your son to leave me and my family alone. I'm begging you."

"You just remember what I said. Not one more person." And with that ultimatum she turned and walked away, leaving Anthony to stare after her and wonder for the umpteenth time if he and his family were going to survive this.

CHAPTER 43

Brandon informed the gum-popping secretary that he was there for his appointment with the D.A., and he then took a seat in the reception area. Looking around he noticed that other than four ratty, crushed velvet chairs with faded flower patterns and the two cheap plastic plants that had been carelessly placed on either side of the double door entrance, there was nothing else in the way of décor besides an old framed copy of the United States Constitution that was hanging at a skewed angle, and probably had been for years. The whole place was badly in need of a paint job. Typical government, he thought, shaking his head. They'll spend millions to study the mating cycle of the spotted snipe but they won't spend a dime on creating a decent work environment for their employees.

"Mr. Hill?" He looked up to see Michael Haas standing before him with his hand extended. He stood quickly and took it. "Thank you for taking the time to see me." he said.

"Well, I have to admit that your call piqued my interest. Let's go talk in my office. Can I get you some coffee?"

"No. I'm fine, thanks." When they were seated the D.A. leaned forward and placed his forearms on his desk, lacing his fingers together in front of him. "So what can I do for you?"

"I want to tell you about a conversation I had with Toby McGrady."

Michael studied him for a moment. "You're representing him. Wouldn't you be breaching attorney/client confidentiality?"

"Yes," Brandon said evenly, his eyes never wavering.

"Are sure you want to do that?"

"Do you want to put him back behind bars where he belongs?"

"You know that's a rhetorical question."

"I presume that you're aware of the Hennessey murder; that guard at the jail?"

"Of course," he said, but his face gave nothing away

"Well I'm almost certain McGrady had something to do with it."

"What makes you think so?"

"The day after it happened he came to visit me at my office, and just as he was leaving he turned around and asked me if I had heard about it."

"It had been all over the news," the D.A. reminded him.

"Yeah, but Toby knew details that he shouldn't have known."

"I don't understand. How would you know what had been released to the public and what hadn't?"

"Actually I have a friend in law enforcement who has access to that kind of information and I had been talking with him earlier that morning."

The D.A. pursed his lips. It was obvious he wasn't thrilled to hear that someone was leaking confidential information, but he let it pass. "Alright, I'll go with it, Mr. Hill. So what exactly did McGrady tell you that he shouldn't have known?"

"He told me that the guy was overweight and that he had been impaled with a stick."

"Are you sure he couldn't have found that out some other way? You did," he said dryly.

"No way. Plus, he was acting very strange. Almost as if he wanted me to know that he had done it. It was pretty unsettling to say the least."

"Even if you're right, this isn't enough to arrest him on."

"I know, but I felt I had an obligation to tell you anyway. This kid is bad news and there's no telling what he's capable of."

"You're not telling me anything I don't already know. Believe me, we're doing everything in our power to nail this creep, but so far he's eluded us and, of course, that injunction you filed didn't help the situation."

"Sorry about that," Brandon said sincerely. "I should have stopped representing him as soon as I became suspicious." He then took a deep breath and glanced up at the ceiling, considering how to broach the next subject. "There's something else."

The D.A. just looked at him, waiting.

"I have to have your word that this will go no further than this office. I need your solemn word on that."

"As long as you're not going to confess to a murder, you have it. What's up?"

"The reason Judge Scalini let McGrady walk on that technicality with the warrant is because he's being blackmailed by Ms. McGrady."

"What? What the hell are you talking about?"

Brandon leaned forward and in a low voice, he recounted everything Judge Scalini had told him. When he was finished the D.A. had to make a conscious effort to keep his mouth from stupidly hanging open.

"That has to be the single-most incredible story I have ever heard in my entire life; absolutely incredible." He watched his hands as they toyed with a pen and considered what Brandon had just told him. Finally he looked up. "Well now that you've made me give my word not to repeat this, what the hell do you expect me to do with it?"

"I don't know. Turn up the heat on McGrady? Put the judge's daughter in protective custody? Nothing? Hell, I don't know. What I do know, though, is that Judge Scalini is a good man who made a mistake when he was a kid. Now his world's being turned upside down and he's scared to death that his daughter's life is in danger. Unfortunately, the fact that McGrady knows about his past has him handcuffed and he can't do anything to protect her."

The D.A. considered this. "He could turn himself in."

"I've thought about that, but what good would it do? He'd lose everything, the circuit would lose a good judge, and more importantly, he'd probably go to prison, and who knows what McGrady would do to his family then?"

"I guess you have a point," he agreed. "Wow. This is one hell of a predicament, isn't it? I guess I'm going to have to reevaluate my feelings regarding coincidences. I mean, think about it: It was a coincidence that Judge Scalini was assigned to the case. It was a coincidence that he had something in his past that could be used against him. It was a coincidence that the other guy involved happened to be the brother of the kid's mother. And it was a flippin' coincidence that he was dying of cancer and decided to spill his guts right at the end. Did I miss anything?"

"Believe me, I've thought the very same thing."

"Well listen, Brandon, I'm glad you told me this and I promise I'll keep it between us."

"I appreciate that."

"I'm definitely going to give this some thought, though, and maybe I can come up with a way that we can use this information to our advantage. In the meantime you better watch your step. Also, is it possible for you to stop representing him?"

"I'm done with him."

"Good. Make sure you file the appropriate paperwork with the court to officially withdraw as his counsel of record. This way we won't have the confidentiality issue moving forward should you find yourself in possession of any new information."

"Consider it done."

"Like I said, let me mull this over and I'll be in touch."

Brandon thanked him again and left. He'd done what he could and now he would just have to hope that either the D.A. figured out a way to use what he'd told him, or hope that Toby made a mistake. For some reason he didn't think there was much chance of the latter happening.

Now he just needed to figure out some way to patch things up with Rose.

◌

Toby had taken Gabby to class this morning and had left from there and headed over to his apartment to pick up some more of his things. On the way he had received a call from his mom saying that she wanted to come over and talk to him about something so he was expecting her any minute. In the meantime he had two suitcases opened on the bed and was busy transferring the contents of his drawers into them.

When the knock came at the door he dropped the stack of shirts he was holding and went to answer it. "Hey, Mom," he said, giving her an obligatory hug. "Nice to see you."

"You too, Toby. Do you have a couple of minutes?"

"Sure, come on in." Rose walked into the middle of the small, studio apartment but made no effort to sit down, turning instead to face him. "Toby," she began, "against my better judgment I told you the secret your Uncle Brett shared with me, and I also told you how I had used that information to get those charges against you dropped. In exchange, you swore to me that you would never repeat it or use it to your advantage. Now I'm here to ask you if you've kept that promise."

"What are you talking about, Mom? Who would I have told?" he asked her, doing his best to look hurt by the question.

"Are you seeing that judge's daughter?" The question caught him off-guard.

"What do you mean?" he said, trying to buy some time.

"I mean exactly what I just asked you, Toby. Are you seeing Judge Scalini's daughter?"

"Well, yeah, I am," he confessed. "But it was just a fluke thing, Mom. Some friends and I went to go eat at this place called Mulligan's and she happened to be our waitress. I thought she was cute so I asked her out. I didn't find out until days later that she was his daughter. By then our relationship had gotten more serious and it didn't seem to matter. Why are you asking me, anyway?"

"Does she know who you are or her father's involvement in your case?"

"Yes, I told her myself."

"And that didn't bother her?" she asked skeptically.

"At first it did, but after she had time to think it over she was okay with it and now we're fine. Her parents know too. How did you find out anyway?"

"Is it supposed to be a big secret?" she tested him.

"No, not at all, but I didn't think any of your friends would have known about it."

"Apparently Brandon was talking to the judge and that's how he found out. He came over yesterday and confronted me about it and asked if I would speak with you."

"Speak with me about what?"

"Well, according to him, the judge isn't as pleased about you seeing his daughter as you apparently think he is, and he would prefer that it stop."

"Isn't that Gabby's call?"

"Is that her name?"

"Gabriella, but most everyone calls her Gabby."

"Yes, Toby, in answer to your question, I would agree that as long as you've been upfront with her and she knows what's going on, then it's nobody's business but your own, and that's basically what I told Brandon."

"Well I appreciate you sticking up for me, Mom."

"Brandon also told me that the only reason the judge was tolerating this relationship was because you had threatened to tell the police about his past. Is that true?"

"Absolutely not – he's lying."

Rose sighed heavily and suddenly she looked sad. "I don't know if you knew this, Toby, but Brandon and I have been seeing each other since shortly after I hired him to represent you. I meant to tell you but the opportunity hadn't really presented itself."

"Yeah, I had an idea," he said, smiling at her.

"Well, for what it's worth, I broke it off with him yesterday and told him I didn't ever want to see him again."

Toby looked surprised. "I don't know what to say, Mom. I'm sorry."

"You've always come first in my life, Toby, and I've always believed in you. I simply cannot tolerate that kind of negativity around me so I think it's better this way." He could see that she was remembering the scene from yesterday and he didn't respond. After a moment she looked up at him. "Don't ever betray my trust in you, Toby. If you do it'll take you a lifetime to earn it back, do you understand."

"I understand," was all he said.

"Is it true that you two are moving in together?"

"Yes, I was packing when you knocked."

"You don't think that's a little soon?"

"It's sooner than we expected, but her roommate was murdered a couple of nights ago while we were out to dinner and Gabby's scared to death to stay alone. It was either we move in together or she was moving back in with her folks, which she didn't want to do."

"Brandon told me what happened to her roommate. It's just horrible. How's Gabriella doing?"

"Not very well."

"Brandon thinks you had something to do with it," she stated, studying his face.

"I just told you I was out to dinner with Gabby. How could I have had something to do with it? That's just a ridiculous accusation by one more person who wants to prevent me from moving on with my life. I'm sick of it," he said, throwing her a very convincing look of disgust.

"He doesn't think it was you but he believes you somehow had something to do with it," she continued, ignoring his outburst. He could see that she was watching his reaction with an inordinate amount of interest. "Do you believe I was involved?"

"Were you?"

"Haven't we been down this road before?" he said, throwing his hands up in disgust.

"Look, I don't want to leave here with you mad at me, okay."

"Then just believe me when I tell you I had nothing to do with it, okay?"

"Okay, I believe you," she said, giving him a reassuring smile. "So when do I get to meet this new love in your life?"

"Give us a few days to get settled and then we'll have you over for dinner one night. How's that?"

"That sounds great. Well, I have to go, Toby. I haven't spoken with your Aunt Sarah in a couple of days so I'm going to stop by and see how she's holding up. I wouldn't want her to think I'm ignoring her," she said, grinning.

"Okay, Mom, well thanks for stopping by and thanks for believing in me when all these other people keep trying to throw me under a bus."

"Alright, sweetheart. You take care, good luck with the new living arrangements, and don't make me wait too long for that invitation, you hear?"

"You got it," he said, relieved this conversation was over.

CHAPTER 44

The pushing and sucking sounds from the ventilator droned on rhythmically, indifferent to the life source it offered to the otherwise lifeless body of Terri Ranes. Her mother and father stood on either side of her bed, each gently squeezing a warm hand that refused to squeeze back.

At least one of them, and most times both, had maintained a bedside vigil since the day she'd been brought here, praying fervently that she would awaken from her coma and flash them one of her famous lop-sided grins, or maybe ask for something to drink. But it was not to be and the doctors had finally informed them that because their daughter was no longer registering any brain activity, she was considered to be in a vegetative state and was being given a zero percent chance for recovery. They needed to make a decision regarding whether or not to keep her on life support.

As difficult as it is for a parent to know that their child is being compared to a potato or a spear of asparagus, finally accepting that this person laying in front of you is just a shell of the son or daughter you knew comes with it an acute sense of betrayal and, unfortunately, there are no medicinal treatments available to eradicate the gnawing guilt from your soul.

The doctor waited for the go-ahead from Mr. Ranes and when at last he received the solemn nod, he reached over and shut off the power. The comforting *Swuuuuhhft* pause *Pffooooooft* they had come to so closely associate with the hope of an escape from this nightmare that had so completely enveloped their lives was suddenly gone, and in its place was a silence so deafening it made you want to scream just to make it go away.

Six minutes later the doctor pronounced Terri Ranes dead and Mrs. Ranes' facade of strength crumbled at last as she collapsed sobbing onto her daughter's chest. Mr. Ranes walked out of the room and into a waiting area where he punched a number into his cell phone and waited.

ᏚᏚ

"Mr. Hill, this is Michael Haas."

"Yes, how are you?" Brandon replied.

"We received a call about an hour ago from the father of Terri Ranes. I'm not sure if that name rings a bell but we're pretty sure she was McGrady's last victim."

"I know who she is," Brandon stated stoically.

"Yes, well anyway, she's been in a coma since she was admitted and today her father informed us that the family made the decision to take her off of life support."

"I'm sorry to hear that," Brandon said sadly.

"So am I, but the fact is that now we have a capital murder charge on top of the multiple counts of rape. I think it's time to turn up the heat on our boy."

"What do you have in mind?"

"How's your grasp of the English language?" the D.A. asked him.

‿◌‿

After carrying the last of his things from his car to Gabby's apartment, Toby spent the next thirty minutes organizing it in the drawers she had reluctantly surrendered to him. When he finally looked at his watch he saw that it was time to go pick her up from school and take her to work, and from there he planned to go hang out with Carl.

When he got out to his car he noticed a plain white envelope that someone had stuck under his windshield wiper and he impatiently tugged it out as he opened the door and got in. When the door was shut he tore it open and inside he found a single piece of paper with a laser-printed note. As he started reading he felt the rage begin to consume him.

Dear rapist (or should I say murderer),

That's right, McGrady, Terri Ranes was taken off of life support today. Remember her? She's the one who ended up in a coma from the vicious beating you gave her. It must take a real man to beat on a woman like that, huh, punk? Yeah, you're a real tough guy. Who's next on your list, Gabriella Scalini, or are you stalking someone else these days?

The good news is that Terri Ranes' nightmare is finally over. The bad news is that yours is just beginning.

We're coming for you, boy. Are you ready?

Toby slowly refolded the paper, placing it back in the envelope, and it would be a fearless man indeed who could have met that calm, dangerous stare without flinching. He picked up his phone and punched in Carl's number.

"It's me. Remember that equipment I asked you about a few days ago? Yeah, that stuff. Get it out, clean it up and make sure it works. I'll meet you at your place in forty-five minutes and I want you there with three or four other guys who can keep their mouths shut. Tell them to bring something to cover their faces. No, I don't give a shit if they're white, black or fucking purple with red polka dots, just have them there when I get there, you hear me?"

"Alright, boys, game on."

∽

"Are you smarter than when I dropped you off?"

"If I get any smarter there won't be enough room for all my brain cells," Gabby teased him as she got in the car.

Here, I picked you up a soda on the way over. Thought you might be thirsty after all that learnin'," he said, affecting his hillbilly accent.

"Why thank you, kind sir," she reciprocated with her best Ellie Mae impersonation. She took it from him and drained a third of it immediately. "Ahhh, that hits the spot," she said, smiling her appreciation.

"Your shift starts in an hour, right?" She nodded as she took another drink. "Mind if I stop by a friend's house to drop something off real quick?"

"Sure, but don't make me late for work. The night manager can be a real jerk."

"Don't worry," he assured her. Fifteen minutes later he was pulling up in front of the shithole apartment complex where Carl lived, smack in the middle of Indianapolis's version of Watts. "Who do you know that lives in this neighborhood?" she asked warily.

"A buddy of mine I grew up with. Don't worry you're safe with me and we won't be long," he assured her as they got out of the car. A couple of bums loitering outside the entrance of the building watched them with interest but quickly went back to sipping their dinner when Toby told them to mind their own business. Carl's place was on the second floor and he took her hand as they made their way up the stairs and down the filthy hallway that stank of mildew, urine and dirty diapers. When they came to Carl's door he rapped twice and some squirrelly-looking black dude Toby had never seen before opened the door immediately.

"Get the fuck out of the way, Buckwheat!" he snarled when the guy just stood there staring at Gabby.

"Toby!" Gabby exclaimed, completely offended by his rudeness.

"Mind your business, Gabby," he shot at her. "This ain't white picket fence suburbia." Buckwheat looked offended as well and started to respond, but then thought better of it and moved quickly out of the way as Toby stepped inside with Gabby. He walked her over to a filth-stained couch and motioned for her to have a seat. When she hesitated he said, "Gabby, I don't have time for this. Just sit down, alright?"

With confusion and hurt on her face she complied and he turned around to survey the room until he spotted Carl tinkering with a video camera he had mounted on a tripod. He also noted there were three other cameras placed strategically around a dirty, piss-stained mattress that had been moved into the middle of the room. To his right, sitting at a table that looked like it still had food scraps stuck to it from last year, were two more guys; both black, both muscular and both looking at Toby as if they were deciding whether or not to say something to him about insulting their friend. "This all you could come up with?" he said, nodding toward the two.

Carl shrugged his shoulders. "I did the best I could on short notice, Holmes." The bigger of the two had had enough and he stood up glaring at Toby. "You know, your attitude be pissing me off, white-boy," he said menacingly. Carl immediately looked up from the camera and seeing the look on Toby's face, just shook his head as he watched him walk over to where the guy was standing and stop approximately a foot away from him.

"Toby . . ." Gabby started, sensing trouble.

"Shut the fuck up!" he barked, cutting her off. Her mouth dropped open but she remained silent. He then found the big man's eyes with his own and they measured one another for what seemed a long time as the silent ritual played itself out. Toby's strange, piercing eyes seemed to almost stare through him, as if they were searching for something that only he could see and it wasn't long before uncertainty crept onto the face of the other man who, in suddenly rethinking his position, allowed his mouth to stretch in a wide smile.

"Hey, man, I was just . . ."

In a devastating blur of calculated motion, Toby drove his fist upward under the man's chin, striking him squarely in the throat and effectively crushing his windpipe. Gabby screamed and as the other three watched, a stunned look of surprise and amazement passed over the man's face as his hands tentatively felt his wounded neck, only to be replaced seconds later with one of panic as he realized he could no longer breathe and began clawing wildly at his throat and chest. When he finally collapsed no one made a move to help, though they continued to watch with morbid fascination for the five minutes it took him to suffocate. Through it all, Gabby sat on the couch alternating between hysterical screams and breathless sobs at the horror she had just witnessed.

When his body had finally stopped convulsing save for an occasional twitch, Buckwheat said, "Where the hell'd ya learn to do that, watching Jackie Chan movies?" Toby ignored this as he walked directly to Gabby and without warning slapped her across the face hard enough to knock her to the floor. He then reached down for a fistful of hair and threw her back on the couch. "I told you to shut your mouth," he said as she lay whimpering in pain and absolute fear of this stranger, this madman standing in front of her.

He then turned to Carl. "So, are we ready to get this show on the road?"

"Oh, we're ready, baby," he said, laughing. The other two just shook their heads and were silently thanking their lucky stars that they hadn't been the one to piss off this crazy white dude. Toby picked up the camera on the tripod and looked through the viewfinder until it was centered directly on Gabby, who had her face buried in her hands. Satisfied, he turned it on. He then walked over to Carl's computer and typed in the URL to a website he'd created a couple of years back but had not used in some time. After a few seconds Gabby appeared live on the monitor.

"Connection's good," he said to no one in particular. He then stood and turned to face Gabby. "I have some friends I want you to meet, sweetheart. This is Carl," he said, pointing toward the mattress, "and this is Heckle and Jekyll." Neither of the remaining two black men commented on the intentional slight.

Gabby recognized Carl from that first night at Mulligan's, but she'd never seen the other two. "W-what are we doing here, Toby?" she asked miserably, holding her hand to the side of her face that still burned from where he had slapped her.

"Well, sweetie, that all depends on your father. It could be that we're just kicking back spending a couple of relaxing days with some friends. Or," he continued, grinning at Carl. "Carl here just might be directing his very first hardcore porn film with you as the star."

Gabby's eyes grew wide with confusion and hurt. "Toby . . . I don't understand. What are you . . ."

"What's to understand?" he said, cutting her off. "Either your father comes through or you're gonna be humping my friends here until we have enough footage for a feature-length movie. Of course if it comes to that, and believe me, Gabby, I surely hope it doesn't, then sadly you'll have to die since I can't have you running around telling your side of the story, understand?" Gabby's mouth was completely devoid of any saliva and her heart felt like it was going to explode through her chest. How could this man who had shown her nothing but kindness suddenly turn into a horrible beast with no warning?

"I don't know yet whether we would tape that part, but it's just bad business to ignore the fact that there are some fucked-up low lifes out there who will pay a king's ransom to see a real-life snuff film, pardon the contradiction." Although his threats were so bizarre it would have been easy to convince herself he was just trying to scare her, she instinctively knew he wasn't bluffing. After all, hadn't she just watched him take a man's life for apparently no reason? "What does my father have to . . . to do with this, Toby?" she asked quietly.

"Oh, that. Well, I hate to break it to you, princess, but it would appear that your old man's not the Boy Scout you grew up worshipping." When he saw the confusion on her face he continued. "On the contrary, it would seem that he and my uncle have quite a past together. Well, *had*, since my uncle croaked a few days ago. But anyway, the story goes that they were friends in law school, and after leaving a party one night they got in my uncle's car all juiced up and smoked some bitch walking down the side of the road, but that's not the best part. The best part is when they decided to just throw her body off in the woods somewhere instead of calling the cops and reporting it."

"Toby, that can't be . . ."

"True?" he asked her. "Oh, it's true alright. How the hell do you think I managed to avoid a life sentence in prison, with my charming disposition? No, my uncle told my mom the whole story before he died and she blackmailed your old man to make him rule in my favor on that search warrant screw-up." He looked around the room and saw that the other three were grinning wildly as they listened to the details of his story for the first time. "Then the next thing you know," he continued, "I'm a free man and I'm banging this judge's daughter. Now how's that for poetic justice?" he laughed.

"Now I'm sure you have lots of questions for me but, unfortunately, I don't have time right now since I have to go meet your dad. See, the police have been fucking with me and either he's going to call them off for good, or his daughter is going on the Internet for the salacious enjoyment of the underbelly of cyber space. Now you be a good girl and don't worry because I've told Carl here that he's to ensure both your safety and your virtue unless I tell him different." He then turned to Carl. "But if she makes any attempt at all to leave that couch without your permission, you and your buddies have a green light to start rehearsing. After all, practice makes perfect, right?" He could hear Gabby beginning to cry again and turned around. "Buck up, sweetie, as long as your old man cooperates you have nothing to worry about. I'll come back to get you and we'll pick up where we left off. How does that sound?" Gabby was too afraid to speak or even look at him and kept her eyes directed toward her lap, which elicited nothing more than a shrug from Toby as he headed toward the door.

"You keep that phone clear until you hear from me, understand?" When Carl indicated he did he said, "Oh, and if I don't call you by tomorrow morning go ahead and do her the same way you did her roommate. And make sure you get it on tape; I hear you can practically retire off of one snuff film." Hearing Toby admit that Carl had murdered Kiley and that he was involved as well caused a low moan to escape from her throat and she began to shake.

"What am I supposed to do with that dead piece of dog shit laying on my floor?" Carl asked him.

"Wait until it's dark and throw his ass in a dumpster down one of these alleys. Some bum looking for scraps will find him and he'll tell the first cop he sees, hoping they'll flip him a fiver for the information. Don't sweat it, he'll be just another dead nigger in a town full of 'em." He stared hard at the other two but they wisely said nothing. He then took one last look at Gabby and left.

CHAPTER 45

As Toby drove toward his apartment he dialed information and asked for the number to the courthouse. When he had it he hung up and quickly redialed. When the switchboard operator answered he asked to speak with Judge Scalini and was put on hold until finally a female voice came on and said, "Judge Scalini's office."

"Yeah, let me speak to the judge."

"I'm sorry but the judge is in court right now. Would you care to leave a message?"

"Tell him he needs to call Toby McGrady as soon as possible."

"What is this regarding?"

"It's none of your damn business what this is regarding, you nosey bitch. Just tell him to call me. No, you know what? Tell him this has to do with Gabby."

"With Gabby?" she huffed.

"Yeah, with Gabby. Do you think you can handle that?"

"I'm sure I'll figure out a way, sir," she responded sarcastically.

"Good." He gave her his cell number then hung up.

A few minutes later his thoughts turned to Gabby and what he had just put her through, and something unfamiliar and slightly unsettling passed through him for just a brief moment and then it was gone. Though he never could have articulated it, the reality was that he had experienced the faintest awakening of the normal emotions that most people are born with and need only to find that special someone in order to stoke them to life. Unfortunately when Toby was born those feelings were buried in a dark abyss somewhere deep within him, destined to lie forever dormant. The fact was, fate had never intended that Toby should feel what most everyone else takes for granted; love, sadness, euphoria, remorse, empathy and guilt. None of these emotions were familiar to him. His was an emotional menu containing but a few items from which to choose.

Anger was one and, of course, that had the potential to turn into a destructive rage in the blink of an eye. There was also the complete and unprovoked contempt he inherently felt for everyone around him. But most of all there was the virulent indifference and complete lack of regard for life that made him extraordinarily dangerous – mostly this.

From birth fate had decreed that Toby would hunt. Like the great white prowling the murky depths of the ocean, he was destined to stalk the dry vastness of his own habitat with a disturbing single-mindedness; his dead and unfeeling eyes searching always for the next target upon which to unleash his savage fury.

Toby was a sociopath born with a blood lust. He was a killer.

༄

Anthony was very concerned as he read the short but chilling note.

Judge,

Call Toby McGrady ASAP.

Regarding Gabby

Ph. 591-1421

p.s. He was a real jerk!

ASAP? What did that mean? Regarding Gabby? Was something wrong with Gabby? Had that son of a bitch hurt her because he found out he'd spoken to Brandon? He forced himself to calm down and then picked up the phone and dialed the number.

"Hello, Judge, how are you?" Toby asked pleasantly when he answered. *Monroe Cty* had come up on caller I.D. so he knew who it was.

"You left a message for me to call. What do you want?" the judge asked in a hesitant monotone, trying not to betray how nervous he felt.

"Kind of piqued your curiosity, did it?"

"The note said it was regarding Gabby. Is she all right?" he asked, ignoring the question.

"Of course, Judge, why wouldn't she be?"

Anthony sighed audibly and said, "What is it then that you want, Mr. McGrady? I can't imagine what else I could possibly do for you."

"You still don't get it do you, Judge? What makes you think it's your daughter I'm after?"

"I'm not following you."

"You will soon enough. I want you to meet me at my old apartment at seven o'clock this evening."

"You think I'm naïve enough to walk into the lion's den just like that?" Anthony asked, not trying to hide his indignation.

Toby laughed. "Relax. I've been called crazy before, but I'm not interested in dealing with the consequences that would come with killing a judge. No, I have something to show you that I believe will be of great interest to you."

"What is it?"

"Now, Judge, if I told you it would spoil the surprise. I'm in the phone book so look up my address and I'll see you at seven sharp." He hung up and looked around the empty room. *"And it begins..."*

❦

After he hung up Anthony had considered calling Brandon, but he had a feeling this meeting was a result of talking to him in the first place so in the end he decided against it, but he'd be lying if he said he wasn't concerned about going alone; especially considering that no one would even know where he was. What choice did have, though? As long as McGrady knew what he knew and was willing to wield it in order to manipulate him, then he basically had two choices: Comply or call his bluff; neither option was especially enticing and either could result in disaster. It did, however, occur to him that if he could get his hands on a gun he could just end this tonight, and though such thinking was foreign to him, as well as exceedingly distasteful, he felt the situation had become desperate and as a result, he was beginning to think like a desperate man. He didn't believe he was quite there yet but he was definitely getting close.

He hoped tonight wouldn't be that final straw that put him over the edge.

∽

"Judge, how nice to see you. Come in, please." Anthony was caught off guard by Toby's pleasant demeanor and at first didn't respond as he cautiously walked by him and stepped into the tiny apartment.

"Have a seat," Toby said as he closed the door. Anthony saw that he didn't lock it and took that as a positive sign. "I'm in a hurry, Toby, what did you want to see me about?"

"Ah, right to the point, huh? Okay," he said, his face turning serious. "I want to know why you found it necessary to bring Brandon in on our little secret? Did you really think he was going to be able to help you somehow?" When Anthony didn't respond he said, "He told my mom, you know. And of course she had to come over here and ask me all kinds of irritating questions, which always puts me in a foul mood. No worries, though. He said quickly, smiling again. "She's always been gullible where I'm concerned so after I gave her my side of the story the end result was that she believed me, she thinks you and Brandon are liars, Brandon no longer has a girlfriend and . . . well . . . here we are." Anthony said nothing as he listened to the rantings of an obviously disturbed young man.

He then walked over to his computer and bent down to quickly tap out a sequence of key strokes, then stood up and waited, though from this angle Anthony couldn't see what he was doing. Finally, appearing satisfied, he punched a number into his cell phone and when it was answered on the other end said, "Are we all set?" Apparently receiving the reply he sought he turned to face the judge and like a circus crier he announced, "Well come on over here, Judge, it's show time," he said with a flourishing wave of his arm.

As Anthony walked toward the monitor all he could make out was what looked like a young girl sitting on a couch, but then as he moved closer it became clear that the girl he was looking at was Gabriella. "What's the meaning . . ." he started to say.

"Just shut up and keep watching," Toby commanded. Then into the phone he said, "Pan it around the room." They both watched as the camera moved away from Gabby and began to reveal the rest of the room. He could see dirty walls with peeled paint that looked like bubbling flesh, two black men sitting at a small table, another one lying on the ground appearing to be asleep, and finally a single, bare mattress lying in the middle of the room with cameras positioned around it. "Alright, put it back on Gabby and hand her the phone."

When the camera returned to its original position they watched as a white guy came from behind it and handed a cell phone to Gabby, which she took reluctantly. When she put it to her ear Toby said, "Hi, Gabby. Do you miss me?" When she didn't respond he said, "Well, we'll worry about that later. Listen, your daddy's watching you right now as we speak, so I want you to look into the camera and give him a thumbs up that you're alright."

Gabby looked absolutely terrified and Anthony felt sick to his stomach. He still had no idea what was going on but had the presence of mind to at least be thankful that his daughter didn't appear to be hurt.

"Gabby, you don't want to make Carl mad, do you?" She immediately shook her head no and slowly raised her arm to chest level and gave the thumbs up sign toward the camera. She then lowered it again and began to cry.

"None of that, Gabby. You've been treated with the utmost respect and you're just going to worry your father, so knock off the tears and give the phone back to Carl." That was the second time Toby had used one of the men's name and Anthony filed it away.

"I want to speak to her," he demanded, reaching for the phone.

"And people in hell want ice water," Toby said, slapping his arm away easily. "You're not calling the shots here, asshole, I am."

Suddenly Anthony attacked. Toby had kind of expected it, but he had to admit he was surprised at how quickly the old guy moved. However, it took him only a split second to recover and when the judge's shoulder hit him in the ribs he pivoted in the direction of his weight and landed on top of him as they hit the ground. Anthony was on his stomach and Toby immediately ran his right forearm under his chin. He then placed his right hand on his left bicep and his left hand on the back of Anthony's head and squeezed, instantly cutting off the flow of blood to the brain. It took less than three seconds for Anthony to lose consciousness.

He came to within a few seconds, but it took longer than that to shake the cobwebs. After a moment, though, the visual of his daughter on the monitor returned and the anger came flooding back. He pushed himself off the floor and got shakily back to his feet just as Toby was turning off the computer.

"Don't rush me again, Judge," he warned. "I told you on the phone that I wasn't crazy about the idea of killing a judge. However, I didn't say I was completely opposed to it. Here, see, I turned it off so you don't have to watch it any longer. Must have been tough, huh?" Anthony just stared at him; wanting him dead more than he'd ever wanted anything in his life. His breath sounded a ragged staccato in his chest.

"Better sit down. You're going to give yourself a heart attack," Anthony didn't move.

"I said sit the fuck down," he said dangerously. After a moment Anthony sat on the couch.

"That's better. Now you be a good boy from now on and I won't have to keep sending you to la la land. Besides, the lack of blood flow can start to cause brain damage," he warned him.

"What are you planning on doing to her?" Anthony asked in a pathetic voice. "What are you planning on doing to my daughter?"

"Ah, now this is where you and I are going to have to agree to disagree. You see, I don't believe that I am the one who's doing anything to Gabby. The fact is *you're* doing it."

"You're out of your mind," Anthony snarled.

"Am I, Judge? Well I'm not sure I agree with you. I mean, you and I had a nice little gig going, ya know? I knew a secret about you and as a result you did what the fuck I said. But now . . . well, now you've screwed all that up by going and telling Brandon about it, who in turn went to my mom and Lord only knows who else, and then I start finding shit like this on my windshield," he said, tossing the note angrily into Anthony's lap.

Anthony read it and the confusion was obvious on his face. "I don't know anything about this letter. I had nothing to do with it."

"It may be true enough that you didn't personally put it on my car, Judge, but it's not true that you had nothing to do with it. If you had just kept your big mouth shut none of this would have happened."

"But what does any of this have to do with Gabriella?"

"What, that?" he asked, motioning toward the monitor. "That's nothing, Judge. Right now she's just being baby-sat by some of my friends, but it could become *something* very quickly if you don't do exactly what I say. And I can guarantee that you won't like what that something is. You saw the mattress, right?" When Anthony nodded he said, "Well unless you and I can come to an agreement your little girl is going to find herself *on* that mattress being violated in all kinds of nasty, despicable ways, all of which will be captured on film and then distributed on the Internet for the sick enjoyment of every pervert out there in cyber-space." Anthony's face contorted and he buried his head in his hands.

"Now I suppose I could have just told you all this and spared you the trauma of having to see it for yourself, but the real thing is so much more effective, wouldn't you agree?" Anthony couldn't speak.

"So here's the deal. Tomorrow you are going to call whoever it is you need to call in order to get everyone to leave me the hell alone. I'm talking about complete immunity here. I don't ever want to see any shit like that showing up on my car again," he said, nodding toward the note Anthony was still holding. "And after you've done that, you're going to turn yourself in for the murder of that girl as punishment for not keeping your mouth shut."

"Not a chance in hell," Anthony growled defiantly.

Toby appeared to consider his words carefully before replying. "Judge, I completely understand you not wanting to go to prison. Hell, I was miserable for the few days *I* was locked up – and that was just jail. But if you don't do what I'm telling you, I'll turn you in myself. On top of that, once you're behind bars I'll film a sequel and it'll be your wife in the starring role next time. Believe that."

"You're a monster."

"I don't do a whole lot of introspective analysis so I won't waste my time disagreeing with you, Judge. However, even if you're right, in a couple of days I'm going to be a monster with a permanent get out of jail free card. You're going to see to that."

"There's one option you seem to have forgotten."

"And what's that?"

"I can just turn myself in tonight and tell the police everything, starting with how your mother blackmailed me. You won't have time to follow through on any of your threats before the police have both of you in custody."

"You could, but here's the problem with that. I may have to ditch plans of making Gabby a star, but one call from this phone and she'll be dead before you can say incarceration. Then I'll make this website disappear and you'll have no way of proving any of it so I'll still be free, your daughter will be dead, and what do you think will be happening to your wife while you're rotting away in prison? I can promise you that whatever you're dealing with behind bars will be a walk in the park compared to what she'll be going through." He paused to let that sink in. "So do we have a deal?"

Anthony knew that he lacked the authority to do what he was being asked, but he wasn't about to admit it. "Okay, give me a few hours to make some phone calls and let me see what I can do. Regarding turning myself in, can I at least have a week to get my personal affairs in order and ensure my family is taken care of?"

"Make the calls, Judge, then we'll talk about the other."

"There's one other thing," Anthony said.

"What is it?" Toby sighed impatiently.

"If I do this for you and then turn myself in, my family is off limits. You take your sick brand of terror somewhere else. Deal?"

"I could probably see my way to doing that, but I expect to hear something from you by tomorrow. Understand?"

"I'll do my best."

"Do better than that, Judge."

In the car Anthony couldn't rid his mind of his daughter's terror-filled face, and for the millionth time it occurred to him that if he had only done the right thing that night and not listened to Brett, none of this would be happening. As far as he was concerned, all the blame rested squarely on his shoulders. However, be that as it may, he knew that he had no intentions of acquiescing to anymore of Toby's demands. He may end up going to prison before this was over but one thing was certain - he wasn't going without a fight.

CHAPTER 46

Brandon was at home trying to compose a brief for an upcoming appeal when he received a call from Judge Scalini informing him he needed to speak with him immediately and asked if he could stop by. After they'd hung up he'd made a half-hearted attempt to return to the brief, but he couldn't stop wondering what the judge wanted to speak with him about. Frankly he was worried. When the D.A. had called him earlier and informed him that they needed to turn up the heat on Toby, they had decided to write the letter in an attempt to bait him into doing something stupid. Now he was concerned that the note had something to do with the call.

"Hello, Judge."

"Brandon," Anthony nodded as he stepped through the door.

"Your call sounded urgent?"

"I just came from meeting McGrady at his apartment and he knows you and I spoke and that I told you everything. Apparently he found this out through his mother. He also showed me a threatening letter that someone stuck on his windshield and needless to say, it didn't go over very well with him. Do you know who might have written it, Brandon?" he asked, searching his face.

Brandon couldn't look at him. "It was me."

"I see. Would you mind telling me why you did it?" Brandon quickly explained his call with the D.A. and told him what had happened with Terri Ranes, and how the D.A. had decided that it was time to go on the offensive. When he finished the judge seemed to be considering the wisdom of such a strategy. He then looked up at Brandon and his eyes filled with tears. "He has my daughter."

"What do you mean he has her?"

"I don't know for sure. Wherever he's keeping her they had a camera with a live feed to McGrady's computer and I could see her sitting on a couch in some filthy room, absolutely terrified. There were at least four other men there and he threatened to film them raping her and then release it on the Internet if I didn't work out immunity for him."

"Shit! I knew he was a bad seed but I had no idea he would go to this extreme."

"Obviously I can't give him immunity, but I didn't tell *him* that. He also wants me to turn myself in for killing that girl."

Brandon was stunned and didn't know what to say. The judge looked miserable and it was obvious that the guilt was eating him alive. "Is there anything I can do?"

"Brandon, I truly believe that the only person with any influence over this boy is his mother. Somehow we have to open her eyes to the things that are so obvious to the rest of us."

"I tried, but she doesn't want to listen to anything negative about her son. Hell, it cost me my relationship with her the last time I tried."

"Then let's stop trying to convince her and show her."

"What do you mean?"

"When I left his apartment I drove down maybe half a block and sat there waiting for him to leave."

"How long did you have to wait?"

"He pulled out less than five minutes after I had, which leads me to believe his computer is still set up."

"So what do you propose?"

"I'm proposing that we get Rose over there and show her what McGrady showed me."

"You want to break in?"

"Yes. Do you know anything about computers?"

"I know my way around pretty well. If he hasn't deleted the history I can find the URL of the last few sites he was on."

"Will you help me do this then?"

"I'm game but I'm not sure how we're going to get Rose over there. Right now she hates me."

"Well, kidnapping worked for her son. Surely she'll listen to reason when we have her undivided attention; don't you think?"

Though Brandon knew he was serious, he couldn't help but grin. "Okay, Judge, let's go."

◌◞◟

Rose was losing her mind in the backseat of the car and Brandon was tiring from the effort of holding her legs that she seemed so intent on using to kick out the side window. When she'd opened the door at her house to ask him what he wanted he had stepped inside and was immediately followed by Anthony. Thankfully she hadn't screamed since she knew both of them, but Brandon saw the unbridled hate on her face and knew they were lucky she hadn't been armed or things would have become a lot more serious very quickly.

As she started to demand they leave, Brandon made his move and took her to the ground, ensuring he kept one hand over her mouth so she couldn't alert her neighbors. Anthony then stepped forward and tied her hands behind her back before securing her mouth with a large piece of duct tape. They both felt ridiculous and were thankful it was dark as they carried her to the car and deposited her in the backseat, and now they were making their way to Toby's apartment, both praying fervently he hadn't returned yet.

"Rose, stop it already," Brandon ordered. This only served to piss her off even more and this time she ignored the window and tried to kick *him* through it instead.

"Rose, knock it off! If you'll just relax for thirty second I'll explain to you what's going on." She continued to flop around for a few more seconds but she was getting tired and after a few more less enthusiastic kicks, she finally relaxed, though he remained on guard. "Look, I'll take the tape off your mouth but if you start screaming it's going right back on. Deal?" She glared at him but finally nodded her head so he reached over and peeled it away.

"You son of a bitch!" she spat.

"I'll put it back on," he threatened. She continued to glare but it appeared that she was going to remain quiet; at least for the time being.

"Look, we're sorry for this but we need to show you something and knew you wouldn't willingly come with us, so unfortunately you left us no alternative."

"This is kidnapping, you bastard."

"Yes, well I suppose it is, but like I said, you didn't really leave us any other option. Now if you'll just listen, the judge will explain what's going on, alright?" When finally she agreed Anthony began bringing her up to date as he drove. When he finished she said, "I don't believe any of it. You both have had it out for Toby since the beginning and you're just trying to set him up."

"I suppose we could argue about that all night," he said.

"Where are you taking me?"

"To Toby's apartment. I'm going to let you see what your son made me look at a few hours ago, and then you'll understand."

"Will you at least agree to let us show you so I can untie you and we can stop with this spy versus spy nonsense?" Brandon asked.

"Fine, but when you're wrong I'm going straight to the police and filing charges against both of you."

"Fair enough."

∽

The apartment complex was old and so were the locks, and Toby's yielded easily to one of Brandon's credit cards. "Okay, let's go before someone sees us," he said nervously.

"It's my son's apartment," Rose stated. "Who's going to bother us?"

"Him if he happens to come home while we're here," Anthony reminded her. Brandon hit a light switch and immediately walked over to the computer and turned it on. As he waited for it to go through the boot sequence Anthony explained to Rose in more detail his conversation with Toby.

"You can talk until you're blue in the face, Anthony, but I'm not buying it," she informed him.

"Well that's why we're here, Rose," Brandon said, motioning them over to the computer. "Toby didn't delete his history and this was the last site he visited, so give it a second to load and let's see what we have." The three of them stood there as the computer worked, no one talking and Anthony barely breathing. After all of Toby's threats he was terrified of what they might see on the screen. And then it was up and there was Gabby sitting in the same exact spot she'd been earlier, looking just as frightened, but appearing to be okay. He exhaled loudly.

At first Rose was silent, but finally said, "How do I know that's your daughter?" Anthony wiped the moisture from his eyes and immediately pulled out his wallet to show her a recent picture of Gabriella. She compared it to the girl on the monitor and by the look on her face it was obvious that she now believed them. "Where is she?"

"I have no idea. All I do know is that one of the three guys there with her is named Carl."

"Take me home," she said.

"Shouldn't we go to the police?" Brandon asked.

"No, absolutely not," Anthony quickly answered. "All he has to do is make a phone call and she'd be dead before the police could get there." He couldn't take his eyes off the monitor and how scared Gabriella looked, though he was thankful it didn't appear anyone had touched her yet.

"Take me home," Rose repeated. "I will call him and ask him to come over to see me. I need to be the one to confront him about this." It was obvious the truth had hit her hard.

"Okay then, let's get the hell out of here before he comes back," Brandon said as he punched the power button on the computer after making a mental note of the website address. Anthony felt an incredible sense of loss when Gabby disappeared from the screen and he almost asked him to bring it up again but knew they didn't have time. The three of them quickly made their way out of the apartment and back to the car, and Rose was the only one to speak on the drive back when she stated what Anthony and Brandon had suspected all along. "He really did those horrible things and I helped set him free."

When they arrived at her house she told them that she would call Toby and invite him over tonight, but she couldn't promise that he would admit anything to her even when she informed him she'd been in his apartment, but for Gabriella's safety they shouldn't do anything until she'd at least tried. Anthony and Brandon agreed and told her that they would be at Brandon's office brainstorming a contingency plan and that she should call them there after she'd spoken with him.

Once Rose was alone she quickly lost the battle she'd been waging with her emotions on the ride back and she collapsed sobbing onto the couch, completely and utterly consumed with the horrible truth of who and what her son really was. She felt helpless and defeated and remained that way for almost ten minutes before finally her concern for Anthony's daughter forced her to get up and start moving. Once she was up she walked over to the phone and punched in a number.

CHAPTER 47

"Come in, Rose, come in," Sarah said, ushering her inside. "You sounded almost frantic on the phone. What's wrong?"

"I'm so sorry to bother you this late, Sarah, but I didn't know who else to call."

"Don't be silly," she admonished her. "You couldn't bother me if you tried. Now please, tell me what's wrong."

"Can we sit down?"

"Of course," she said, leading her into the kitchen where Rose took a seat at the table. "Can I get you some tea?"

"That would be great," she said, taking off her coat. While Rose watched her prepare the tea she again considered the wisdom in coming here. She had no idea what Sarah knew, if anything, and hesitated to tell her anything that could potentially tarnish her memory of Brett. However, at this point she didn't know who else to turn to.

Toby was a rapist and maybe worse – that much she now knew. The thing she was struggling with the most, though, was how he had changed into this monster right before her eyes and she hadn't even seen it. Wasn't it her responsibility to know what was going on with her child? And because she had missed it, didn't she now bear some of the responsibility for everything that had happened?

When Sarah returned to the table with two cups of hot tea she could see the pain in Rose's eyes. "What's troubling you, Rosie?" The diminutive use of her name got her attention since only Brett had ever called her that. She looked up and smiled. "I miss that."

"I miss him too," Sarah replied. "Now why don't you tell me why your pretty eyes are all red from crying."

Rose took a deep breath. "Do you remember when Toby was first arrested and I came here to talk with Brett about it?"

"Of course."

"Well Brett was the one who picked up on the fact that the police had improperly served the search warrant. Did you know that?"

"I don't think he specifically told me that but I assumed he had. He was always very sharp like that," she grinned.

"Yes, he was," Rose agreed. "He also told me that that technicality probably wouldn't be enough to have the evidence ruled inadmissible." She searched Sarah's face as she said this but it betrayed nothing so she continued. "Are you aware that Brett and the judge that was assigned to Toby's case were good friends during law school?"

"Yes, he mentioned that to me."

"Really?" Rose asked, surprised. "Did he happen to tell you anything else?"

"Like what?"

"Anything."

"No, I don't believe so," Sarah said, appearing to think back to the few days leading up to his passing.

"Well suffice it to say that Brett knew something about the judge that he thought I could use to ah, influence him shall we say; to rule in our favor."

Sarah appeared to carefully consider this. "And did you?"

"Yes," Rose said simply.

"Well, I always trusted Brett's judgment so I assume his intentions were noble."

"Ordinarily I would agree with you, Sarah, but I believe he knew that losing him to cancer and my son to prison both at the same time would have been more than I could bear. I think it convinced him to divulge something to me against his better judgment." She shook her head pathetically. "Trust me, if he had had any idea that things would turn out the way they have I don't believe for a second that he would have told me anything. It's just gotten out of control, Sarah. People have been hurt and I feel like it's all my fault and I don't know what to do about it." She began to cry again.

Sarah watched for a moment and then reached across the table for her hands. "Look at me, Rose, and tell me what's happened."

Rose wiped her eyes and leaving out Brett's secret, she described how she had met the judge in the parking lot and threatened to expose him with what she knew if he didn't rule in Toby's favor, and how Toby had later convinced her to tell him everything Brett had confided in her. She then recounted Brandon telling her how the judge was now concerned for his family because Toby was seeing his daughter, and how mad she had been at him for implying that Toby's intentions were anything other than noble. She took a deep breath at this point and sipped her tea. After a moment she continued.

"Toby has kidnapped Anthony's daughter and is threatening to do horrible things to her unless he can promise him complete immunity from the police. Right now wherever he has her he has a camera set up because you can see her over the Internet."

"Was it the judge's daughter?"

Rose nodded. "Anthony showed me a picture and it was definitely her. There's supposedly four other men watching her and Toby's threatening to have them rape and kill her."

"Oh, my God," Sarah said. "Are you saying that it's likely Toby *did* rape those women?" Rose nodded again.

"And this poor judge is basically being held hostage by Toby, who is threatening to take this supposedly awful secret to the police and have him sent to prison if he doesn't give him immunity? Does that about sum it up?"

"Yes, that's exactly what's happening."

Sarah got up from the table and walked over to the sink, peering out into the darkness. And with her back still to Rose she said, "Do you trust me, Rose?"

Rose was taken aback by the question. "Of course I trust you. That's why I'm here."

"Good," she said, turning around. "Then call Brandon and get him and this judge over here right now."

"What? Why?" Rose asked her, confused.

"You said you trusted me, right?"

"Of course I trust you, Sarah, but . . ."

"Then call them, Rose," she said, setting the phone in front of her. "Tell them Brett Mitchell's widow has something very important to tell them. That should be enough to get them moving."

"What's this about, Sarah?"

"Let's just say that Brett was a big believer in contingency plans."

"I don't understand?"

"You will. Just make the call and I'll explain everything to you when they get here."

Rose had to remind herself to breath as she dialed Brandon's number.

CHAPTER 48

By the time Brandon and Anthony pulled up to the Mitchell house they could see that Rose was already there and were somewhat relieved since neither of them had ever met Sarah Mitchell. Rose answered the door and Brandon noticed that the hardness in her face had been replaced by something else. Hurt? Betrayal? Sympathy?

"Anthony," she began. "I . . . ." Her eyes filled with tears as her voice faltered. "I cannot begin to tell you how sorry I am for what my son has done to your beautiful daughter. I want you to know if I could change all of it I would. I'm just so sorry."

"Thank you," he said softly. He then turned and met the intelligent gaze of Sarah Mitchell who had joined them. "It's a pleasure to finally meet you, Anthony," she said, shaking hands. "Brett told me a lot about you toward the end and it was obvious he held you in high regard." This revelation caused Rose to look at her funny.

"Recent events would probably call that statement into question, Mrs. Mitchell," he stated flatly.

"Yes, well, I suppose you're right about that," she said, "which is why I had Rose ask you both to come here this evening. And I know you must be curious so if you'll all take a seat in the living room, I'm going to run upstairs and I'll join you momentarily."

When the three of them were seated and the silence had become uncomfortable, Brandon looked at Rose and said, "Did you get a hold of Toby?"

"No, I called Sarah first and when I told her what had happened she immediately told me to call and get you both over here. Believe me, I'm just as in the dark as the two of you."

As Sarah was returning down the stairs someone rang the doorbell but she intentionally walked right by the door and continued into the living room. "Do any of you know who that might be?" she asked with a concerned look on her face.

"Yes, I do," Brandon declared as he heaved himself up from the couch. He conducted a quick visual through the peephole and appearing to be satisfied, opened the door. Anthony and Rose's mouths dropped open as he ushered in none other than the District Attorney, Michael Haas. After quick introductions Sarah said, "I'm confused. Did you invite him here, Brandon?"

Brandon looked embarrassed and when he hesitated, Michael looked directly at Anthony and said, "Brandon came to me a few days ago and told me everything, Your Honor."

Anthony looked like he wanted to jump out of the nearest window and he gave Brandon a hurt look that communicated exactly how he felt about this betrayal. "But how did he know about this meeting?" he asked, "I was with you tonight."

"Right after Rose called us I told you I needed to go to the bathroom, remember?"

"You can relax, Judge. Brandon made me give him my word that I wouldn't repeat anything he told me, and so far I've kept that promise."

"But I don't understand why you're here," Sarah said.

Brandon spoke up. "Mrs. Mitchell, I wasn't sure why you asked us to come here tonight, but I was certain it had to do with Toby, and since the D.A. knows everything that's happened thus far, and some things about Toby that none of you even know yet, I thought it was prudent to have him here. I trust him and I'm asking all of you trust him as well."

They looked around at each other and finally Sarah said, "It's fine with me if everyone else is okay with it." When both Anthony and Rose indicated that they were, Sarah directed the D.A. to a chair and readied herself to begin.

Nothing could have prepared them for the bombshell she was about to drop.

CHAPTER 49

"The first thing I want to say is directed to Anthony," Sarah began. Anthony looked up from his hands and met her eyes.

"You and my husband made a terrible mistake when you were young, and I can't imagine what it must have been like to live with that guilt all these years. I know that you and he had made a promise to never speak to anyone of what happened, yet he broke that promise to you by telling Rose. I don't know if it makes any difference to you, but he wanted you to know that he felt horrible for doing it, but you have to understand that besides me, Rose was the only family he had and he felt an obligation to protect her at all costs; even if that meant betraying your trust. However, I also want you to know that Brett wasn't naive. He knew how powerful this secret was, and that he was leaving you and your family vulnerable should the wrong person learn of it."

"Someone like Toby," Michael said.

"Exactly," she said, looking toward Rose as if to say she was sorry.

Anthony didn't say a word but Rose looked confused. "Sarah, are you saying that Brett told you about that night?"

Sarah nodded her head. "Yes, Rose, except I'm happy to say that he told me a story with a much happier ending than the one he told you." Now everyone in the room was confused and they all leaned in a little closer in anticipation of where she was heading with this. Sarah then stood up and extracted something from her pocket then walked directly to Anthony and held out her hand to him. "Does this look familiar to you, Anthony?" she asked him, smiling.

Anthony looked stunned at what he saw lying in the palm of her hand, and at first couldn't forge a response. "That's my class ring."

"Yes, it is," she confirmed.

"But . . ."

"Brett gave it to me before he died. He said it was insurance in case things got out of control." She then looked at Rose. "I'm sorry to have to tell you this, Rose, but he was never as sure of Toby's innocence as you were." Rose just nodded sadly.

"So if the ring is here, then that means he never put it in the girl's pocket," Brandon said, stating what they were all thinking.

"No, *he* never did, but you're welcome to if you want," Sarah said with a sly grin.

"I don't understand," Anthony said.

"I don't know of any way to break this to you gently, so I'm just going to say it." She looked at each one of them individually and finally her eyes came to rest on Rose.

"Rose, honey, you *are* the girl that Brett and Anthony hit that night."

No one said a word as their minds tried to assimilate the ramifications of what she had just said. So stunned were they that had a soft summer breeze drifted through the room, it would have swept every last one of them out of their seats and deposited them on the floor in one big, confused pile. Finally, after what seemed like an eternity of silence, Rose said, "That isn't possible, Sarah. What you're saying isn't possible. They killed her that night. Brett told me himself. He checked for her pulse and couldn't find one. Isn't that right, Anthony?" she implored.

Anthony was as dumbstruck as everyone else and it took him a moment to recognize that Rose had directed the question toward him. "Uh, yeah. Yes, that's exactly what happened," he agreed. "I admit I'm not a doctor, but she certainly looked dead to me; she wasn't moving, that's for sure."

Sarah walked over to her china hutch and extracted a legal sized envelope from one of the drawers. She then turned around and held it up for all of them to see. "This envelope contains everything you'll need to substantiate that what I'm telling you is the truth. You see, Rose, Brett told you the same story that the judge here would have told you if he'd been so inclined. He had to if Anthony was going to believe you. Thankfully, though, the outcome of that night was much different than what he led you to believe. Of course, only he knew that."

She sat back down but held on to the envelope. "After he dropped you off at the campus that night, Anthony, he *did* continue on to hide the girl's – Rose's - body, but when he opened the trunk to take her out he decided to check her pulse one more time and lo and behold, this time he found one. And since Brett was no murderer, there was no way he was going to just leave you and walk away. However, he was still afraid of what would happen if he went to the police, so he rushed you to the hospital and told them that he was your brother and that you had been in a bad car accident. You were in such critical condition that they didn't really ask many questions."

She paused here to make sure everyone was keeping up. When she was fairly certain they were, she continued. "It was touch and go for a few days but you finally pulled through and started to get better. Brett would go visit you every day and he told me that each time he walked through the door he would hold his breath, expecting you to ask him who he was. You never did, though, because although your body was healing, your memory was not. You had severe amnesia and your entire past had apparently been wiped clean. The doctors told him there was a slim chance you might regain some of it, but you never did. And since you hadn't been carrying any identification with you the night you were hit, he had no idea who *you* were either.

He told me that he would spend hours, day after day, scouring the local and national news channels and publications for anything that might mention a missing girl that fit your description, but he never saw anything. It was then that he decided he was going to have you move in with him and take care of you as best he could. The fact that his parents were deceased just made it that much easier to pull off. No one in southern Indiana knew him besides Anthony, so who would question him about suddenly having a sister, right? Of course, the situation demanded that he distance himself from you as much as possible, Anthony, since you were the only one it would raise a red flag to."

She looked at Rose. "That's where you really got those scars from, Rose, not the story he'd always told you."

"Oh, my God," Anthony said, shaking his head. "Why wouldn't he have told me any of this? Why keep it a secret?"

"Because he was trying to protect, Rose. By the way, that was the first name that popped into his head when they asked him your name at the hospital, and you've been Rose ever since," she told her, smiling. Rose was too bewildered to respond.

"He knew if it ever got out that she wasn't really his sister that she'd more than likely be put in a foster home, and he didn't want that to ever happen hence, the reason why he never told anyone, including Rose."

"This is unbelievable. Absolutely unbelievable," the D.A. remarked, echoing everyone else's feelings. "You say you have proof in that envelope?"

"Yes," she said, holding it up again. "In here are all the records of your time in the hospital, as well as the results from two different DNA tests. One proves that you and Brett are not related by blood. The other was done on a sample of dried blood taken from your ring, Anthony. It confirms that it belongs to Rose."

Rose buried her face in her hands and began to cry softly and Brandon walked over and knelt down next to her to offer whatever support he could. Of course, Anthony still had a daughter whose life was in danger and he was contemplating the significance of all of this. He looked at Sarah. "So all of these years that I've had to live with this guilt, it was for nothing? Is that what you're telling me; that I was blackmailed and my daughter has been put through hell, all for something I didn't even do?"

"I don't know what to say, Anthony. If I had known what was happening, I would have revealed all of this sooner. I am so terribly sorry for what you and your family have had to endure, and I know for a fact that if Brett had thought for a second that things would get this out of control he would have taken this to the grave with him." Anthony just nodded as he rubbed his temples.

"Rosie, there was one other thing Brett wanted me to tell you, and it was important to him that you understand it." Rose raised her head off of Brandon's shoulder and looked at her expectantly; tears tracking down her beautiful face.

"He told me to tell you that he never thought about the fact that you weren't related by blood; that he couldn't have loved you more if you were. You and he had an amazing bond and he didn't want anything to ever change that." She paused for a moment to get her emotions in check. "Anyway, he wanted you to know that."

Michael Haas stood up. "Look, I understand that we've all been blown away tonight by this, and it will no doubt take some time to come to terms with it, especially for you, Rose, but I think we can all agree that we have a much more pressing problem facing us right now."

Without hesitation they nodded as one.

CHAPTER 50

"How is my daughter?" Anthony asked Toby.

"She's fine, Judge. You know, just hangin' with the fellas."

Anthony took a deep breath. "I'm sure you would agree that what you're requiring me to do is not an easy thing for anyone. After all, you're basically asking me to forfeit the remaining years of my life."

"Cry me a river, Judge. You should have thought of that before you killed that girl."

"Toby, your Uncle and I made a grave error in judgment that night and believe me, not a day goes by that I don't wish I could turn back time and do it all differently."

"Your nostalgia is very touching, but what's that got to do with why you're here?"

"I came here to tell you that in order to protect my daughter I will turn myself in like you've asked. However, I will only do it if you promise to leave my family alone. I do this and you never have contact with them again, understand?"

"I don't think you're really in a bargaining position, Judge."

"You know, I could have just walked in here and put a bullet between your eyes. I don't think there're many who would miss you."

"Yeah, you could've, but you didn't."

"No, you're right – I didn't. I guess I'm not a killer like you."

"There aren't many like me, Judge, that I can tell you for sure," he said, grinning. "So what's up with the immunity? Did you get that worked out?"

"The paperwork is being drawn up as we speak."

"Damn, you judges do have a piss pot full of power, don't you?" he laughed.

Anthony ignored him and began moving absently around the apartment, appearing to be lost in thought. "I need to know something, Toby."

"Yeah, what's that?"

"I need to understand why you did this to my daughter? You already knew enough about my past to get me to concede to just about anything, so why did you have to go after Gabriella?"

"It's no mystery, Judge. I just didn't think you'd take me as seriously as I needed you to so I created my own insurance. All in all I'd say it was pretty effective, wouldn't you? Plus, that note on my windshield pissed me off. Bad move. Whose handiwork was that, anyway?"

"I honestly didn't know when you first showed it to me, but I've since found out it was Brandon."

"Brandon?" he said, surprised. "Huh, maybe he's got bigger balls than I gave him credit for. He was banging my mom, you know."

"No, I didn't know."

"Think she'll still want him after I castrate him?"

"You mean you're not going to use a stick like you did on that guard?"

Toby chuckled. "Come on now, Judge, did you come here to go fishing or pull your daughter's head out of the lion's mouth?"

"You're not in court, Toby, it's just you and me here. I figure if I'm going to die in prison you could at least satisfy my curiosity. And who would I tell, it would just be your word against mine and who's going to believe me after I confess to what I did, right? I have to admit that I'm actually impressed with how you've had the police pulling their hair out."

"That's because they're a bunch of morons who can't find their ass in the dark with both hands."

"But what is it exactly that you get out of hurting people? Is it a control thing? Is it sexually stimulating? Are you just psychotic and can't control yourself? What is it?"

"It's presumptuous for you to think that you could ever understand someone like me, Judge."

"But what changed? I mean, I know now that it *was* you who raped those women, but what made you suddenly change your M.O. and beat that last girl into a coma?"

Toby just looked at him, trying to figure out why he was asking all these questions. "Are we done here, yet?"

"She died, you know."

"Who?"

"Terri Ranes. The one you put in a coma. It was her blood they found on your shirt. That means you're now guilty of capital murder. They can execute you for that."

"Then I guess I'm lucky you ruled that it was inadmissible."

"I suppose you're right. But why beat on her, Toby? Why not just rape her like the others and then leave?"

Toby was growing tired of the questions. "Okay, Judge, you think you can handle being a spectator in the front row of the mind of a mad man? Fine, but it's only fair to warn you that you could lose your sanity."

Anthony nodded somberly. "I can assure you the loss of my daughter's innocence is infinitely worse."

"Have it your way then," Toby began, as a demented smile crossed his face. "I know you want to hear something like she managed to get a hold of a knife and I had to defend myself, or she hit me in the head with a vase and started running around the apartment screaming, but unfortunately it wasn't anything nearly as dramatic as that. I beat her for no other reason than the fact that she bit me. I had already warned her about what would happen if she made any noise, so to keep herself from screaming she bit me on the arm." He frowned as he remembered it and then looked at Anthony. "So there you have it, Judge. Do you feel better knowing? No? I didn't think so. Now get the hell out of here and I expect to have those papers in my hands by the end of the day if you want to see Gabby in one piece?"

"Wait a minute. She was afraid you'd hurt her if she screamed so to keep from screaming she accidentally bit you in the arm and you beat her to death?" Anthony asked in disbelief.

"My world ain't your world, Judge. You have your pet peeves and I have mine. I suppose eventually we'll both meet in hell and our differences will be irrelevant, but until then . . ." He just shrugged.

"But what about the guard at the jail? What could he have possibly done to deserve to die like that?

"He was sport," he said, his eyes beginning to radiate like heat reflecting off the desert floor.

"Sport?"

"That's right, Judge – sport. Someone pisses me off, I wait for the day that I get that itch, and then I go scratch it. You know . . . with a long stick or whatever's handy," he added, laughing.

Anthony thought he might get sick. "And Jeanine Brandt? Is that why you decided to go back for seconds – sport?"

"Her mother had no manners, Judge. Someone had to pay. But like I said . . . your world ain't mine." His eyes were disturbingly devoid of any emotion.

Anthony stared at him, his face flush with hate and disgust. "You and I aren't even in the same galaxy, you sick son of a bitch, and you're fooling yourself if you think you're going to hell. I am supremely confident that there's a special place set aside for animals like you; someplace so evil and abominable that it defies the most vile of imaginations;

a place where the predators become the prey and where you'll beg for insanity from a God who's no longer listening," he snarled through clinched teeth. "Rest assured that you and I will not be meeting there, lad."

"Wow, that was quite a speech, Judge. Good for you. However, I have things to do and I'm cautiously optimistic that Gabby will be feeling well enough to give Daddy a little lovin' tonight provided, of course, you produce that paperwork. If not, she'll be giving a *lot* of lovin' to some fellas who don't share my sunny disposition so I suggest you get a move on."

"Show me my daughter, Toby."

"What?"

"I said show me my daughter. Do whatever it is you did last night to that computer and show me that she's alright."

"You ain't running this thing, Judge."

"Toby, if you think I'm going to prison for nothing you're sadly mistaken. I'm only agreeing to do what you asked in order to ensure the safety of Gabriella. Now show me that she's okay or you can go to hell and I'll take my chances with the police. Personally I don't think you know where that girl's body is anyway."

"Don't push me, Judge."

"Maybe it's you who better not push me. Now you show me that Gabriella's okay or I promise you I'll take my chances and walk out of here right now and you can kiss your immunity good bye," he said, starting for the door.

Toby watched him for just a moment. "Okay, Judge, okay. I was just a joshin' ya," he said when Anthony turned around. "I was wondering when you were going to ask to see her. I'm surprised it wasn't the first thing out of your mouth when you got here." He walked over to his computer and typed in the website's URL and Anthony stood next to him as they waited for it to load. "I'll bet you been missing your little girl, huh?" he asked him sarcastically.

"You know what, Toby, I actually haven't been missing her as much as I thought I would."

Toby looked at him with raised eyebrows. "What did you say?"

"I said I didn't miss her as much as I thought I would," Anthony repeated. "After all, I spoke with her right before I came over here to see you."

Toby looked at him like he had a screw loose. "What the hell are you talking about? Did you hit your head on the way over?"

"I'm talking about that," Anthony said, pointing toward the monitor. The website had come up and what Toby saw caused him to do a double take.

"What the fuck?" he exclaimed. He couldn't believe his eyes. The scene was exactly the same; same couch, same apartment. But this time instead of Gabby sitting in the front of the camera it was his mother, and she was staring into the lens with a look of such disgust and bitter disappointment that it was obvious she knew he could see her. Anthony had moved a few feet away but Toby stood where he was.

In an eerily calm voice that shouldn't have surprised Anthony at this point but did nonetheless, he said. "How does she know I'm looking at her right now?"

"Because the police were listening to our conversation, as they are even now, and when they knew you were logging on they placed a phone call to their counterparts who were waiting at Carl's apartment with your mother."

"You're wired?" he asked, without looking at him.

"Yes."

He continued to stare at the monitor as if he were waiting for the channel to change back to his show. "And Gabby?"

"Gabby is on her way to the hospital with her mother. Luckily she appears to be fine." He could see that Toby's mind was working now.

"What if I had logged on right before you showed up? I would have known something was up?"

"The police have been staged since last night and they were monitoring her through your website. If any of your buddies had touched her they would have moved in immediately. Of course, then we would have had to count on one of them testifying against you since we wouldn't have had your confession on tape as we do now."

"So you're saying the police are outside my apartment listening to this right now?"

"Yes."

"Then why aren't they breaking down my door?"

"It would only take a word from me."

Toby wasn't looking at him but from this angle he could tell he was grinning. "This doesn't solve all your problems, Judge. You know you're going down with me."

Anthony hesitated before answering, unsure how to answer. Finally he decided that he wanted him to know. "There's no girl, Toby."

"Say what you need to say while the cops are listening, Judge, but you and I both know what you did, and we both know I can prove it."

"Don't get me wrong, Toby, I thought we had killed her too, but come to find out your mother is actually the girl we hit that night. Apparently we were a little presumptuous in our assessment of her condition. I won't bore you with the details but suffice it to say that she was as shocked as the rest of us since your uncle had never told her either. He did tell your Aunt Sarah, though, and thankfully that nasty bit of business has finally been laid to rest, so I'm afraid you're going to have to walk alone to the execution chamber."

Most people would have been blown away if they'd been broad-sided with something like this, but Toby never flinched. Anthony did note that the grin had disappeared, though. "So are they coming in here or are we going out there?"

"Whichever you prefer."

He stood where he was for another minute before finally turning to face him. "So you win, huh?"

"There are no winners here, Toby, just shattered lives and years of healing ahead." He then leaned his mouth toward his collar. "Come on in, gentlemen, I think you have all you need." The door opened immediately and the room was instantly filled with police. Toby made no attempt to resist as they put him on his face to handcuff and search him. When they had him back on his feet and moving toward the door he looked over his shoulder and said, "I just have one more question for you, Judge." The two policemen escorting him looked toward Anthony and he held up his hand for them to wait as he walked over and positioned himself directly in front of him.

"What is it?"

"I'm just curious; how'd you know I wouldn't go after you once that website came up?"

"I didn't."

He seemed to consider this. "But you were alone. Weren't you afraid I'd kill you before they could get in here?" he asked, nodding toward the cops.

"To be honest, Toby, I was hoping you would try." He then reached down and lifted up his shirt to reveal the handgrip of a nine millimeter stuck in his waistband.

Toby whistled in admiration and grinned like a Cheshire cat. "Do you think you could have used it?" he asked tauntingly.

"With absolutely no hesitation or remorse, young man," he stated matter-of-factly.

Toby's eyes found his and held them as he appeared to be searching for something. "You know, Judge, I think I may have underestimated you because I'll be damned if you don't look like you're telling the truth."

"Get him out of here," Anthony said, heading for the door. "I have my family waiting for me."

CHAPTER 51

(One month later)

Neither Brandon nor Rose said anything for a while as they lay listening to the rain sound a drum roll on the roof, announcing spring's arrival.

Finally Rose broke the comfortable silence. "Do you think Anthony will one day be able to forgive me? After all, if it wasn't for me none of this would have happened."

"Give him some time, Rose. He'll eventually come to realize that you were just doing what any mother would have done for a child they were sure was innocent. Your brother gave you a surefire way to save him and you took it. Who could blame you?"

"I guess so."

"Anyway, right now I'm sure their main concern is their daughter."

"I pray for her every day."

"So do I, Rose, so do I."

Another few moments went by without either speaking until Rose turned to look at him.

"How do you not see your own child go bad, Brandon?"

"It wasn't something that happened overnight. The psychiatrists that have managed to get him to talk say that he exhibits an extraordinary number of sociopath, as well as narcissistic traits, and it was only a matter of time before he snapped. Believe me, it wasn't anything you did."

"They'll sentence him to death, won't they."

"More than likely."

"I suppose a person who's done what he's done deserves to die."

"I suppose you're right," he said, moving his hand to stroke her face. "Anyhow, it's out of our hands now."

After some consideration he took a deep breath. "Have you thought about the fact that you may have an entire family out there that has never had closure?"

"Of course."

He continued to strum her face. "Will you try to find them?"

"I haven't decided yet. I recognize that I have some healing to do before I can begin that journey." The drumbeat grew more furious as the clouds unleashed their final assault on winter.

"Secrets are never a good thing, are they, Brandon?"

"No, I don't suppose they are."

"Promise that we'll never have secrets between us."

"I promise."

This seemed to comfort her and she settled closer into him. "I'm glad you came back," she said softly.

"Believe me, Rosie, I never left."

The End

Made in the USA
Columbia, SC
10 September 2021

45266021R00226